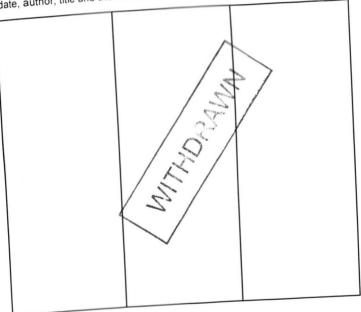

Cataloguing and Publication information is available from The Canadian ISBN Service System, Library and Archives Canada.

ISBN paperback: 978-0-9952968-0-0
Website: www.stellamaclean.com

Editor Services: Patricia Thomas
Cover Artist: The Killion Group, Inc.
Formatting Services: Author E.M.S.

This book is dedicated to Bev Boutilier

A caring friend and a discerning reader.

CHAPTER ONE

Terra Cameron would remember this moment for the rest of her life.

The soft light of the moon spread over their naked bodies as she snuggled next to her husband, Sean. Happy didn't begin to describe how she felt. "Honey, what are you thinking about?" she asked, trailing her fingers over his jaw, feeling the beginning of light stubble growing there.

"That the sooner you're pregnant the better. I want a house full of kids."

"Sean!" She pretended to be shocked. "We've been married all of eight months."

"So?" he asked, his mouth caressing the soft skin between her breasts.

"So does this mean you don't want dessert?" she asked, her body melting under his touch.

"You *are* dessert," he said, his voice a husky whisper as he kissed her neck. "Not that the dinner you made wasn't spectacular. It was." He smoothed her hair away from her face, his eyes dark and impenetrable in the soft light of the bedroom.

She loved Sean Cameron with every fiber of her being. He was her life, her future, and now with a baby on the way, they had a whole new experience to look forward to. She'd made dinner, planned every part of it down to the last bite, all to make the night ahead the most wonderful night of their lives. She couldn't wait to see the happiness on his face when she told him she was pregnant. "If we're going to spend the rest of the evening in bed, I'd better close up the house."

"I'm here, ready to make love to you, and you're worried about locking up?" he asked, his dark blue eyes focused solely on her. "I already checked. Every door in this house is locked."

"But did you put the alarm system on? I need to have the alarm on, you know that."

Taking her hand in his, he kissed each finger, slowly and deliberately. "Some day I'm going to cure you of your fears…all of them," he whispered.

She'd like to simply curl up next to him, lose herself and for just one whole night, not think about anything, including the past. "I'll be right back," she said, pulling her hand away from his lips and reaching for her white robe.

"Just you remember what's waiting for you right here," he called as she headed down the hall toward the door to the garage and the security system keypad.

She passed the living room and dining room where the high ceiling reflected the shimmering light from the back garden fountain. She imagined this space filled to overflowing with baby things, lots of baby things… In the kitchen the dishes from the evening meal were scattered over the counters, the cluttered stovetop stood quietly in the semi-darkness. "I'll clean this in the morning," she whispered into the silence.

Reaching the back entrance, she punched the 'stay' button on the pad. 'System failure. Door ajar' displayed on the screen.

"Shoot! One of us must have left the door to the lower deck open," she muttered, smoothing her tangled hair off her face as she went down the stairs leading to the lower level. She was sure she'd closed the door after they came in from the deck…so sure… And Sean had said he'd locked all the doors.

Reaching the bottom of the stairs, she hit the switch and the room was bathed in soft light from the ceiling pot lights.

This was Sean's favorite room in the house, one he'd spent hours planning and designing. He called it his man cave—and it was, with its home theatre and general all round space for her husband. As she made her way around the corner, past the wall-mounted television and the wet bar she saw the French doors that led to the stone patio.

They were open. The motion detector light cast a hard blaze of light on the outdoor space. Her heart tripping wildly against her ribs, she closed the door and locked it before moving back toward the stairs.

Just then someone moved out from the shadowy space beside the bookcase next to the French doors.

Gasping in surprise, she stumbled back, nearly falling.

Another man appeared beside her, his face covered in a black mask.

"Don't move," he said.

A scream started in her throat, extinguished immediately by a large hand covering her mouth.

Powerful arms pulled her backwards, crushing her chest. "What have we here?"

Terrified she struggled against him. His grip tightened.

"You utter one sound and I'll kill you," the intruder said, his voice soft and sure. "Where's your husband?" he demanded, yanking her back against him, lifting her feet off the floor.

Panic clouded her vision, trapping her mind, her body trembling. "Bedroom," she choked out the word, pointing toward the ceiling.

"Nice, real nice. That's where we're going." He dragged her across the floor. His fingers squeezed her left breast—her yelp of pain was muffled by his hand.

"Like I said, shut up. We're not here to hurt you. We're looking for that bastard you married. He's going to die for what he did."

Sean had watched his wife leave, his eyes following the flow of her robe around her body, her easy stride. He was the luckiest man alive. He'd dated a lot of women while ignoring his mother's plea to get married. He'd almost given up on finding the perfect woman—a woman who would put him first and be there only for him and their children—when Terra had literally walked into his life. He'd seen her with a friend along the trail that followed the river. He'd been on his way from a meeting, using the park as a shortcut to his office. To this day he still wondered how it was that they had found each other. Meeting Terra, who hung on his every word and encouraged him in everything he chose to do, was exhilarating. Terra wasn't a member of his family's social set, and he didn't care. She was everything he wanted and needed. He had fallen in love with her, surprising him and his family.

Terra was a nurse in Langford Hospital's Surgical Intensive Care Unit in the city center. He'd wanted her to give up her job and simply enjoy being his wife.

Running Cameron Industries consumed most of his time, but he promised to change all that if she agreed to leave work. An old-fashioned notion, but one he believed in with all his heart. He wanted Terra to be happy at home raising their family.

Yet so much of that would change if his suspicions about what was going on at Cameron Industries were true. He had been quietly looking into operational issues at the office and their plants spread across the Midwest. He had hired a private investigator, Neill Baxter, to help him. The investigator had gone to all four plants, hung out with the workers and learned that at each plant they expected the facility to close any day. Production numbers were down, according to the shift managers the investigator had talked to. The rumor mill at all four plants said the company was bankrupt, and yet the actual financial statements seemed sound enough. He hadn't mentioned it to his twin brother Shamus because he wasn't sure whether his brother was involved, and until he knew more he hadn't wanted to start a fight with him, one that would ultimately pull his mother into the discussion.

Sean had no idea who was behind it, but a couple names

kept coming up. He had a meeting with his PI tomorrow to go over the report the man had written. Once he'd read Neill Baxter's report he'd talk to Shamus about what the investigator had found.

So maybe it was just as well that Terra remained working at the hospital, just in case the situation became dire. A phone call from the PI that afternoon, and the packet of papers he'd delivered, convinced Sean that he had to talk to Terra tonight. Worst of all, he might have to ask Terra for the money he'd given her after their wedding, money he could need to keep their lifestyle afloat.

The soft ping of his cell phone alerted him to a new message. He leaned across the bed, picked up his phone and saw a message from BBTAY, a person he knew only through a chat room. He stared at the message, his breath catching in his throat. It seemed BBTAY wanted to meet him in person.

So far it had all been simple fun, no attachments, only the occasional hook up on a chat room. He had never intended to take it further, and he certainly had no intention of meeting up with whoever this was. He loved Terra, would always love her. This was just a diversion. Thankfully no real names had been used and he assumed BBTAY had no idea how to find him.

Regardless of what the message said, he had no choice but to ignore it for the moment. He had more urgent issues to deal with, starting with how he was going to tell his beautiful wife that they could be in serious financial difficulty.

He shut the phone off and shoved it to the back of the drawer on the bedside table. He'd worry about BBTAY in the morning.

The man's palm pressed hard into Terra's pelvis as he dragged her up the stairs to the kitchen. He smelled of pizza and beer and sweat. She tried to twist away, which made him crush her to him even harder. *What if he was hurting her baby?* The thought terrified her.

And what had the man meant about killing Sean? I

couldn't be true. Her husband didn't have an enemy in the world.

The man suddenly let go of her. She stumbled as her feet hit the floor.

"Terra, honey," Sean called from the bedroom. "What's keeping you?"

The rough fabric of her attacker's stocking mask scraped her skin as his face pressed close to her ear. "Listen and do exactly as I tell you." There followed a threatening pause. "You're going to walk into the bedroom and pretend that everything is just fine. If you don't, I'll kill you *and* your husband. Is that clear?"

Her body trembled. Fear flooded her mind. She swallowed, not daring to look at him.

The other masked man appeared in front of her. "You will do what we ask," he added, his words a harsh drawl. He took her by the shoulders and marched her down the hall. Leaning close, his rank body odor wafted around her. As they approached the door he hissed in her ear, "Now. Walk in, act normal, or your husband dies."

Terra managed to walk into the bedroom where Sean rested against the headboard, a sheet covering his lower body. He had a broad smile on his handsome face.

An eerie sound hummed in her head and she couldn't seem to breathe. It was as if she were trapped in a nightmare waiting to wake up, wanting to hear Sean's soothing words when she told him she'd had a bad dream. She gripped the corner of the dresser, her knees threatening to buckle. "Run!" she mouthed, her eyes pleading with him, her hands shaking so hard her fingers slid off the smooth wood.

"What is it, darling?" Sean asked, a look of concern clouding his face as he got out of the bed and came toward her.

"One more step and your husband's a dead man," the masked man muttered behind her.

"No! Sean!" She put her hands out to stop her husband from coming closer.

She swung around and kicked out hard against the man behind her. His surprised grunt told her she'd hit the mark.

"You bitch!" he growled through his mask.

"Terra!" Sean yelled, reaching for her.

The second man pressed past her into the room, a knife in his hand. His huge frame filled the space. "You get the hell back against the wall. Don't move or I'll kill her."

Sean's eyes flooded with fear. "Don't harm my wife. Whatever it is you want, take it. We won't tell anyone. Take whatever it is you came for and leave us alone."

"We came for you," the bigger of the two men said, his tone hard and hate-filled.

The other man grabbed Terra and dragged her toward the bed. "We both have a little business with this happy couple. You look after him. I'll look after her," he said, his startling blue eyes glinting as he tossed Terra onto the bed so hard the air *whooshed* from her lungs.

"Hey! We came here for the husband, remember? What do you think you're doing?" the other man demanded, his knife still pointed at Sean.

The masked man unzipped his jeans as he stood over her. "I've always wanted to do this, just like in the movies." He dropped his pants to the floor and climbed onto the bed.

"Don't touch my wife," Sean yelled, and his words were followed, almost immediately by a grunting sound.

"Sean!" Terra screamed, jerking her head sideways as her husband doubled over in pain.

"Shut up!" the man said, towering over her, yanking hard on her hair, and pinning her arms over her head.

With one swift movement he tore her nightgown from her body, opening her up to his hard gaze. His breathing changed. He gripped her hands in one of his, as he squeezed her right breast, making her scream in pain.

"A yeller," he chuckled. "I like that." He reached down and forced her legs apart.

Terra felt faint and dizzy and scared; for her, for Sean and the baby. Her mind struggled to understand what was going on. A dizzying array of images flashed across her mind. This man would hurt her; damage her in ways that could harm her baby. The last thought trumped all the rest. She had to protect her unborn child.

Gulping air, she grabbed his mask but failed to pull it off

his face. In an instant, she snaked her foot up, landing a kick into his soft belly. Mind-stopping pain careened up her leg, breaking her concentration for a few seconds.

He gasped and swore, but released her hands as he reached for his gut. She kicked again, then drove her fingers into his eyes. He cursed, swinging wide, his fingers spread, searching for her.

Terra scrambled away from the man and fell off the bed onto the floor. She hit the corner of the bedside table so hard her head exploded in a rain of stars.

"Sean!"

Sean lunged at the man holding the knife. "Run! Terra! Run!" The man stepped sideways, his hand coming up, the blade slicing across Sean's chest. Sean grabbed at the hand holding the knife, but missed.

Terra scrambled across the floor toward her husband, frantic to reach him. Struggling to her feet, she kicked out at Sean's attacker and missed. The man ducked, raised the knife and slashed downward, catching Sean in the neck. Terra shrieked in horror as her husband slid to the floor, his hand on his neck, disbelief in his eyes, blood spattering everywhere.

"*Shit*! Let's get out of here," one of the attackers said.

"Damn right," the other one said.

Terra sank to the floor beside her husband, intent on holding her hand on his throat. The rush of blood from the knife wound seeped through her fingers, trailed down his neck onto the carpet. She pressed harder into his soft skin, pleading for him to stay with her while she watched a red stain bloom on the carpet beneath his neck.

Sean's eyes clouded over. She was losing him. Galvanized by fear, she remembered the panic button in the bedside table. Would help get to them in time? She prayed as she scrambled across the floor to the drawer, her fingers searching while her eyes remained on her husband. Her bloody fingers curled around the button. She squeezed hard on the plastic disk.

A loud blaring sound, like car horns, echoed around the outside of the house, penetrating the bedroom with is powerful wail. Somewhere she heard a door slam. In minutes there would be police and an ambulance at her door.

Terra crawled back across the floor and cradled her husband in her arms. Frantic, her fingers made contact with his throat. She felt the flow of blood sliding over his skin. Trembling, terrified and desperate to stop the blood she pressed her shaking fingers hard against his neck, willing him to survive, to stay with her and the baby. Gradually the flood became a trickle...

"Sean! Sean! Stay with me!" she pleaded, holding him close in her arms, sobbing into his hair, stroking his face.

CHAPTER TWO

Detective Derrick O'Leary had been enjoying a night off when he got the call he would never forget. He was to report to twenty-two Magnolia Drive. The residence belonged to Sean Cameron, and his wife Terra, members of the powerful and influential Cameron family, the town's greatest success story. Four years ago he'd loved Terra Cameron, and he'd made a poor decision and hurt her. A time that stood out in his memory as one of the stupidest periods in his life. Derrick hadn't seen Terra over those four years. They didn't travel in the same circles.

But his past was not relevant to the situation at hand. The officers answering the house alarm had been on the scene in minutes, sirens blaring and attracting a press core hungry for sensational news; the knifing of an upstanding member of the community being fodder for the late night evening news.

His cell phone blared. Call display showed it was from his partner, Detective Meaghan Wilson.

He picked up. "Yeah."

"I'm on the scene. Sean Cameron is dead. Robbery doesn't seem to be the motive. No electronics, TVs, or computers missing—that we know of. Mrs. Cameron's purse was sitting on the kitchen counter, untouched as near as we can determine. The part-time housekeeper, Selena Shepard, is on her way over here to confirm that. Terra Cameron is suffering shock, and she's been assaulted. The ambulance is here. The ME just arrived."

"I'll be there in five," he said and hung up, his foot slamming the gas pedal, his body humming with fear for Terra.

Derrick parked along the street in front of the house, dodged past the reporters and walked briskly up the walkway. Meaghan met him inside the back door, her red hair doing its usual wild thing around her face. Although they'd been working together as detectives for about a year, he could honestly say she was the best partner he'd ever had. She was smart, thorough and knew her job well. "What a hell of a mess."

"No kidding. The wife is in the bedroom, barely able to speak. I understand two masked men gained entrance to the home through the French doors off the backyard on the lower level. Sean Cameron is dead, knifed to death by one of the assailants. Although his wife was in the room at the time she couldn't give much of a description. I've sent two officers to interview the neighbors; see if anyone heard or saw anything." Meaghan shrugged. "I have an officer staying with Mrs. Cameron until they can collect any evidence off her skin before they take her to the hospital."

Angst and a sense of foreboding gripped him as he remembered Terra had been the victim of a home invasion when she was a teenager, and that had made her very security conscious. "Did they try to kill Terra as well?" he asked, a sick feeling rolling through his body. He jammed his hands into the pockets of his jacket to hide their trembling.

Meaghan stared at him in surprise. "Terra? How'd you get to be on a first name basis with this woman?"

"It's a long story," he said, physically backing away from his partner and any personal discussion about the woman of the house. The sooner he got to the bedroom, the sooner he'd know how Terra was doing.

"I need to see the crime scene and talk to the ME. Let me know if the officers learn anything useful from the neighbors." Derrick stepped around his partner and headed into the house.

"Will do," Meaghan said, her eyes assessing him.

The long hall leading to the master bedroom was decorated in soft cream tones, and covered with artwork that Derrick assumed was expensive. A man of Sean Cameron's stature would have only the best. Including the woman who had become his wife.

He reached the door of the bedroom and was suddenly assailed by the coppery smell of warm blood. He glanced in and saw the ME carefully assessing the body of a man lying on the floor.

How would Terra face a scene as monstrous as this? How would she ever get over the horror of watching her husband die?

His eyes searched the massive bedroom, coming to rest on Terra curled up against the large armoire along the wall, a blanket over her naked body, her face white with shock and God knows what other emotions. He wanted to go to her, to pull her into his arms, tell her that everything would be all right. His years of training as a police officer and a detective held him back. He couldn't touch her and risk further contaminating the scene. He had to remain focused on finding the bastards who'd done this.

He'd seen this look many times before on other victims, but never on the face of someone he'd loved, like Terra. Someone he'd planned to marry and then abandoned for the sake of a lying, cheating woman he'd been foolish enough to get tricked by. He'd always prided himself on being smart where grasping women were concerned, but he'd fallen for the biggest con of all—a claim of paternity against him. Shit! Life could be a bitch.

Yet, despite the horror surrounding him, he couldn't help but look at Terra. Her tangled hair hid her high cheekbones. Her face devoid of makeup still held a loveliness he hadn't been able to get out of his mind for three years, eleven months and—*Stop this!*

He waited, hoping to have a few words with the ME, away from Terra. Whatever her state of mind, it would not help her to hear the clinical assessment of her husband's demise.

His heart pounded slow and hard in his chest as he surveyed the rest of the room from the door—the cooling body, the pooling blood. A young female officer talked in quiet tones to Terra, whose eyes remained on her husband. Derrick signaled the Medical Examiner to approach him.

"The man's throat was slit. Time of death, about a half hour ago, based on the wife's description of events."

"Two assailants?"

"The wife says yes. She'd gone to set the alarm before going to bed. She discovered the door open on the lower level, and two men in ski masks overpowered her. They dragged her upstairs and into the bedroom, threatening to kill her if she tried anything."

"What else did she tell you?"

"Only that one of the men tried to rape her. She tried to tear off his mask, but didn't see his face. She couldn't remember if either of them wore gloves."

Derrick's chest tightened. His eyes moved to Terra again, wishing he could help her, maybe ease the emotional pain that would haunt her for a very long time. "She looks like death," he said, trying to contain his anger.

"We need to get her out of here, away from the scene. We're going to send her to the hospital for a rape kit, and to gather any forensic evidence on her skin. She says she kicked the man who tried to rape her in the stomach," the Medical Examiner said.

"When you give the go ahead, I'll take her to the hospital."

"Oh… Do you know her?"

"I do."

The ME cleared his throat and squinted at Derrick. "There's an ambulance waiting to take her to the hospital."

After what had happened between them, going with Terra to the hospital was the least he could do. "You need the ambulance to transport the body. I'll let Detective Wilson know I'm leaving with Mrs. Cameron."

From her position on the floor of her bedroom Terra felt numb, disoriented as if she were watching a horror movie.

"Breathe slowly, in through your nose, out through your mouth, Mrs. Cameron," the officer said soothingly. But Terra was beyond listening. Sean was dead. He'd died in her arms, his blood seeping through her fingers as she watched in a blur of agony and disbelief.

She remained immobilized against the hard wood of the armoire. Vaguely aware that someone had put a blanket around her to cover her nakedness, she tried to focus on the room where Sean had been killed.

There was a man working around Sean's lifeless body. The room felt cold and empty. She felt afraid and alone. The female officer with her seemed so kind, her words sympathetic, but the woman didn't understand. Sean would never look at her again. Would never smile or laugh. Never make love to her. Her eyes were drawn to the king-size bed, the spill of sheets over the side, and suddenly she was back there—kicking at the man trying to rape her. She could see him as if he were still in the room, the hate in his eyes, the rancid smell of body odor washing over her. She gasped at the memory.

"Come on," the woman said, reaching for her hand to pull her up. "Let's get you out of here."

"I can't leave him," Terra whispered, her heart slamming into her chest at the thought of leaving Sean alone.

"He is going to be moved in a few minutes. It would be better if you weren't in the room."

She glanced up at the officer who was holding out her hand. She looked vaguely familiar, perhaps from the hospital where she worked. This time she took it and eased herself to her feet.

"Come with me," the officer said gently and led her from the room toward the bedroom across the hall. "You sit here for a minute while I go back in and get you some clothes."

Terra sat on the edge of the bed, hugging the blanket close to her body. Her legs trembled as the images flooded her mind again… Sean's face…

She clutched the blanket tighter around her.

The woman came back in with her clothes. "Do you need me to help you get dressed?" the officer asked.

"No," Terra said, as she held the blanket against her trembling body.

"Then I'll wait outside," the officer said, turning to leave and closing the door behind her.

Terra's fingers fumbled as she fastened her bra, pulled on a shirt and squirmed into a pair of jeans. The fabric felt rough against her legs and her hip pained from the force of the kick she'd landed on her attacker.

The officer returned a few minutes later. "You're dressed. That's good."

"What happens now?" Terra asked.

"You'll be taken to the hospital for an examination. For purposes of the investigation we need to see if any of the assailant's DNA was left on your body when he tried to rape you."

The word smashed around the room, tearing at the quiet space, obliterating her thoughts. "He didn't rape me. I fought him off."

"Even so, we need to check for any trace evidence that might still be on you," the officer said softly but firmly.

Terra swallowed. She didn't care what they did. Her reason for living lay dead in the room across the hall. The baby they conceived together would grow up without a father.

"Wait here," the officer said.

Terra remained sitting on the side of the bed, trying to block out the chaotic memories that flashed across her mind. Tears eased over her cheeks. She didn't know how long she sat there. It was as if time receded, as if life had stopped.

The door opened quietly. She glanced up.

"Terra, I'm so sorry for your loss," Derrick O'Leary said.

What was he doing here? What cruel twist of fate brought him into her house, into her private space? The last thing she wanted to do was share her grief with this man... His appearance was an intrusion, and for a second, anger flared.

Derrick couldn't help but stare at the woman from his past. The woman he'd realized he loved—but too late. Though still beautiful, she looked as if she'd been tossed from a moving vehicle. He wanted to pull her to him and block the images he knew were terrorizing her mind. Two things held him back: He had a duty to see that she got to the hospital and he knew, without a doubt that him touching her was the last thing she wanted. Her eyes said it all. He was not welcome.

Yet he had no choice but to do what needed to be done. He had to get her to the hospital. Gently he helped her up and led her down the hall. They left the house through the door next to the garage so he could get her into his vehicle as quietly as possible. As he opened the door, a reporter shouted from beyond the yellow tape, "Mrs. Cameron, can you tell us what happened in there?".

Seeing the fear on Terra's face he reconsidered taking her in his car. The ambulance would provide protection from the relentless intrusion of the media.

Another reporter shouted out a comment. Terra stumbled, her gaze flying to Derrick's face. He steadied her as he moved toward the waiting ambulance. He was about to help her up into the vehicle, when someone in the crowd of onlookers shouted. "Terra Cameron. Is your husband dead?"

Terra gave a soft cry and collapsed toward the hard concrete of the driveway. Derrick's arm shot out, catching her as she slid toward the ground. Acting on instinct he picked her up in his arms, his eyes locked on hers as he held her tight against him.

"Derrick!" Her single word held so much pain, so much desperation he wanted to take her somewhere safe, away from the reality of the night. But he had no choice except to keep going to the waiting ambulance.

As she was helped inside, Derrick stood shielding her from the flashing cameras and cell phones, willing the two EMTs to move faster. At the moment, he couldn't look at Terra let alone interrogate her. He regretted that she would have to face his questions later, would have to recount what had happened tonight, not only for him, but for a jury during the murder trial.

He settled her then returned to his car and keyed the ignition. Calmly he followed the ambulance through the winding streets, relieved that Meaghan was at the crime scene while he followed Terra.

Though it had been four years, seeing her again felt as if he'd never lost touch with her. Other than the obvious stress on her face, and the pallor of her skin, she looked the same to him.

As the two vehicles approached the ambulance entrance, he parked along the curb. He intended to prepare her for what happened next. He approached her stretcher as the ambulance doors were opened. "Terra, you'll be examined and a rape kit done. I'll be present—"

She raised her head and glanced at him. "I know why I'm here. They're going to do a rape kit. I was attacked. I wasn't raped, but they're doing a rape kit. My husband is dead! I just want to go home." Her voice broke.

"That won't be possible until we finish processing the scene and gathering evidence."

"I don't care. I want to go home. I want to go…" She glanced toward the ambulance bay as if she hadn't seen it before. Yet he knew she had worked there at one time.

"I don't care," she repeated, her voice empty as her eyes moved back to her hands, resting in her lap.

He followed her stretcher into her assigned room, away from the others, a cubicle with glass walls and privacy curtains. When they entered the space, Terra was moved from the stretcher to the bed: She didn't say a word, didn't glance in his direction. He understood how much she didn't want him there.

The EMT's left the room. "Can I get you anything? A glass of water, maybe?" he asked as a nurse brushed past him with an examination tray in her hands.

She stared at her hands. "Nothing."

He eased away from the entrance to the cubicle, waiting just outside until the doctor arrived. When Dr. Allen came down the corridor toward him, Derrick nodded, relieved that someone he knew and who was extremely competent was going to do the examination. The doctor glanced at the chart in her hands. "Terra Cameron?"

"Yes. She's the victim of assault and attempted rape. Her husband Sean Cameron is dead from a knife wound."

"Oh!" Dr. Allen's face reflected the shock in her voice.

Without another word, she went into the cubicle. He could hear the doctor's words of introduction and explanation, and Terra's soft words of compliance with the doctor's requests.

But he wasn't so interested in that, as he was in the three people coming down the corridor toward him. "Oh, shit!" he muttered, walking toward them and away from Terra, intending to keep them from barging into her room.

"We're looking for my sister-in-law, Terra Cameron. Are you the police officer assigned to protect her?"

He wouldn't have used those words, but he did want to protect Terra as well as her right not to be disturbed by the arrogant man standing in front of him. Terra's brother-in-law stood, blocking Derrick's view of Olivia Cameron, mother and matriarch of the Cameron family—another force to be reckoned with. He knew the story of the Cameron boys: They had been twins, Shamus and Sean, so the mousy woman trailing behind them was likely Shamus's wife, Bethany.

"I'm Detective Derrick O'Leary. I'm part of the team investigating the incident at your brother's home this evening."

"Incident! My brother's dead!" Shamus thrust his face forward, his intention clear. "I want to see my sister-in-law," Shamus ordered.

"You can't see Mrs. Cameron yet. She is being examined

by the doctor. You'll have to wait," Derrick said, matching the other man's tone and inflection.

Inside the cubicle Terra lay on the stretcher waiting for the exam to be over. The doctor had been kind, the nurse efficient. Terra didn't recognize the nurse, and wondered why. Terra worked in the surgical intensive care unit she usually made it out to coffee and lunch breaks, yet she couldn't remember ever seeing this nurse before. But at a time like this, what difference did that make? It was suddenly a relief to simply focus on the present.

The doctor had done a thorough examination, asking questions, about what had occurred between her and her attacker. Terra answered her questions, telling her that she and Sean had been intimate that evening, and that they were expecting a baby.

"Is my baby okay?" Terra asked, placing her hand over her abdomen.

"Everything seems to be fine. Although I suggest you get in to see your obstetrician as soon as you can."

The doctor asked more questions about her general health and what, if any, prescriptions or supplements she was taking. Terra had trouble focusing on the doctor's questions, the fear of the past hours bubbling through her, making her feel lightheaded, as if she weren't a part of what was going on.

"By your description and the pain you describe from kicking at your assailant, you will probably have some pretty sore muscles by tomorrow morning. I want you to know that what you did, the strength and presence of mind demonstrated, almost certainly saved you from being raped. Have you taken any training in self defense?"

"Yes. I learned to kick box, and I'm working on my black belt in karate."

"Impressive. What made you decide to do that?"

"Because I felt I needed to."

"There are days when I wish I knew how to kick box.

It's a zoo around here, particularly when the moon is full."

Dr. Allen pulled off her rubber gloves and dropped them onto the open tray while the nurse gathered all the samples, labeled them and put them into plastic bags to be taken to the lab.

"We're finished here. The detective is waiting outside." The doctor touched her arm, a touch both clinical and caring. "You've been through a horrible experience. Be kind to yourself. And if you have any issues, like not being able to sleep, or anxiety call your family doctor."

The curtain closed behind the nurse and Dr. Allen. Terra lay back against the raised head of the stretcher, her mind numb. She'd like to go to sleep for a little while…

The rattle of the rings against the curtain rod startled her. Expecting to see Derrick O'Leary, she glanced over.

"When did you plan to tell us that Sean had been killed?" Shamus demanded, striding into the room toward her. Olivia followed behind him, her expression like stone, eyes dark, her body rigid and unyielding.

"I've…I… The police have been at the house since it happened. They were questioning me—"

"Why didn't you save him? You're a nurse, for God's sake! Why didn't you do something?" Shamus said.

Olivia moved to the other side of the stretcher, the Cameron family bracketing Terra, closing in on her. She wanted to run home, to lock the doors and never come out again. "Terra you can understand why we're upset," Olivia said.

"My twin brother dies and I have to hear the news from the police chief?"

Olivia glanced quickly at her son, and back at Terra. "Why are you in here? Were you hurt?"

"I was attacked by one of the men. He tried to rape me."

"Where was Sean?" Shamus interjected.

"The other man was holding a knife on him."

"Did Sean try to stop your attacker? Is that it?"

"Sean couldn't move. I managed to fight the man off. By the time I got free of the man, Sean was lying on the floor, his throat…bleeding." She sobbed, once again seeing the pleading in Sean's eyes as he slowly died in her arms.

Shamus stepped back, disbelief registering on his face. "You were there. You're a nurse. Why didn't you stop the bleeding?"

"I tried. When I got to him he was lying so still…"

"You weren't able to help him?" Olivia asked, her tone disbelieving.

Shamus clenched his fists at his sides his eyes bright and speculating. "You could have stopped them."

"No! They grabbed me, forced me to go to the bedroom with them. They were looking for Sean."

"Like hell they were! They were looking for money. That's what was going on. They wouldn't have killed Sean if you'd used your karate skills on them. You let my brother die."

"No! I didn't. I was trying to protect…" Her voice jammed in her throat. She had been trying to protect her baby. She had been looking out for their child.

She stared at Shamus, then at Olivia. Did they really blame her for Sean's death? Surely they knew how much she loved him.

CHAPTER THREE

Outside Derrick was making small talk with Bethany, a woman clearly in awe of the Cameron family. "How long have you and Shamus been married?" he asked, more as a distraction than anything else. His was a losing battle to keep his thoughts away from Terra.

"Our second anniversary is in two months and seven days," she said, twisting the wedding band and diamond solitaire around and around on her finger. The repetition of it would have been damn near hypnotic if Derrick hadn't had something more important on his mind.

"I met Shamus when I was working for Mother Cameron. I was her assistant during the huge fundraising campaign for the new wing of the hospital. We got along really well; became friends sort of. I was so lucky to get that job. I mean it was such a good job. I met a lot of important people, and Olivia came to rely on me to do just about everything around her office. She often told me that I'd be perfect for her son Shamus. She wanted him to settle down, become more serious about his life and his career. While she was running the campaign, she had an office in the same building as Cameron Industries, and one day Shamus dropped in to see her." She gave a triumphant smile. "We started dating, and like they say, the rest is history."

Derrick stared at her for a minute, trying to figure out what Shamus could have seen in this mousey woman. The wealthy, eligible Shamus Cameron had dated a lot of women, or so the story went, and then one day the whole town was buzzing with the news that Shamus Cameron was going to marry a woman from New York that he'd met on a business trip. A couple of months later the relationship ended. No one knew why, or if they knew, they weren't saying. Later people speculated that Shamus had to have been on the rebound when he married Bethany. Or maybe he did it to please his mother. Who knew? And at this point, who cared? Derrick certainly didn't.

Bethany sniffed, wiped her cheek and shifted from one foot to the other. "Sean is. I mean *was* a wonderful man. We all loved him. How could you not?" She shrugged. "He and Shamus. They…" She hesitated. "They were close."

"They worked together as well," Derrick said, giving her an encouraging smile hoping she'd continue. Family relationships often held the key to solving a crime.

"Yeah." Bethany smoothed her hands over her hair. "Shamus is the head of… operations, I think it's called, but Sean had the more responsible job. He was CEO of Cameron Industries." She smiled up into his eyes. "You can imagine that most of our family dinners were all about the business. Mother Cameron didn't object though because she loved to hear her sons talk about the business her daddy and her husband had started."

Mother Cameron. Who says that anymore?

"Is the Cameron family a member of any church?" Derrick asked, wondering what part of his brain that question came from.

Bethany's eyes lit up, her face animated. "The Cameron family have been Catholic for generations. But Sean and Shamus haven't been involved in the church, although I'm sure they donate a lot of money," she said, her smile twisting downward as her gaze moved beyond Derrick. "I wonder how much longer they'll be? I wanted to go in, but Shamus said no." She moved a little closer and looked up into Derrick's eyes. "Do you think it would be appropriate for me to pray with Terra? I really believe that in awful times like this, prayer is the only answer."

Derrick eased back a bit. "You'll have to ask Terra." He was pretty sure Terra wouldn't care one way or the other.

"I really love Terra. She's like a sister to me. We share everything. I want to help her—"

A sudden outburst from behind the curtain fueled Derrick's rush to step inside the space. Terra was crying. Olivia stood at the end of the stretcher, her face a mask of pain and sorrow. Shamus stood next to Terra, his wide hand braced on the headboard, his face red.

"Okay. I think it's time for everyone to give Mrs. Cameron a little space." Derrick held the drape aside for them, indicating that they were to leave.

Relieved they were gone, he turned his attention to Terra. "How are you doing?" he asked, approaching the bed.

"Awful." She gulped for air. Swiped at her wet cheeks and pulled the sheet closer to her chest. "I want to go home."

"I'm not sure that's the best place for you right now. There will still be police tape up. The press will almost certainly be waiting there."

She reached for a tissue from the box on the table next to the bed. Derrick noted that her hands were shaking. "Terra. Is there anywhere else you could go for tonight?"

"Yes. My sister, Carolyn's."

Derrick remembered Carolyn well. She was older than Terra, a librarian whose life was devoted to her job and her parents until they passed away. Derrick always had a niggling suspicion that Carolyn was jealous of Terra. If so, having Terra married to one of the richest men in the city must have been a sticking point between the two of them.

"I'll call your sister for you right now."

Terra swung her legs over the side of the stretcher. "Then I need to get home and pack a bag."

"I'll go with you. I have questions about what occurred tonight."

Terra frowned. "But Officer Wilson already asked me a whole lot of questions. Can't this wait?"

He saw tears flood her eyes and wished he weren't a police officer.

They drove in silence except for the occasional clicking of the lane change indicator and the sounds of the car's engine. Terra rubbed her arms, as if touching her skin would wipe away the memories circling her mind, memories that confused her with their intensity. She couldn't close her eyes without seeing Sean's face, his eyes pleading with her to save him: And as they replayed, her fear blocked any rational thought as it had during those indescribable minutes before he died.

Why hadn't she been able to save him? She had worked an Emergency Room nurse for years and now was an intensive care nurse accustomed to responding instantly in an emergency, saving the lives of countless patients with her quick thinking and quicker reflexes.

The sky, bracketed by the avenue of trees leading to her home, held a hint of pink, signaling the dawn of a new day. Her first day without Sean. She couldn't imagine what this day would feel like, how she would cope without her husband to turn to, to seek his advice, laugh with him, but most of all to tell him the secret that would have made their life together perfect. She clutched her hands and buried them in her lap to keep from crying.

"Is either of your garage bays empty?" Derrick asked.

His words, the first since they'd left the hospital startled her. "Ah…yes. Sean's car is at the dealership for something. I don't remember what."

"Do you have your house keys?"

Her fingers felt around the bottom of her bag. "Yes."

"Okay. A police officer will be at the house. If anyone is waiting outside, you duck down. I'll pull into the driveway, go into the house and unlock the garage door, then I'll drive the car in so that you won't be seen."

He pulled into the driveway, empty except for a patrol car. "I'll just be a minute," he said, getting out of the car and going toward the house. She watched him as if in a dream. She was back at her home, back to where it all happened…to where she'd lost everything.

When Derrick returned to the car and drove into the garage she felt the panic begin to rise in her chest. She gulped air as she tried to focus on getting out of the car. What was she going to do when she got inside the house?

"Terra, it's okay. I'm here and I'll stay with you if you need me."

She glanced across the seat at him. "I can do it," she said, opening the door and getting out before her courage abandoned her. In seconds she was standing in the hall where the stairs led to the lower level, where the house alarm keypad glowed green.

Suddenly the memories rushed back, filling her mind. "The alarm display said that there was a door ajar in the house. I went downstairs to check. I turned on the lights, saw that the motion detector light outside on the patio had come on and the patio door was open. I locked the door, and before I could do anything, a man grabbed me from behind, told me he'd kill me if I made a sound. He stunk so bad, and his hands were so rough."

"What then?" Derrick's words were gentle.

"He dragged me upstairs. When we got here, I remember thinking if I could get my legs up, kick out against the wall… Then I heard Sean's voice calling to me from the bedroom."

She walked into the kitchen, past the open concept living space toward the hall leading to the bedrooms. "The other man stepped past and got to the door of the bedroom first."

"Did they say anything about what they planned to do when they got there? Do you remember if they said anything to each other?"

She stood still, her eyes searching the cavernous kitchen, her head aching, her body trembling. "They said they were looking for Sean."

She sank into the closest chair. "They said they were

going to kill him. They were going to kill my husband." Her sobs were hard gasping sounds. She couldn't breathe.

Wanting to help her, Derrick took a glass from the cupboard, filled it with water and gave it to her.

Holding the glass with both hands she took a sip before putting it down.

Despite his anger at what had happened to her, he organized his thoughts. At first glance what happened here would look like a robbery gone wrong. But if the two men came looking to kill Sean Cameron, it would explain why nothing seemed to be missing. Why had Sean allowed the attacker to hold a knife on him while a man tried to rape his wife? Was the man with the knife a lot bigger than Sean? "Terra, can you describe these men? Were they tall?"

"Yes. They were about the same height. Both taller than me, both heavy set, I think."

"So, you got to the bedroom, what happened then?"

"They told me to keep quiet." She stared at her hands.

"Did one of them have a knife?"

"I didn't see one… Not until we were in the bedroom. No. That's not true. I didn't see the knife until I fell onto the floor. The other man—"

"Not the one trying to rape you, correct?"

"Yes. He was near the bathroom door, holding the knife." She closed her eyes, reaching out as if to catch something. "He was bent over Sean. Sean was on the floor. There was blood all around Sean. I tried to get to him, stop the blood. It wouldn't stop."

"Where were the men?"

"I… I don't know. They were somewhere in the room I think." She pressed her fingers to her forehead. "No. They must have gone. I heard a door slam. We have a panic button. I had to leave Sean, get the button out of the drawer and press it. I left Sean bleeding, bleeding so much. But I couldn't think of what else to do. If I hadn't left him…"

Derrick wanted to hold her and comfort her. Instead he took her hands, sandwiching them between his own. Her hands were cold. She stared at the ceiling, pools of tears shimmering beneath her lashes. He'd seen shock and fear many times in his career, but this time it was different…personal. "Terra, it wouldn't have mattered what you did. Sean was bleeding too quickly from the knife wound to his throat. You couldn't have saved him. No one could."

"But I'm a nurse. There should have been something I could have done." She looked straight at him, daring him to deny her statement.

He shook his head. "You're lucky they didn't kill you. Remember, you're the only witness to what happened last night."

"A witness who doesn't remember much."

"Not true. Here's what we're going to do. Once your sister gets here, you'll take a few things from your room and go with her. It's not unusual for a witness to remember things once the initial shock begins to ease. If you remember anything, anything at all… A color. A smell. Their eyes. Anything. Call me." He dug a pen out of his pocket and put his personal cell phone number on the back of his business card.

"I want you to call me." He studied her face. "And Terra, you'll get through this. I'm here to see that you do." He wanted to say more, to offer his apology for the stupid way he'd behaved toward her, years before, but now was not the time.

The officer on duty came into the kitchen. "There's a Carolyn Billings claiming that she's here to pick up Mrs. Cameron."

"My sister," Terra said, relief evident in her voice. "She'll help me get my things."

Derrick watched her leave the kitchen to the jingling tones of his cell phone.

"O'Leary."

"It's me," Meaghan said.

Derrick waved the officer off. "What's going on?"

"No forensics yet, but it's early. The neighborhood canvas didn't turn up much. Sean and Terra were quiet neighbors, no big parties, no noise. No one saw anything out of the ordinary during the time in question."

"So the men who did this were careful not to draw attention to themselves, maybe passing themselves off as repairmen or deliverymen…suggesting that the murder was planned."

"The question is by whom," Meaghan said.

"Ideas?"

"Well, we could start with the wife."

"Why?" Derrick asked, surprised at what his partner was suggesting.

"We have no other witnesses to the events inside the house, and no one outside that saw anything. We have no reason to believe Mrs. Cameron's version of events."

"But we have no reason *not* to believe her." He wanted to say more, to defend Terra, but decided not to. Now was not the time to argue with his partner.

"Let's wait and see," Meaghan said. "In the meantime the press is calling for a story."

"You passed them over to media relations, I assume," he said.

"I did." There was a long pause accompanied by the background noise of the squad room.

He knew that silence. When Meaghan was concerned about something it took her a little while to say what she was thinking. "Something on your mind?" he asked.

"This might be the time for us to talk about your connection to Mrs. Cameron," Meaghan began.

"Why would my connection, as you call it, matter? She's a friend."

"Are you sure that's all?"

He wanted to tell her to mind her own business, but Meaghan was usually sympathetic to female victims. Had she heard something about his past with Terra? Something she wanted to get out in the open? "What's going on with you?" he asked.

"Will you be biased toward Mrs. Cameron? I need to know."

Surprised at Meaghan's question, he was about to respond when he decided against it. They were on the same team. She had his back as he did hers. "There's nothing for you to be concerned about. Let's just do our jobs. I'm finished here. Mrs. Cameron is going home with her sister."

~~~

Terra was so relieved to see her sister, to feel Carolyn's arms around her. Her sister's words of consolation and caring rushed into the bottomless void created by Sean's death.

"I'm so sorry, Terra. I love you, and I'm here for you," Carolyn whispered as they hugged and swayed in the middle of the living room.

Carolyn held Terra's shoulders and looked into her eyes, her expression highlighting her concern. "Why didn't you call me sooner? I would have been here."

"I've been… They needed to test my skin, take my fingerprints, move Sean. I had to go the hospital to be examined."

"It's okay, the police told me. I'm here now, and I'm taking you home with me. That's okay, is it?" Carolyn asked, her gaze moving from her sister to Derrick.

"Absolutely. Your sister needs to rest. To feel safe."

"I'll see to it." She hugged Terra close again.

Moving as if in an awful dream Terra went down the hall, stopping at the bedroom door. She cried out at the sight of her husband's blood still darkening the carpet.

Carolyn clutched her hand. "I'll get your things for you." She crossed the room, passed the spot where Sean had died and returned with jeans, shirts, nightie, underwear and shoes.

"You're doing fine," Carolyn said as she helped her fill a small suitcase taken from the top shelf of the closet. Her movements were hurried, and she spilled the contents of Terra's makeup bag onto the floor. "Darn!" she said, scooping things up, snapping the suitcase closed.

"Please be careful," Terra warned, suddenly fearful that Carolyn might step on the spot where Sean had died.

Carolyn led Terra out of the house to the car then opened the back door and put the suitcase on the seat. "Get in, Terra. We have to get you away from here as fast as we can."

Terra slid into the front seat, snapped the seatbelt in place and stared at her sister.

"Are you okay?" Terra asked her sister.

"No. I'm not." Carolyn brushed her hair off her face, sniffed and looked across at Terra. "Someone killed your husband last night. They might be waiting around here for you," she said, her lips compressed in a tight line, her hands gripping the wheel. "I'm getting you out of here. I told you a long time ago that marrying someone like Sean Cameron was a mistake. Now, someone's killed him. I'll call the police tomorrow morning and tell them you need protection."

The engine roared to life.

Carolyn's house was on the other side of town, a neat blue-and-white story and a half, about a block from what had been the train station when there were still passenger trains servicing the area. Terra hadn't been to her sister's house in months because their relationship had been strained ever since their mother died. Carolyn had inherited the family home, in part because she'd moved home to look after Doris Billings. Carolyn had refused to put their mother into a care facility, opting instead to care for her in the home.

Terra hadn't agreed with that decision, her experience and training dictating how she felt about it. She knew that with a steady decline in her mother's mental health, a professional institution was the better choice, and a safer choice. But Carolyn saw Terra's position being in favor of abandoning their mother to some nursing home where caregivers would have been indifferent, at best.

Yet as they sat in the familiar living room with Carolyn's collection of folk art paintings, Terra vowed that somehow they would repair their relationship. She didn't want to be without her sister in her life ever again. "Thank you for picking me up."

"That's what sisters do," Carolyn replied. "And I meant it when I said you need protection."

"Please, let's not argue tonight," Terra pleaded. "I'm exhausted."

Carolyn relented. "I know you are."

"I'd like to lie down. I'm so…so tired," Terra said, feeling as if a heavy weight was pushing down on her.

"Sure. Do you need anything to eat or drink before you go up to bed? I could fix you a bit of breakfast, toast maybe?"

Terra hadn't eaten anything since the dinner she'd shared with Sean. "No. I couldn't touch food right now. But thanks. I just want to lie down."

They climbed the stairs together, Carolyn leading the way and carrying Terra's small piece of luggage.

Somewhere in the recesses of her mind a headache rose slowly, gaining her attention, making her feel nauseated. By forcing her feet forward she made it into the bedroom at the top of the stairs.

Carolyn went to the closet and brought out a cotton nightie. "Here, put this on. You can unpack your clothes later."

Just then the phone rang. Carolyn picked up and answered in a quiet voice before looking across at Terra. "You-know-who wants to talk to you."

It had to be Kevin… How had her friend figured out where she was so quickly? But then, Kevin Jackson had been there through every part of her life. Of course he'd be there for her now. "No surprise, I suppose," she said as she reached for the phone.

Terra put her ear to the phone. A deep voice cut across the early morning quiet. "I heard what happened. I'm coming over."

"Kevin, this isn't a good time to talk."

"I'm not leaving you alone in the middle of this. What a mess! Peter is really worried about how this will end. He has the mayor on his case, and he doesn't have a suspect."

Terra tried to focus on what her friend was saying. She and Sean had been two of the very few people that knew Kevin's boyfriend was the police chief. Kevin insisted on keeping his personal life private. Those who knew the truth had respected their wishes.

"Terra, what can I do?"

"Nothing. There's nothing anyone can do. Sean's dead."

"Peter says they think someone was sent to kill him?" Kevin asked.

Hearing her friend say the words made it so real. Unbidden, images of horror and loss invaded her mind. She clamped her hands tighter around the phone and focused on the chest of drawers at the foot of the bed. She studied every curve of the wood, noting the color—anything and everything to keep her mind from charging back to those moments in the lower level of her house, and the terrifying scene that unfolded in their bedroom.

"Kevin, I can't talk right now. Don't come over. I've been up all night. I have to go to bed."

"I understand completely. So sorry for your loss, Terra. Please stay safe, honey. Call me when you wake up. I'll come over to Carolyn's house later and keep you company if you need me. Right now you're in shock. I would be."

"Thanks, Kevin."

When she hung up, her sister was standing near the door with a steaming mug in her hands. "I brought you a cup of chamomile tea. You need to sleep, to forget what happened. This will help you relax, maybe even get some sleep."

Terra looked up into her sister's face, saw the caring in her eyes, and realized that her sister would almost certainly remain near her while she slept. "Please don't worry about me. There's no need for you to babysit me."

"Not worry? You can't expect me not to worry. Someone killed Sean and hurt you."

It felt as if her sister was talking about someone else's life, not hers. As Terra sipped the tea she heard the worry and anger in her sister's voice. But she couldn't think about that now, or anything else. She was too tired, too heartsick and too lost to concentrate on anything. Closing her eyes, she sank into the bed, pulled the duvet up around her shoulders and turned toward the wall.

Later that morning Derrick was about to leave for the

precinct when a call came in from the police chief's secretary ordering him to a meeting at eleven.

Derrick checked in with Meaghan before heading upstairs to the chief's office. Once there he stood in front of the police chief's desk, trying to contain his annoyance with the man in the chair. It was clear that Peter Lynch was angry and had decided that Derrick was a safe target for his anger.

"Okay, let me get this straight," Peter Lynch said, his voice heavy with sarcasm. "You're escorting Terra Cameron to the waiting ambulance when she collapses. You help her avoid injury when she collapses by gathering her in an embrace."

"Not an embrace, sir. I was the only one close enough to break her fall."

The police chief moved out from behind his desk, picked up a remote and clicked a button. The TV mounted high on the wall next to his desk was flooded with a news clip showing Derrick holding Terra in what could be misconstrued as an ardent embrace if someone didn't know the circumstances. "Sir, what would you have wanted me to do? Let her fall?"

"I don't care for your tone, but I'll ignore it for the present. What matters here is that a member of my police force had a relationship with Terra Cameron, and was seen holding her in a very intimate way, immediately after the murder of her husband. Do you know what the press will do with this if they find out your connection to this woman?"

"Are you saying you want me off the case?" Derrick asked, surprised by where the conversation was going.

The police chief turned off the TV and circled the room, coming to stand at the window, his hands clasped behind him as he gazed out at the street. "What I'm saying is that the optics aren't good on this. Cameron Industries is a major employer in this town. Olivia Cameron has a lot of influence, and I've already had a long, unpleasant chat with Shamus about what we're doing and where the investigation is headed. It would seem that Shamus, and probably Olivia, believe that Terra was somehow involved in Sean's death—and they're pointing fingers."

"But sir, Terra was nearly raped. How could she be considered a suspect?"

"Things are not always what they seem. We can't jump to any conclusions, but at the same time we have to do our jobs. That means we have to find the two men who did this as quickly as possible. I want you to consider all options. I want you to report directly to me. And Detective Wilson will be given a major role in this investigation should it become necessary to remove you. Your history with Mrs. Cameron might be misunderstood. I have to keep this investigation free of any form of controversy. You understand that."

Cautionary words straight out of the protect-your-ass handbook as far as he could see. But he had to go along with his boss. He had no choice.

"Officer Wilson and I will share everything. She's my partner and I trust her completely, sir. And she trusts me," he added hurriedly.

"Then, you'd better get going. Remember, keep me informed," he warned.

Derrick went back to his office, closed the door and tried to think. Something about the details of the crime stirred a memory of another crime that happened a few years before. Glancing outside his office to see who might be watching, he pulled his private cell phone out of the inside pocket of his leather jacket and dialed a number he'd memorized a few years ago, but had never had a reason to call. Until now.

CHAPTER FOUR

When Terra woke, the sun sketched a long low line across her bed. She was back in her bedroom, in the home she'd grown up in with her sister and her parents. In the same room where Carolyn had announced she was going to be a librarian and teach children to read. Terra remembered it well. Carolyn had also announced that she wanted to write children's books and biographies, and wrote her first children's story in high school.

But why was she in the bedroom of her childhood in her parents' house? She squinted at the walls that now held different photos than she remembered. *How could that be? Why was she here? What had happened that brought her back here?* She gasped as she spotted the small suitcase that Sean had given her. Like an avalanche causing blocks of memories to careen over a cliff face, it all came back to her. Trembling she sat up, tears running down her cheeks, her breath coming in short gasps.

Sean was dead.

She clutched her abdomen, willing her baby to be safe. But that only led to more tears and sorrow, knowing that Sean would never know, let alone hold his baby—never see how wonderful their life would have been as a family.

A phone ringing somewhere downstairs startled her. It

was answered immediately. She could hear her sister talking low in a muffled but earnest tone to someone she obviously needed to speak with.

She drifted off to sleep again, lulled by the mumbled sounds of her sister's voice. She was talking to someone, her tone urgent, but Terra couldn't make out any of the words. Later, she stirred at the sound of the phone ringing again. This time she heard Carolyn clearly. "Just a minute. I'll see if she's awake." Terra could hear her sister climbing the stairs, heading toward her room.

"It's Derrick O'Leary. He needs to talk to you," she said as she poked her head through the doorway. "Are you up to it?"

Terra sat up, her head swimming for a few seconds. "I'm not sure," she said, her stomach churning.

A few more steps and Carolyn was beside Terra's bed. "He sounds pretty concerned," Carolyn said, holding out the phone to her.

"Yes?" she asked, holding the phone to her ear, forcing her eyes to remain open.

"Terra, I checked on you a couple of times during the night and you were asleep."

"Last night?" She must have slept all day and through the night. Had Sean died almost two days ago? How could she have slept that long? All she had going to bed was a cup of chamomile tea. So why did she feel as if she'd been drugged?

"Yeah, it's nearly eight in the morning."

Terra pushed the hair off her face in resignation, wishing she could just go back to sleep. But there were things to do: By now Sean's family would be anxious to arrange the funeral, an event that would need a lot of planning. And she'd slept all this time.

"Why are you calling?"

Derrick had called twice the day before and both times he'd been told that Terra was sleeping. That was really hard to believe because when they'd been together, Terra seldom slept through the night. Maybe she'd taken a sleeping pill. He would have.

After he talked to the chief, he'd begun to pull the available evidence together—which wasn't much as yet. Luckily the cause of death was clear. But the neighbors offered nothing: There were no eyewitnesses and the ME report would take days.

He'd called Shamus's office requesting an interview and had been given the name of his lawyer. When he met with Shamus and his lawyer, he asked Shamus about his whereabouts for the night in question. Shamus said he'd been home with his wife and seemed affronted by the police questions. The man had been aggressive during the interview, raising Derrick's hackles and making him suspicious. But since he had nothing to go on that would implicate Shamus he had no reason to question him further—for now.

His gut told him that Shamus was involved somehow, but with good lawyers and an alibi it would take time to figure out how. Derrick knew that without good reason they wouldn't be able to obtain a warrant to get into Cameron Industries.

He and Meaghan had been working for over an hour with all the available information spread out in front of them. They looked at each piece from every angle possible, starting with the idea that it had been a home invasion gone wrong...

Derrick didn't buy that...mostly because of what Terra had described when he took her back to the house. The intruders had stated, clearly, that they went into the house with the intention of killing Sean Cameron.

Meaghan's theory was that the wife had hired the two men to kill her husband. He'd need some pretty strong evidence implicating Terra before he'd see that scenario as the most likely. Besides, Terra wasn't capable of killing another human being. He remembered the day her gold fish died—the flood of tears over a fish, of all things.

Then there were the police chief's insinuations about his relationship with Terra: He had to be scrupulous in his investigation or face being removed from the case. But after listening to Meaghan's theory about Terra being a prime suspect he was out of sorts. He decided to leave the office and go for a walk to clear his head.

Meaghan had volunteered to go with him, but he turned her down. He didn't want his partner encouraging and listening to his thoughts about Terra and his belief that Terra wasn't involved in any way. Once out of the office he dialed Carolyn's number. He had to warn Terra that she needed to protect herself; just in case Meaghan's theory received consideration.

He dialed the number and Terra's sister answered immediately. She assured him Terra had slept long enough and it was time to wake her. He waited until Terra was woken up and could take the phone.

"Terra, it's me." He took a deep breath, suddenly aware of how he'd come across sharing this with her, or how she might take his warning to protect herself. Yet he felt he had no choice but to say what he had to say. "As your friend… As the officer in charge of the investigation, I think it would be in your best interest to call a lawyer who specializes in criminal law."

"What! Why should I do that?"

"Because this investigation is looking at all possible scenarios. You need to protect yourself."

"From what? Am I a suspect?"

What could he say to that? "We… No. You're not."

"Then why are you telling me to get a lawyer?" she demanded.

"Everyone will be interviewed to determine the facts of the case. After what you've been through it would simply be better for you to have someone with you who is accustomed to the process involved in conducting an investigation."

After a short pause, Terra asked, "Have you identified either of the men who were in my house?"

"Not yet."

"Then, I don't see the point in getting a lawyer. Besides, I have Sean's funeral to arrange. I need to get in touch with Olivia."

"I understand that. But I've learned, over the years, that things can turn on a dime and it's good to be prepared," he said, wishing he could make her see how vulnerable she was.

"Is that all?" she asked.

"Yeah."

"Can I get into my house this morning? I need to find a few papers before I go over to the Cameron mansion."

"Sure. If you like, I can pick you up in about an hour and take you home. I don't think you should go in there alone, certainly not today."

"Carolyn will take me," she said, making it clear to him that she didn't want him with her.

"Fine. Is there anything else I can do for you?"

"Will you keep me informed about police progress in finding the two men?" she asked. Her formal tone placed further distance between them. He was the policeman on the case, nothing more.

"We're working on finding them, but if you should remember anything more, would you call me?" he asked.

"I will. I have to go now," Terra said, her voice low.

"I'll be in touch," he said and with those words he felt a strange loneliness bearing down on him and his gut ached with foreboding. Terra didn't seem to understand the seriousness of the situation and he'd done a poor job explaining it. Perhaps he wasn't the best person for this job...

He knew enough about human behavior, that if she became a suspect in the death of her husband the Cameron family would close ranks, and Terra would be on her own.

Once off the phone from speaking with Derrick, Terra went downstairs. His words still echoed in her head. She had hoped his call was to tell her they'd found the attackers. Instead he'd suggested she hire a lawyer. Her head still felt fuzzy when went into the kitchen where Carolyn sat reading the paper at the kitchen table.

Glancing up, Carolyn folded the newspaper before

putting it down. "Coffee's on. I baked cranberry muffins. Your favorite."

"I feel as if I've been drugged."

"I put extra honey in your tea before you went to sleep. Maybe that was it."

"Why did you let me sleep so long?" Terra stifled a yawn.

Carolyn got up and poured them each a cup of coffee. "Thought you needed rest more than anything."

Terra glanced at her sister, noting the high color in her cheeks. Terra was momentarily distracted by the physical changes in her sister—her hair color was different; it was lighter and cut in a softer hairstyle and her arms were tanned. *Had Carolyn started using a tanning bed?*

"You're probably right. I feel better this morning after getting some sleep. Thanks for looking after me, sis."

"You're welcome," her sister said, pushing aside the folded paper revealing an article about Sean's death written by a reporter for the newspaper.

Terra averted her eyes, hoping to hold back the tears forming under her eyelids.

Seeing her distress, Carolyn flipped the newspaper over. "Oh. Sorry. You didn't need to see that."

Feeling so alone and still reeling from Derrick's call, she tried to eat a muffin but left most of it crumbled on the plate. Instead of eating more, she settled for a second cup of coffee. "I'd better get showered and dressed before we go over to the house."

"You're sure you want to do that?" Carolyn asked.

"Of course. I need to get started on the funeral arrangements."

Once she was dressed, they headed over to the house. There was still yellow tape, but there didn't seem to be anyone around. Terra climbed out of the car, and went to the door. Inside the house everything looked normal. She'd seen movies where police searched a house, leaving a mess behind. So, she guessed they hadn't searched hers, or they'd been careful to put things back.

In Sean's study she checked her voice mail. Maybe Olivia had already called. There were a dozen messages, words of condolence from friends, and a message from the reporter, Tim Martin, but no message from any of the Cameron family.

There was an urgent message from a Mr. Neill Baxter, claiming that he needed to talk to Sean, that he'd come by the house yesterday and no one answered the door. She wondered who the man was, but for now she couldn't focus on anything other than checking her home, seeing if everything was all right.

She hung up the phone and scanned the desk for Sean's laptop. He had all his business contacts on it. She'd need it when she went over to Olivia's house to talk about the funeral plans.

The laptop wasn't there. And neither was the brown envelope she remembered seeing on the edge of Sean's desk. He'd come home last night—no, two nights ago—saying that he wanted to talk about the information in the envelope.

"What is it?" her sister asked.

"Sean's laptop and a brown envelope are missing."

"Maybe someone moved them or took them as evidence. I'm betting the police. If they did, maybe you can get them back today."

Terra put a call in to the number on Derrick's business card. A woman answered. "Officer Megan Wilson, how can I help you?"

"It's Terra Cameron. Is Derrick, I mean Detective O'Leary there?"

"Not at the moment. Can I help you?" the officer repeated in a cooler voice.

"My husband's laptop is missing, along with a brown envelope from his desk. I'm trying to locate them."

"Are you at the house?"

"Yes. I needed to come back for a few things and a list of Sean's contacts."

"Understandable. Look, I'll check for those things, and

either Derrick or I will get back to you, Mrs. Cameron."

Feeling deflated because she couldn't reach Derrick directly, she glanced around the den at all the sailing trophies and the photographs of their life together. On the wall next to the bookshelves there was a painting of the sailboat Sean had owned. He'd sold the boat when they decided to start a family. He said he'd wait and get a smaller boat when his children were old enough to learn to sail.

The room doubled as her husband's home office and had been a place he really enjoyed working in. He'd always said that his home office was so much better than the one at Cameron Industries. Everywhere she looked, she was reminded of her loss, and the end of the life they'd been so excited about only days ago.

Leaving the room, she headed down the hall toward her bedroom. "Wait for me," Carolyn called out. "You shouldn't go near that room alone."

They walked down the hall together, past so many paintings that Sean had purchased with such care. They had both shared a love of art. At the door to the bedroom she gasped in revulsion. There was blood spatter along the wall and a huge dark stain of blood on the pearl carpet—a gruesome sight. Suddenly nauseated Terra backed away and raced to the bathroom down the hall, losing the breakfast Carolyn has made for her.

When she came back out, her sister was waiting, a curious expression on her face. "Are you okay?"

"Yeah. The sight in there—"

"Maybe we should leave now."

"No. I've been sick lots of times before this."

Carolyn squinted at her. "What do you mean?"

She smiled, waiting for Carolyn's reaction. "I'm pregnant."

"What?" Carolyn's face suddenly paled: her eyes widened, her mouth opened. And shut. "That's great news." She pulled Terra into a hug. "When were you going to tell your older sister that she was about to be an auntie?"

She clung to her sister, her heart pounding with regret. "After I told Sean. I was going to do that the night he was killed," she said, her body convulsing in sobs.

"Oh, honey, I'm so sorry. So sorry."

They stood for a few minutes longer, holding each other. Terra soaked in her sister's warmth and caring, feeling the bond of sisterhood like a physical force. "I've got to get going."

"Okay. Here's what we'll do. I'll go into the closet with you, help you find what you need. After that, I'll drive you to the mansion to face down the Cameron family. How's that for a plan?"

"Sounds perfect."

When they arrived at Olivia's house Alice, the maid, greeted them. She was a fixture in the house, a woman who had trouble keeping a smile off her face. But not today. Today she looked like someone had walked on her grave, her expression tense, her eyes downcast.

"Mrs. Cameron will see you now," She led Terra and Carolyn down the marbled hallway.

As they entered the room Olivia stood up and came toward them. "I've been expecting you," she said as she glanced from Terra to Carolyn. Olivia's hair wasn't quite as perfect as it normally was. Instead of the usual neat-as-a-pin pants and elegant brightly colored blouse, she wore a black sweater and pants.

Terra saw the ache in her eyes, the sag of her face, and hurried over to her. "I'm so sorry, Olivia," she offered, putting her arm around her mother-in-law, creating an awkward moment for both of them.

Olivia patted Terra's back. "We all are. It's a very tragic time." She moved to the sofa. "Let's sit down. We need to talk about the funeral. Did Sean and you…ever talk about?"

"Yes. We did." Terra went on to explain.

"That sounds like Sean; always prepared. He was a wonderful Boy Scout. He had every badge Scouting ever offered. And he will be buried in the family plot at Gravenhurst."

Terra never imagined that she'd be discussing her

husband's funeral plans. They'd talk about it more as a joke than anything. Now it was real. "Of course. Sean wanted that."

"Mr. Cox from Cox Funeral Home will join us in about an hour. I told him we needed to work things out before we spoke with him. Alice will bring coffee."

As they sat next to each other, Carolyn waited at the door. "Maybe I should come back later to take you home, Terra."

Olivia smiled at Carolyn and looked at Terra. "If you like, Terra, someone here can drive you home after we finish."

Terra didn't want to be left alone in this house with people she wasn't comfortable with and who she really didn't trust. Every time she and Sean had gone to Olivia Cameron's home, Terra felt she was assessed and found to be not quite up to whatever standard the Cameron family used to determine worthiness. The house itself always felt a little creepy, and never more so than today, with his high ceilings, ornate woodwork and dark recesses. As she glanced around, it felt as if grief had added a thin layer of despair to the house. "No. If you don't mind I'd like my sister to wait for me."

"Then, let's get started," Olivia said as Bethany entered the room. "I've asked Bethany to help me. She was a huge help during the hospital fundraising campaign. I've come to rely on her."

Bethany slid onto a chair near Terra, sitting forward, her face eager. "I want to help. I'm here for both of you." She smiled fleetingly at Terra, saving her biggest smile for Olivia.

They were just about finished making preliminary arrangements when Shamus came into the room, his eyes dark as he removed his jacket and threw it on the chair. "Bethany called me. Why are you meeting without me?" he demanded.

He turned on his mother. "I told you we could make the arrangements. We don't need Terra here."

"Shamus, she was Sean's wife, she has a right…and this is not the time." Olivia fixed her gaze on him.

Bethany stood up, smoothing her skirt nervously. "Your mother's right, Shamus. We all need to get along."

Shamus ignored his wife, moving to the other side of the room next to the fireplace that dwarfed the rest of the room. For the first time, he directed his attention toward her. "Terra, you will not inherit one penny of the Cameron family money. I know because Sean and I drew up our wills together. Besides that, until they catch the men you hired to kill my brother, you're not welcome in this house."

Terra gasped in shock. "Shamus, I'm not here for money, nor did I want my husband dead. I loved him. I'm only here to make arrangements—"

"Sure. Sure." He waved off her comment. "I just wanted to make that clear. Once the funeral is over, we're finished—"

"Shamus! Stop now!" Olivia, well up in years, crossed the room so fast that she took everyone by surprise. "Terra is your brother's wife. Try to remember that."

Shamus stared at his mother, but said nothing.

Unwilling to talk about Sean's funeral service under such awkward circumstances, Terra stood up. "I think it would be best if I leave," she said, wanting to lash out at Shamus but knowing the futility of trying to reason calmly with a man who had always used anger to get his own way. As much as she loved Sean, the one bright spot in all this was that after the funeral she wouldn't have to deal with these self-absorbed, arrogant people ever again.

She'd have her baby, and live her life somewhere other than in this town that worshiped at the Cameron Industries' altar.

Bethany hurried out behind them, reaching for Terra's hand. "I'm so sorry for your loss, Terra. Really sorry. I want you to know that I'll do anything I can to help you. I'm praying for you. And you're on my prayer list at church."

Bethany's anxiety was clear on her face, anxiety and something else...

Terra wasn't sure exactly what was going on with Bethany and she really didn't care. She was no longer part of the Cameron family. Terra looked past her toward the room she'd just left. "Thank you, Bethany."

Bethany squeezed her fingers. "Please try to understand. Shamus doesn't mean to talk like that. This is a great loss for him and he's under a lot of stress."

"You don't need to apologize for him."

Bethany looked surprise. "Apologize? Hardly. My husband is grieving. His twin brother is dead. He's angry at the world."

Terra looked at the woman, at the unsettling stare, the fluttering hand movements, and wondered if Bethany might be ill.

"I'll see you at the funeral," Terra said as she moved toward the door.

Bethany followed her. "Terra. Where will you live?"

"What do you mean?"

"Is the house really yours? Do you own it now?" Bethany asked, smoothing her hair across her forehead.

"Of course. Why would you ask such a thing?"

Her eyes widened. "Shamus says the house isn't paid for, that there's a big mortgage."

What was wrong with this woman? They didn't have a mortgage, but that was none of Bethany's business. "Shamus obviously doesn't know what he's talking about."

Bethany touched her arm. "But I can't help but worry. We're almost sisters, don't you see? After what happened to Sean, you need me."

Terra couldn't think of any response. They had never been close, and Bethany was the last person she needed in her life. "I'm leaving now," Terra said, then turned and walked out the door with her sister.

On the way to the car, Carolyn said, "What a weird woman. If she wants to pray for someone, I think she should start praying that her husband gets some anger management training, don't you?"

"I've thought that for a long time," Terra said, waiting for her sister to unlock the car door.

As they drove through the security gate leading to the street, reporters were standing along the sidewalk, their cameras aimed at the car. Terra tried not to look at them as Carolyn drove past…the faces blurred—all but one. A man seemed to be staring more intently than anyone else, right into the car. *Did she know him?* There was something in the way he looked at her... No, there was something off-putting in the way he looked at Carolyn. "Did you know that man we just passed?"

"Who?" Carolyn asked, her eyes focused on the narrow pathway created by the line of people, their faces framed by their hands blocking the sun, as they tried to see into the car.

"One of the reporters was looking directly at you as we drove past. You didn't see him?"

"No. I was concentrating on my driving. Besides, why would he be looking at me?" Carolyn asked, genuinely baffled.

"Maybe he wasn't..." Terra said, relieved to see they were about to turn onto the roadway and away from the whole mess.

"Let's go back to my house. We need a strong cup of tea and a little time to celebrate something positive—your great news," Carolyn said. "We're going to have a baby in the family."

"You know, I've hardly had time to think about what it will mean to have a baby in my life. I learned only a few days ago that I...we were expecting. Yet the shock of Sean's death has made me feel as if the baby isn't real."

Carolyn glanced across at her. "I think your morning sickness is pretty real."

"Yeah, that part. But the idea that in seven months there will be a baby in my life hasn't really had time to sink in."

"Well, I can't wait to start knitting. I like yellow, so be ready for a load of yellow baby things."

"Now, that I'd like to see," Terra said, her heart lifting at the image of her sister contentedly filling her evenings with the click and clack of knitting needles.

When they got to Carolyn's house there was a familiar car in the driveway. "I'm surprised Kevin wasn't here when you woke up. He's always around," her sister said.

"He wanted to be," Terra said responding to the doubt registering on Carolyn's face. "He wanted to come over right away but I told him no." She had wondered why Kevin hadn't spent the night at Carolyn's house while she slept.

"Kevin cares. He just does things his way," Terra said as they climbed out of the car.

Kevin ran to her and wrapped his arms around Terra. "I'm so sorry for your loss. Where have you been?" He peered down at her, his deep blue eyes questioning, his expression one of concern. "Oh, yeah, funeral arrangements. How did that go?"

"It went okay, I guess," Terra hugged him, feeling comforted by Kevin's presence. She'd seen him through his terrible time in high school when he made the decision to share his news with the world: He was gay. He'd worried about telling his parents his news, unsure of their response.

Since then, Kevin had become a very successful interior designer who lived between an apartment in Chicago, a condo on Lake Michigan and a house in Florida. He practiced what he called site-specific "outing," meaning that his friends in Palm Beach knew he was gay but not his friends here at home. He and his partner, Peter Lynch wanted it to remain that way.

The three of them walked arm in arm up the walkway toward Carolyn's house. "I'll make coffee for all of us," Carolyn said, unlocking the front door.

Once settled at the table in the kitchen, Kevin turned his full attention to Terra. "I'm here to talk you into coming on a jaunt with me to my condo on the lake."

Terra looked at him, surprised. "I don't think—"

"Hear me out. A little bird tells me that there is a manhunt on for the two attackers; the press is hounding the police for information and of course they're looking for you," he said. "I mean, seriously, you must have seen them camped out along the roadway leading to the Cameron mansion?"

"I did."

"Trust me. I'm going to get you organized and take you away with me. The press can go to hell. How's that sound?" He looked from Terra to Carolyn and back.

"Maybe he's right," Carolyn offered.

Kevin took Terra's hand. "You know I'm right. You and

Sean have always been so good to me, so protective. What if the police have a breakthrough in the case? The press will be looking for you to comment. Do you want to be around for that?" he asked.

Terra sighed, her shoulders slumping. "You're right. I need a little time and a little space."

"Then let's go. Do you need any clothes?"

"If we're just staying a night or two, no. I packed a bag before I came here."

"Then that's it." He got up and made for the door.

"Can I finish my coffee?"

"Do you want anyone to figure out you're here with your sister? Her life would become a circus as well."

"You're right." Relieved to have Kevin take charge, Terra gathered her things, hugged her sister and headed out the door.

~~~

The powerful Mercedes hummed along the highway leading toward the lake. Cars whizzed past. Rain splattered the windshield. Inside, Terra sat hemmed in by the seatbelt, her thoughts a jumbled mess. It didn't seem possible that Sean, the love of her life, was dead. Nothing seemed real except for Kevin's presence next to her.

When they arrived at the lakefront condo, a feeling of calm settled over Terra. "As usual you were right. Getting away for a couple of days will make a huge difference," she said as the car rolled to a stop.

He took her overnight bag from the trunk. "Terra I know how awful this must be for you. I loved Sean too."

"I know. We've had good times together over the years, haven't we?"

"We sure have," Kevin said, putting his arm around her shoulder as he led her into the condo. The massive open area led from the front door to the windows that showcased a beautiful view of the lake.

"This feels like my second home," she said. "Staying here will be so nice, especially when my home is such a mess," she said, her throat tightening against the memory of the blood stained carpet.

Once settled in the house, Kevin began to prepare dinner while Terra watched the light change on the water, the easy lift and sway of the branches of an oak tree outside the window. "Are we expecting a storm tonight?" she asked.

"Not that I know of."

"There's a dark line of cloud out there." She pointed toward the horizon.

"Hmm…possibly. In the meantime I have a wonderful merlot and two rib steaks going on the barbecue in a few minutes. How does that sound?"

"Okay. But I'm not sure how hungry I am."

"It doesn't matter. Eat what you feel like," he said, passing a glass of wine to her.

She shook her head.

"You don't want a glass of wine?"

She wasn't ready to tell him her news. Kevin was always so dramatic about anything that took him by surprise, and she simply wasn't ready to share her news, face all Kevin's concern coached in excitement, at least not this evening. "Wine would only make me feel more tired than I already feel."

He put the bottle down on the table. "If you say so," he said, his brow furrowed.

By the time the meal was finished Terra could hardly keep her eyes open. She stifled a yawn then saw the smile in Kevin's eyes. "I slept for hours at Carolyn's house, but I'm still sleepy."

"You get to bed. I'll clean up."

She didn't argue. "Thanks." She headed up the winding staircase that championed a spectacular view of the lake, making her way to the room she and Sean had always slept in.

She stopped abruptly. She couldn't go in there. It was too hurtful to remember all the great times they'd shared, the fun, the late night chats, walks on the beach before climbing into the wrought iron bed—an antique Kevin had purchased just for them.

"Kevin…" she called down the stairs as she reached the landing.

He started up the stairs toward her. "Yes. You can take one of the other guests rooms."

"How did you know that's what I wanted?"

He reached the top and put his arms around her. "Because I love someone as much as you loved Sean. I get what's going on with you."

"Are you serious?"

He leaned back and peered into her eyes, his face suffused with delight. "Yes. Peter and I love each other. I'm ready to go public with it, but Peter isn't. He's afraid it will affect his job."

"But he's the police chief."

"Sure. Everyone would appear to be accepting on the surface, but we all know that bias still exists, that there would be people who would be happy if somehow he screwed up. He wants to run for governor some day, which means he has to manage his private and public life much more carefully than your side of the sexual divide does."

"I guess so. I'm sorry Kevin, that you found someone to love and who loves you, and you can't show the whole world how you feel."

Kevin shrugged. "We all have things that force us to be someone we're not. Look at you. You married someone whose family gives a whole new meaning to the word dysfunctional."

Kevin had been so impassioned in his objections to her marrying Sean that they didn't talk or see each other for a year. "Kevin, do not go there."

"I'm sorry. This isn't the time or place. I'm sorry," he repeated.

"It's okay. It's always been okay between us… At least most of the time."

"Yeah, like the day you beat me at the spelling competition. Grade Four. I'll never forget it. I still haven't settled that score. You will pay," he said in his best version of Darth Vader's voice.

"You're good for me, you know that."

"I've always known it. Now go to bed." He kissed her cheek.

Terra slept fitfully, and finally got up around five and went for a walk along the beach. A stiff breeze out of the east had her huddling inside her jacket; one she'd left at Kevin's condo for mornings like this when she and Sean would go for long walks together. Her throat tightened at the memory. She huddled deeper into the jacket to ward off the desperate feeling of loneliness that assailed her. She looked down the shoreline toward Kevin's condo and saw him wave as he started toward her.

"You didn't have to walk out here alone this morning. I would have come with you," he said as he approached.

"I know you would, but somehow walking alone out here this morning felt right. Sean loved walking along the water's edge, skipping stones and talking about his plans for the company."

Kevin took her hand as he walked beside her. "You and Sean were a great couple in every way. He loved you so much."

"And I loved him," she said, as they approached the deck of the condo.

Kevin slid the patio doors open for her. "Thought maybe you'd like your favorite breakfast this morning. I've got French toast with whipped cream and strawberries," he said, heading for the kitchen.

The food was delicious. Sitting quietly sipping her coffee felt so normal, and it was a relief that she didn't have to think about anything for a little while. Being with Kevin meant she didn't have to explain anything, didn't have to talk if she didn't want to, or think, or do anything. They settled in across the table from each other, their plates heaped high with French toast.

But she did have something she should attend to. Despite her reticence to deal with Derrick O'Leary, one thing was unavoidable: He had advised her to get a criminal lawyer, obviously based on something he knew but couldn't tell her at that time. She thought back to their breakup, years earlier. It had been very difficult for her, but one thing she could say about Derrick; he always spoke the truth, no matter how painful.

"Kevin, I need to find a lawyer."

"Well, Cameron Industries has a battery of them at your disposal."

"No. The way Shamus has been behaving I doubt I'd be welcomed at the office, or offered legal counsel. Besides, I need to feel that the lawyer would be working just for me."

"You mean Shamus might go behind your back, use his influence with the company lawyers to undermine or interfere with what is going on should you be faced with any form of litigation?"

"Exactly. Besides I think I may need a criminal lawyer."

"Why?" Kevin's face registered surprise.

"I had a call from Detective O'Leary, and he suggested it might be a good idea for me to hire one. And when I met with Sean's family, Shamus went on a rant accusing me of having Sean murdered. He's insane."

"Derrick's among the best detectives in the city. If he thinks you need one, he may be right. Funny, I always liked him. When you were seeing each other I thought he was perfect for you."

"Kevin. Don't go there. That's over and done with."

"Okay, so let's see." He tapped the screen of his cell phone. "We need to identify a few good criminal lawyers back in the city. And believe me there would only be a few." He tapped away for a few minutes longer. "I've located four five-star lawyers who are identified on several sites as reputable criminal lawyers."

"Give me their numbers, please."

"You're going to call now?"

"Yes. I want this over. Besides, I'd rather be prepared than not. Maybe I could get an appointment with one of them sometime after the funeral."

"If that's what you want to do, I'll jot them down and

leave you to it while I check my email and make a couple of calls myself. I'll use my cell."

Terra made the first call, got through to a lawyer specializing in criminal law who seemed pleased to hear from her, offered her his condolences before asking what he could do for her. When she told him what she needed, he hesitated before telling her he'd just been placed on retainer by Cameron Industries, meaning that he couldn't act for her.

Terra was shocked. Why would Cameron Industries offer a retainer to a legal firm specializing in criminal law when they already had in-house lawyers they could call upon?

She thanked the man and hung up.

Three phone calls later, not one of the major firms in town would take her case, all citing the same reason as the first one. "Damn!" she yelled, hanging up.

"What's wrong?" Kevin asked coming into the room, a look of concern on his face.

"None of the firms will take me on as a client."

"That's insane."

She explained to him what had happened. "Ah." Kevin nodded his head slowly. "I know what's going on here. Your instincts were correct. Shamus doesn't want you to have good counsel should you need it. He has paid a retainer to all the qualified lawyers, which means that they can't work for you. It would be a conflict of interest, and put them in an impossible situation."

Frustration burned through Terra. She did not need this. Her life was complicated enough as it was. "I've got to find another good lawyer who practices criminal law."

"Can you ask Derrick for a name?"

"No!"

"You're sure," Kevin said, his head tilted in question.

"Absolutely. Stop trying to push me into his life. I mean it." She gave Kevin a gentle push. "Don't you know anyone? Surely Peter would have a few names."

"He might, or might not…" Kevin sighed.

"I'm going to ask Carolyn. Maybe she knows someone."

She made a quick call to her sister who gave her a name.

Dennis Sparks was a sole practitioner who worked out of a small office in the downtown core.

Terra called. Dennis Sparks, offered to meet with her later that day. She put her hand over the phone. "He's offering me an appointment. Should I take it?"

"You'd better before Shamus throws money at this one as well."

She jotted down the appointment time and the lawyer's address. Getting off the phone she turned to her friend. "Kevin, I can't do this. It's too hard. What am I going to say to this lawyer? That the police might be about to charge me with something? What could they possibly believe I could have done? Will you talk to Peter? As chief he must know where they're looking for suspects. Hopefully, not at me."

"I will, honey, but whatever is going on—if there *is* something going on where you're concerned—it may be out of Peter's control."

"I feel as if I'm in some awful dream, that I'll wake up any moment and Sean will be beside me. I can't do this alone." Tears stung her eyes. She took a deep breath and tried to get her emotions under control.

"You're not alone."

"But I have to face a complete stranger later today, and see if he is willing to take on my defense should I need one. I'm scared."

When Kevin's landline rang it startled both of them. "I didn't think that phone ever rang," she said, looking at him.

"I should give it up, but I like the idea of having a number that only a select group of people know about." Kevin jumped out of his chair and went to the phone. He listened for a few minutes without a word. When he hung up there was an apologetic look on his face. "Terra, I'm sorry. I have to go to Chicago this afternoon. One of my design jobs has run into a snag and the owners are demanding that I be there to resolve the problem. I don't want to leave you here alone in case someone figures out that you're here. I'll drive you back to town, but we have to leave now."

Terra was disappointed but understood the demands of work. Sean had been completely devoted to Cameron

Industries, while she loved her nursing job at the hospital. "I'll gather up my things."

She pulled her cell phone out of her purse. "I'm going to make a quick call and see if I can get my handyman to meet me at the house. I need to get the carpet in our bedroom replaced, the walls painted—" At the thought of dealing with repairs as well as her grief, she started shaking, her fingers wrapping the edge of the dining room table for support.

"Hey that's all right; we don't need to rush. Take your time," Kevin offered kneeling next to her.

"Yeah. It's just so hard to imagine my life without Sean. We had so many plans." She looked into her friend's eyes, and saw his concern. "I didn't get a chance to tell you."

"What?"

"Sean and I are…" She gulped back tears. "I'm expecting a baby."

His eyes glowed. A smile lit up his face. "That's so wonderful…so wonderful." He pulled her into his arms, hugging her close. "I am crazy happy for you."

"Me too. I didn't have a chance to tell Sean. I was going to tell him that night." Her body shook. "We were so happy. He had something special to tell me, and I had something special to tell him. And now neither of us will know what the other one wanted to say."

"Life is so damned unfair!" Kevin said, holding her at arm's length, looking into her eyes. "But you have friends and a sister who love you, and we will see you through this." He arched his eyebrows. "I want you to know I'd be happy to be a godfather, if you need one. Don't know how you feel about that sort of thing."

She saw the expectant look on his face. He had stood by her through every upsetting event in her life. And now he was willing to stand by her once more. Feeling her first moment of joy since Sean's death, she hugged him. "Oh, Kevin, I would love that. Sean… Sean…" She swallowed hard. "Carolyn will be the godmother and you can be the godfather. How's that?"

"Exceptional. But for now, maybe we should get on the road. I hate to pressure you," he said, his expression anxious.

"Not a problem. Give me a couple of minutes, and I'll be ready."

She climbed the stairs, feeling as if there was a bright spot in all this. She knew, without reservation, that Kevin would be the best godfather any child could have. She was feeling better as she gathered her clothes and toiletries, zippered her bag and went back downstairs.

Kevin waited at the door. "You're going to make a great mom, Terra. And from now on, I'm going to drive very carefully whenever you're in the car," he said, taking her overnight bag, and putting his arm around her as he opened the door.

Suddenly a whoop went up. Someone yelled Terra's name.

From somewhere near Kevin's car, someone called out. "Mrs. Cameron, can you tell us what you're doing here? Is Mr. Jackson a friend of yours?"

Kevin swore. "Get away from here now," he yelled as he led Terra to his car, tossing her bag in the backseat and opening the door for her.

"Just asking. Someone told us you were up here. Alone. All night long," one of the people in the milling group replied as cell phones clicked and video cameras whirred.

"Are you having an affair?" one of the reporters standing next to the car yelled.

Kevin glared at the reporter as he opened the driver's door. "Get lost."

Safely inside the car, her heart pounding, she clung to the seat. "Who was that reporter? I've seen him somewhere before."

Kevin started the car. "Tim Martin. Once upon a time he was a good investigative reporter. Now he's just a gossip jock."

CHAPTER FIVE

"What am I going to do?" Kevin asked as he roared along the lane and up onto the road, glancing in his rearview mirror as he did so. "I have to call Peter. As if he didn't have enough on his mind," he muttered, accelerating.

Terra gripped the seat as Kevin's heavy vehicle swerved onto the access ramp of the Interstate. "Remember what you said about driving super carefully. Please, slow down," she pleaded.

He glanced across at her, before edging into the lane of traffic. An eighteen-wheeler sped past them, spraying water from an early morning rain shower. "Sorry. I'm just worried."

"That makes two of us."

"I've got to get back to work and see what the issue is, and I'll have to tell Peter about this before the video hits the news."

"Oh, Kevin. If I hadn't come out here with you, none of this would have happened."

His glance swerved to her. "This is not your fault. Those reporters are after a sensational headline, not the truth."

All the way to the city she gripped the seat, partly out of fear because of her friend's erratic driving and partly because she was genuinely afraid of what would happen next. Kevin kept glancing in his rearview mirror. "I think I lost those bastards. I'll drive more carefully. All we need is for me to be stopped for speeding, right?"

As they reached the off ramp leading to her part of town, Kevin turned to her. "I'm going into the house with you."

"You don't have to. You need to get to your office."

"I'll just do a quick walk-through, and see if everything's okay. Then I'll be off."

When they arrived at her house, there were two vehicles parked in the driveway. She recognized her sister's car, but not the other vehicle. Once in the garage, she raced into the house, her heart pounding. What could have happened?

Carolyn met her at the door. I've been trying to call you on your phone. "There's been a break-in."

"A break-in?" Terra repeated the words as if she didn't understand what they meant.

"The police were called when a neighbor saw a strange man in the backyard. Derrick called me, and I came right over."

"What did they take?"

"I'm not sure. Every piece of Sean's clothing was tossed out of the closet and scattered over your bedroom floor," Carolyn said in a worried voice.

Derrick appeared behind Carolyn. "I'm sorry to have to ask you this, Terra. But I need you to walk through the house with me and tell me what's missing."

"Why would anyone break into my home?" She bit down hard on her lip to keep it from trembling.

"It's not that unusual after a headline in the paper: Sometimes after a death or even a wedding, people's houses are empty and there are always people ready to take advantage." He glanced at Carolyn. "And you say Sean's clothes are scattered around your bedroom? That's bizarre, to say the least. Maybe whoever was here the last time came back looking for something your husband had in his possession or that caught their eye before they ran off. Until we know more I'm going to assume that Sean's death and this break-in are connected."

"How did they get in?" Terra asked, willing herself to remain calm, to focus on Derrick's words.

"We're not sure. There's no sign of forced entry."

"Are you saying that the person who did this had a key? That's not possible."

"Terra, how many keys do you have?"

"Sean, myself, the housekeeper, Selena Shepherd, and a spare hidden in the garage. Sean's keys and wallet are here." She pointed to the bowl on the kitchen counter. Mine are in my purse, and I'll show you the spare in the garage." She walked with him out into the garage to the metal box hidden under Sean's workbench. She opened it, displaying a key inside.

Derrick pulled a glove and a plastic bag from his pocket, picked up the key and placed it in the bag. Terra watched him as if in a trance. Everything seemed so out of focus, frightening and strange, as if she were seeing things from a distance. She clutched the top of the workbench, drawing in a deep breath in an attempt to gain control of the fear rushing through her. "Derrick, who would break in here and scatter Sean's clothes around? He's dead. He can't harm anyone now. What are these people after?"

"Who has the security code for your alarm system?"

Her eyes widened. "Sean. Me. Selena. That's all."

"What about Sean's family? Any of them have the code?"

"No. Shamus seldom came here unless it was to see Sean about business. Bethany has been here more than Shamus, but I never gave her keys or the code, and I'm sure Sean didn't either."

"And there is no one else?"

"I have a key and the security code, Terra," Carolyn said, coming into the garage.

"And so do I," Kevin said, walking behind Carolyn.

"What is wrong with me? Of course you both have keys and access to the house. Am I losing my mind?"

Seeing the look on Terra's face, Kevin hurried to her, his voice filled with caring. "This is so unfair! Why is this happening to you?" He turned to Derrick. "What are the police doing about this?"

"We're investigating every possible scenario. Forensics will be here as soon as possible. You can help by telling us where you were this morning," Derrick said to Kevin.

"Carolyn must have told you already. I was with Terra at my condo on the lake."

"He was with me," Terra confirmed, glancing at her sister.

Kevin turned to Terra, cupping her shoulders in his hands. "I have to leave. I'm overdue at the office, and I have to return an urgent call. Sorry to leave you this way, sweetie."

"You go, and we'll talk later," Terra said.

"Believe it," he replied, heading for the door.

"I'm going to make tea. Anyone want some?" Carolyn asked.

"Not me," Terra said, trying to contain her fear. She couldn't give into the panic charging through her. Feeling as if her life were spiraling completely out of control she turned to Derrick. "Who is behind all this?"

Derrick saw the desolation on Terra's face. "I wish I knew," he said. "But believe me we will find out, I promise."

The fear in her eyes cut through him. "I'm afraid, Derrick. But I can't let these evil people take control of my life. I can't. Tell me what I can do to help."

He knew it wasn't his business, not at all, but he was damned proud of this defiant woman standing there after such a devastating incident when many people would have succumbed to their fear and demanded the police protect them.

It didn't take much to figure out what had to be going on inside her head. To have your husband killed one day and someone break into your house three days later, would leave anyone reeling with fear and anger at the senselessness of it all.

"Follow me." He led her through the kitchen into the hallway toward the den. "We'll walk around and you can tell me if anything looks different to you, or if something is missing. I don't want you to touch anything, just tell me if you see something that doesn't seem right to you."

He followed her into the den. The desktop was empty except for a very expensive-looking clock. He pointed to the clock and looked at her.

"It was my Christmas present to Sean the first year we met. I spent way too much money on it. Sean loved it. But that was Sean. He loved every gift I ever gave him."

Terra walked around Sean's desk, stopped and asked, "When Sean came home the other night he had a large brown envelope with him. Did you find it among the things the police took away from here?"

"I don't recall anyone mentioning it. Do you know what was in the envelope?"

"No idea. Sean brought it home that night. I asked him about it, but he said he'd explain later."

Something urgent enough that Sean had brought the envelope home with him and planned to talk to his wife about it that night. Strange coincidence? Worth looking into… "I'll check up on it, and get back to you."

"When can I get Sean's computer back? I really need it. All his family and friends' contact information is on it. He didn't use the laptop for work," she said, her look imploring him to understand. "Did Detective Wilson not tell you I called you earlier to ask you about it?"

Meaghan hadn't told him Terra had tried to reach him at work. "About what?" he asked stalling for time, annoyed that Meaghan hadn't mentioned the call. But maybe Meaghan had been busy tracking down leads.

Derrick wasn't about to tell Terra what they already knew. Sean had been using a chat room, one frequented by men and women looking to hook up. Meaghan believed that Sean had met someone on the anonymous chat room site. She was looking for proof that he'd been involved with someone there, believing that Terra had found out and was so jealous she decided to do something about it. Derrick believed that if Sean had hooked up with someone online, it was someone who wanted more from Sean, had found out who he was and went looking for him. "The laptop's part of the evidence. It won't be returned for a while."

While Meaghan pursued leads involving the chat room, Derrick was convinced that Sean's murder had to do with something related to Cameron Industries. Shamus's aggressive behavior toward Terra at the hospital suggested that he was angry about something that involved the family.

Terra sighed. "Without that laptop I will have to talk to Olivia again. She would have the family names, but not Sean's work associates. Shamus would know…"

Which reminded him. "You made the news a little while ago."

"I did!" She stared up at him, her cheeks flushed, her eyes wide.

"One of the news channels showed footage of you coming out of a condo—"

She gasped. "That fast? It only happened a couple hours ago. Why are the press doing this?"

"Because you're news. I hate to say it, but Sean's death is big news." He saw her elegant shoulders sag and wished he could do more for her. He couldn't imagine what it must be like to be a woman and lose the man you loved in such a horrific way. Although he'd seen it many times in his line of work, he never had it happen to someone he knew.

"Will the reporters show up here at the house again?"

"Almost for sure."

"What should I do? I want to stay here. This is my home, but if I have to go past reporters asking questions every time I leave the house…and even when I attend the funeral." Tears pooled in her eyes, ready to overflow and run down her cheeks. He wanted to comfort her, more than anything. To hug her and console her. But he had to remain impartial, keep his distance. Doing so was the only way he could help her. He couldn't give his boss any reason to believe what Meaghan said, that he was biased and would not be able to maintain his emotional distance from the person Detective Wilson believed was the prime suspect in Sean Cameron's murder.

He ordered his hands to remain at his sides. He could not touch this woman. He had no right to show her anything other than professional courtesy. "We'd better finish going through the house. I realize this isn't easy, and having to do it for the second time…"

She looked up at him, a forlorn expression on her face. "You're not telling me everything, are you?"

He didn't answer. He couldn't. But the good news was his urgent call to an old partner from his early years on the police force had been returned. They were meeting for coffee in a few hours. His niggling suspicion had blossomed into a very real possibility about who the attackers might be. He just needed to start building the case. Mike Fenton was the one person who never forgot a detail of a case and he only hoped he was free and willing to help with a case that otherwise, was headed in a very wrong direction.

She drew in a deep breath. "Okay. Let's finish looking through the house."

He led her down the hall toward the bedrooms, where he stopped, wishing there was some way to shield her from what she was about to see. "We found this." He pointed to the interior of the room.

Sean's walk-in closet was empty. His clothes, underwear, every item of apparel had been tossed around the room. A couple of socks clung to the curtain rod. In the bathroom his toiletries had been smashed and trashed, the room reeking of his expensive aftershave and cologne.

Terra's hands went to her throat; her cry of anguish filled the air. Her eyes wild with fear, she clutched the doorframe.

"What? Who? Who would have done this?" Her gaze locked on Derrick. She swayed for a moment. Derrick reached for her.

She stepped away from him, her skin pale, her eyes wild. "No! This can't be happening!" She ran from the room and down the hall to the kitchen where she took a glass from the cupboard and filled it with water, her hands shaking so badly she could barely bring the glass to her lips.

Derrick took the glass from her shaking hands. "You need to sit down somewhere. We need to talk."

Apparently calmed by his reassuring tone of voice, she

sat on the edge of the kitchen chair closest to the sink. "What do we need to talk about?"

Derrick needed to ask Terra about the past months, about her marriage but wasn't sure how she'd view his questions. "Terra, did Sean change in any way over the past few months? Have any business worries? Any unexplained things? Anything that caught your attention?"

"Like what?"

"Maybe he was staying at the office later. Or maybe he seemed preoccupied when he came home?"

"What are you suggesting?"

She hadn't answered and he didn't want to push her. *Damn!* He didn't want to ask her questions about her marriage or any other part of her life. He had no right on a personal level, yet every right as an investigating officer in her husband's murder. He didn't want to know about her happy life with her husband. He still wallowed in self-pity over the mistake he'd made. And Marylou had definitely been the biggest mistake of his life. Wanting to redirect the conversation away from anything personal, he said, "You asked about an envelope. Why?"

"Because it was on Sean's desk before the two thugs entered the house, and he said it was important."

"And he didn't say anything about what it contained?"

"We didn't get to talk to each other that night. I had news I wanted to share with him, and he said he had something he wanted to talk to me about." She rubbed her forehead, her face crumbling. "How could anyone have killed Sean? He was a good person. People at work liked and respected him. He was a good husband."

The phone rang. Terra jumped, swiped her hair off her face and answered it. Derrick watched helplessly as her eyes filled with tears, her gaze coming to rest on his face.

In that instant his need to hold her nearly overpowered him again. He wanted to shield her from any more pain, provide her a shoulder to cry on, and tell her how damned sorry he was for what he'd done. Instead, he forced himself to lean against the counter.

"That was the florist." She pushed her hair from her

face in frustration. "Why do people feel they have to talk about my loss? It's my loss, not theirs." She closed her eyes. "Sorry. I'm being mean, aren't I?" she asked.

It was his turn to say nothing.

"The florist is coming here to help me make a choice for the flowers on Sean's casket, something ostentatious and expensive, no doubt."

It was time for him to leave. Besides he had a lot of work to do, and the forensics team had arrived. He needed to get back to the office. "I'll be in touch. Call me if you need anything, or remember anything however small, that might help us."

"I will. And thanks for the advice about the lawyer. I can't believe that I'll need one, but I appreciate your concern." She looked up at his face, her gaze moving slowly to his eyes. A jolt of low voltage current raced through him, slowing his pulse, making him wish he could stay with her.

Shit! He had to get out of there.

He walked to the door and didn't look back. He couldn't. Terra still fascinated him more than any woman he'd ever met. Or ever would meet. But there was nothing he was going to do about it now. The woman deserved his professional help and support. Nothing more. Nothing less.

He deserved nada.

With a cup of coffee from his favorite java boutique in his hands, his one indulgence, Derrick had made it into the police station just as his cell phone rang. "I'm coming up the stairs. What is it?" he asked Meaghan as he took the last flight, two steps at a time. He always took the stairs because the exercise helped lower the stress of his workday.

Right now, he'd like to find a way to give Terra a break from all the anguish he'd seen in her eyes and what surely lay ahead. He certainly couldn't help her with her grief, but maybe with enough time he might be able to provide information about what happened to bring about her husband's death.

He reached the top of the stairs, pulled open the door and walked into the open room lined with desks, chairs and randomly placed computers. People were standing in groups, sitting at desks, focused on a computer screens, or staring off into space. A typical day at the police station.

Meaghan came toward him. "You've got a problem."

"What now?"

"The chief wants to speak to you. As in, yesterday."

"What about?"

"I would guess that it has to do with the Cameron case, and the press coverage."

He put his coffee cup on his desk. "I'm on my way," he said.

When he reached Peter Lynch's office the man was pacing back and forth across the room. As he entered he stopped, turned and faced him.

"Sit down."

Derrick did so, bracing for what came next. "What did you want to see me about?"

"When did you plan to update me with what's going on in the Cameron investigation?"

"As soon as I had anything to report, anything concrete."

"That's not good enough. Did you watch the news?"

Derrick had stayed late the night before, trying to piece together what little description they had of the assailants and correlate the attack on Sean Cameron with any similar attacks in the area. "No I didn't."

"The press photographed Mrs. Cameron coming out of a lakefront property with another man." The chief clasped his hands together as he paced, his frown digging deeper into his forehead as he clicked on the TV behind his desk.

The screen lit up with a full face view of Terra looking startled and terrified, and then moved to Kevin Jackson's face, a man who looked angry and defensive. A man telling the reporters that what Mrs. Cameron did with her time was none of their damned business. The questions hurled at Terra suggested that they thought she was having an affair.

The police chief shut it off and sat down, his eyes boring into Derrick. "This cannot happen again. Do I make myself clear?"

What couldn't happen and what was the chief so upset about? "With all due respect, we can't stop the press from following a story."

"Maybe not. But we can't have the media involved in, or dictating how we carry out this investigation. We have to be completely open and unbiased. Do I make myself clear?"

Where was the chief coming from on this? It had only been a couple of days. Every avenue was being investigated. He and Meaghan had logged a lot of hours, and would continue to do so. There was no reason to think that two of the best detectives on the force would not build a careful, concise case against whoever was found to be the involved. "Understood."

The chief's gaze never left Derrick, making him feel exposed, out on a limb, waiting for what would come next.

"I'm aware that you had a relationship with Terra Cameron a few years ago."

What the hell was going on? "Yes, I did."

"I need to know that you are going to be unbiased in your efforts, that you will pursue every avenue of investigation."

What was the chief getting at? Did he believe that Derrick wouldn't do his job because of his past relationship with Terra? Or was he anxious to avoid problems with the Cameron family? Whatever his reasons, Derrick couldn't sit there and have his reputation called into question.

"Sir, I can promise you that my investigation will uncover the facts, then follow where they lead. So far we have little to go on about these two men, only a vague description of them from a woman who had been traumatized. The only other witness is dead.

"We are waiting on the forensics from the scene, and hope to have something concrete to further our investigation very soon. In the meantime, we are searching the Cameron neighborhood to find anyone who saw a suspicious vehicle in the area or two men near the Cameron house. The attackers had to have driven to the neighborhood. Their vehicle probably wasn't an upscale one, probably a service van. Our only witness gave a very general description except for the fact that her attacker reeked of body odor and wore dark clothing and ski masks. So far we have little to go on, but it's early in the investigation."

"It's never too early to bring in the only witness and question her, is it?" the chief asked, his voice too loud, too overbearing, so unlike the man's usual demeanor. *What was going on here?*

"I wanted to give her a little time to recover from the attack, and hope that her memory will improve. She remembered some details, but I'm hoping she remembers more as the shock wears off."

The chief snorted. "Or are you giving her time to prepare her story?"

Angry at the chief's words, his suggestion that Terra was somehow involved in this, he said, "You want me to bring her in here, giving the press a new story. Allow them to harass her, and for what? We have no evidence that she was involved, other than as a victim, in any of this."

"None at the moment, but maybe in talking to her you will learn something, get a lead maybe. Having her go over it again might be helpful," the chief said, his tone softer than before.

Derrick counted to ten, slowly and methodically. "We will do our job, and do it right. But at the moment we have no reason to consider Mrs. Cameron a suspect."

"Or maybe you don't want to see her that way."

Clearly this conversation was going to end on a bad note. Remembering the work he wanted to get to, the calls he needed to make, his old partner to meet, Derrick moved toward the door. "I will keep you informed."

"You will. But in the meantime, I want you to bring Mrs. Cameron in for questioning. And be sure she brings her lawyer with her."

Derrick strode back to his office, angry and yet, intrigued. What in hell was going on? The police chief had been concerned and apprehensive the first time they talked. This time he seemed afraid. But afraid of what? Was the press hounding him? Had Shamus Cameron called looking for answers—or favors?

Meaghan was waiting for him, her red hair swirling around her head, her green eyes brimming with questions. "So?"

Derrick settled into his chair, his fingers tapping the edge of the desk. "He wants us to bring Terra in for questioning."

"Why? We don't have anything on her. In fact I have discovered someone who might have seen those two men earlier in the evening. He works at the convenience store, two blocks west of the gated entrance to the subdivision. Two men fitting the description were seen buying two of those high energy drinks there."

"That's good news," Derrick said, relieved that all the police work might be about to pay off.

"I'm heading down there now. The store has security tapes we can look at. Want to come with me?"

He sighed. "No. I have to bring Terra in for questioning."

"Derrick, you be careful. Once the press find out about your past with Terra, they could drag you into this."

He started to speak.

She stopped him. "Listen to me. Let me do the interview with her, and let me see if there's anything else she can tell us. If I get the video surveillance from the convenience store, maybe it will help her remember something more about the two men."

Meaghan slipped into the chair beside his desk. "Look, Derrick, I know you care about her. When Sean Cameron was killed, it was all over the station that Terra and you had a history. I don't want the details. You're my partner and my friend. I want to help you. You're a good detective. Everyone here knows that. But the press doesn't really care what you are. They'll only care about your story, the part that involves Terra. Let me conduct the interview."

He met her gaze and saw the caring and concern in her

eyes. "Thanks," he said, checking his watch. "Oh! I gotta go. I've got an appointment, and I'm already late."

"With who?" Meaghan asked, indignation adding emphasis to her words.

"I'll tell you when I get back," Derrick said, heading for the stairs.

CHAPTER SIX

Derrick pulled into the parking lot of Joey's Diner; he and Mike Fenton had used this place as their second office for years. As detectives, Mike had a phenomenal memory for detail and Derrick loved setting the scene. Together they'd solved a lot of cases… That is until Mike's alcoholism got the better of him.

Derrick opened the door, his gaze going immediately to the booth at the back of the diner. Mike sat there, cleanly shaven with a smile of welcome on his face. Derrick waved to Callie Parsons behind the counter before heading to the booth.

They shook hands as Derrick slid in opposite Mike. Mike wasn't the hugging kind, and neither was Derrick—women being the exception, of course.

"So, you need my help," Mike said.

"I do."

"And I need sugar and caffeine." Mike waved Callie over and placed an order of coffee and doughnuts for both of them. Stirring four spoons of sugar into his coffee, Mike said, "Fire away."

"The Cameron killing."

"Ahh… Wouldn't I like to be in your shoes. Retirement sucks. Any suspects?"

"Not yet."

"So what made you call me?"

Pushing his cup of coffee aside, Derrick rested his elbows on the table. "Two attackers dressed in ski masks enter the home of an elderly woman, and beat her to death."

"The Pickering Case—2010. Ellen Pickering lived alone in a quiet neighborhood. Two men broke in, wearing ski masks and killed her. Buddy Edson was arrested, and charged. Got off due to a break in the chain of evidence, allowing the defense to raise reasonable doubt. Lennie-the-Crotch Taylor had an alibi—his wife, Shirley. Called him the crotch because he stunk up the holding cell. Remember that?"

"Yeah, I do." Derrick tipped two creamers into his coffee.

"You think they're your suspects?"

"It's possible. The only witness said the one who assaulted her stunk really bad and he wanted to hurt her. I just don't want to waste time on a false lead. What else do you remember about the two men?" Derrick asked.

"Buddy and Lennie started out robbing convenience stores. Both liked to use their fists, brought up on charges of wife beating, but the wives wouldn't testify. Any prints you can use?"

"So far only Sean, Terra, Carolyn and the part-time housekeeper's prints."

"Oh. Terra Cameron? My. God… Is this your Terra?"

"She's not *my* Terra."

"You can't fool me. Remember? I'm the person you spent your time with after the mess with that other woman. What was her name?" Mike tapped the table.

"Mike. You know her name. You knew her brother. Don't pull that stuff on me. You never forget a name."

Mike gave a wry grin. "For the record I won't say her name." He held up his coffee cup and nodded to Callie who came around the soda fountain counter over to the table with the coffee pot.

"You guys having a good reunion?" she asked.

"You could say that," Mike offered, stirring in another four teaspoons of sugar.

"Great to see the two of you back here together. Just like old times."

Derrick nodded and smiled at Callie, though his mind was on Buddy and Lennie as possible suspects. A hell of a lot safer to keep his thoughts on them than on Terra.

Mike returned his assessing gaze to Derrick. "I know how painful that breakup was, how you hated yourself for what you'd done."

"Leave Terra out of this. She's just lost her husband. She's grieving and facing the Cameron family who, I'm told, believe she's nothing but a gold digger."

"Have you checked to see where those two hooligans are living?" Mike asked.

"Buddy married a woman nearly twice his age. Lennie left his apartment with no forwarding address. I'm going to see if I can find either of them today, see what they're up to. There have been no arrests since the incident in 2010, which means they could have moved away, been arrested or are in another jurisdiction."

"Anything else that strikes you about the Cameron case? You've always had great instincts," Mike asked.

"It's a feeling that I have about the whole thing. This picture-perfect couple was on everybody's invitation list. Yet, the attackers told Terra they were there to kill Sean."

Mike brightened. "Hey! You left the best for the last. Now all you need to do is find someone who hated the man, who wanted him dead for some reason. Greed, love gone wrong, hatred. What about Shamus?"

"He has an alibi for the night in question, thanks to his wife. But he could have hired people like Lennie and Buddy to do the job. If I'm going to investigate him I need to tread carefully, get all my ducks in a row. I can't investigate a pillar of the community without something to go on that suggests he is guilty."

"True."

"You can see that I need a new set of eyes on this," Derrick said, his stomach burning from the coffee. He wished he could give it up, but knew there wasn't a chance in hell that he would. He fished an antacid tablet out of his jacket pocket.

"Anything else you want to talk about? Anything else

about the case?" Mike asked, rubbing his palms together, a motion Derrick knew from long experience. It meant that Mike would spend a lot of time thinking, turning ideas over in his mind and then go to work.

Mike, as a retired detective, couldn't be involved directly, but he knew his ex-partner's ability to look at the facts and find the connection—and hoped his curiosity would draw him in to help. "Another odd thing is that sometime earlier today someone broke into the Cameron house. Forensics is once again in there looking for evidence, including fingerprints. This time a neighbor reported seeing a man in the backyard of the house."

Mike scratched at his beard his eyes bright with interest. "Wait a damn minute. Didn't we investigate a similar incident with the Ellen Pickering case? Wasn't there someone in her backyard just days after her death?" He rubbed his beard harder. "Yes, we did." He pointed his finger at Derrick. "Remember? We got the next door neighbor to describe him, but the description was too vague to place either Buddy or Lennie at the scene."

"Maybe they just like to revisit the scene of a crime. Only in Terra's case they had reason to go back into the house days after they killed Sean. His clothes and personal things were scattered all over the master bedroom," Derrick said, his heart beginning to pound as he remembered Terra's reaction to the mess in the bedroom. "If they were looking for something specific, what might it be?"

"His cell phone maybe?"

"We didn't find one."

"Who lives without a cell phone these days? Especially an executive of a large company."

"Color me stupid," Derrick said embarrassed at such an obvious oversight. "I'll look into it."

"I wonder if there's any connection between Lennie, Buddy and any member of the Cameron family? Those two wannabe thugs, smart enough not to leave prints, would be poster boys for the break-in set. Anyone looking for someone to break in and leave no prints behind would be looking for people like these two," Mike said.

"Given that Sean is dead, if there was a connection to the Cameron family it would most likely be through Shamus or Olivia. Neither one makes much sense though, unless there was something big at stake." Derrick rubbed his jaw in thought.

"Like money? A love triangle? Could Sean have had something on Shamus? Something Shamus didn't want revealed? I've heard that Olivia Cameron is one tough customer. She was involved when the workers at Cameron Industries tried to unionize. I remember because my brother was one of the organizers trying to get union certification. She mobilized every person of influence she could find, even went and spoke to the workers on the shop floor, encouraging them to think twice about unionizing. It worked. If I were a betting man my money would be on the idea that if someone in the Cameron family were behind this murder it would be her. I wouldn't want to take her on without one hell of a good reason and great odds," Mike offered, a half smile on his face.

"You could be right. I wouldn't be surprised if she had a hand in Shamus's choice of wife."

"How so?" Mike asked, looking interested.

"Something Bethany said a few days ago about having Olivia's support in her marriage to Shamus. Maybe there's a connection we haven't thought about," Derrick said, digging out his cell phone and dialing the precinct number. Only he wasn't calling Meaghan, he was calling Lucy in records. He needed every piece of information he could find on Lennie and Buddy.

As he spoke to Lucy, he could see the look of longing on Mike's face, and vowed that when he retired—unlike Mike sitting opposite him—he'd have a life that included more than work.

If that's what you want O'Leary, you'd better get on it.

"Gotta go," he said as he hung up.

"Keep me posted, will you?" Mike asked, a wistful tone in his voice.

"I will."

"Coffee's on me," Mike said.

Derrick, headed toward the door, looked back to see Mike in deep thought. If he got stuck on figuring this out, or if Meaghan thought his theory was crazy, he'd be back to Mike.

Finally the florist left but not before Terra had agreed to more flowers than she wanted. But she didn't really care about flowers. She cared about getting through the visitation and the funeral with some level of dignity and control.

Carolyn glanced around the large kitchen area. "Are you going to be all right staying here? You can always come back to my house."

"No. I want to clean the house up, organize Sean's things. I can't postpone the inevitable. Plus I need to finish the arrangements for Sean's funeral."

"I worry about you being here alone after everything that's happened in this house. You could always come to live with me," Carolyn offered.

"But I need to be here, to look after things." Terra knew that most people would assume she didn't need to do much of anything for the time being, but she really wanted to be here in this house with her memories. She felt closest to Sean right here. "Why don't you move in with me?" Terra asked.

"I… I could I suppose. If it would make things easier for you."

"It certainly would."

"Then I'll do it. I'm not sure I can be here with you every day." She shrugged. "I have a job but I could help when I'm able and when you need me."

"I don't expect you to be here every minute," Terra said.

Carolyn nodded. "I have to drop back over to my house, check my messages and pack a bag." She scooped up her purse from the island. "I'll be back as soon as I can. Then I'll help you tidy the house up. The police said it was okay to put things away, and you need to deal with Sean's death in your own way, doing those things that matter to you, don't you?"

"Yes. So much."

"By the way there's another message on your phone from that guy. I think his name is Neill Baxter, or so it said on the call display."

"I don't know him, and I don't have time to find out what he wants," Terra said.

"Well, if he really needs to get in touch with you, he'll keep trying." Carolyn looked around the room, her mouth turning up in a smile. "I've always loved this house. Sean and you did a beautiful job of putting it all together. A great family home."

Terra gulped back the sudden rush of tears.

"Darn! I'm so sorry. I didn't think—" She put her arm around Terra's shoulders. "It will be okay. Listen, when the funeral is over and you can concentrate on your baby, we'll go shopping for all the baby paraphernalia we can find. You'll need maternity clothes pretty soon."

Terra returned the hug. "Thanks for reminding me that I have something special to look forward to."

After Carolyn left, Terra went from room to room, noting all the places that had been disturbed by the police search of her house, a search conducted to learn more about what happened here. They certainly hadn't meant to leave things out of place, and they probably thought they'd put things back as they found them. But she was accustomed to everything being in its place, and couldn't stop herself from carefully putting things exactly where they belonged.

Coupled with that was the mess in the bedroom—Sean's personal things were scattered about. All of it added up to a terrible invasion of her privacy. This was the only place in the world that meant anything to her, the one place she felt protected and safe. Now, all of that was gone, gobbled up in the rush to learn who could have murdered her husband, what might be missing from the house and what additional evidence the police could find.

These rooms and everything in them were part of her dream to raise her children here. Of living a happy, love-

filled life. Yet, now all that remained of the dream was
silence.

Terra couldn't face the bedroom alone, so she went to the
den where she began to tidy and straighten Sean's desk.
Finding the silence depressing she searched for a CD to put
into the CD player that Sean had on his credenza. He'd
always preferred to CD's to playlists on his cell phone,
stating that the music sounded so much better. She was just
about to play a Coltrane CD when the doorbell rang. She
wasn't expecting anyone. Glancing out through the side
panes of the front door she couldn't see anyone. Tiptoeing
to the door, she waited, not certain what to do.

"Terra?" a voice called from the other side of the door.

"Bethany?" *What was she doing here?* Terra opened the
door. "I didn't expect to see you. Is something wrong?"

"I was in the neighborhood, and thought I'd drop by to
see how you're doing."

Shamus and Bethany lived near the Cameron mansion,
in a whole different part of town. There wasn't any obvious
reason for her to be here, but maybe Bethany simply wanted
to be kind. Terra didn't know very much about her sister-in-
law, except she'd come from a family with limited means and
was deeply religious. Both qualities seemed at odds with
Shamus's view of life and his privileged upbringing. But
maybe Shamus was a very different person inside his
marriage—she hoped so.

Terra held the door wide. "That's very sweet of you.
Come on in."

Bethany hesitated. "You're sure it's okay?"

"Why wouldn't it be?"

"I wasn't sure you would see me. I mean after the way
Shamus behaved at Mother Cameron's house."

"Shamus is going through a difficult time," she offered,
not really caring how Shamus was making out. *Just a small lie
for the sake of the next few days.* "We are all stressed at the
moment."

Bethany came into the house, glancing around the foyer. "Terra, I… Are you going to stay here? I mean after what happened in this house, will you be able to live here as if nothing happened?" She peered down the hallway leading to the bedrooms. "How will you ever—?"

"Bethany, I'm sure you didn't come here to remind me about Sean's death. You're too kind to do something like that." She raised one eyebrow in question.

"No. Of course I didn't. I'm really sorry. I'm not normally like this." She wrung her hands and stared at the floor. "Terra I came here to tell you that Shamus is really, really angry at you. At me as well."

"Why?"

"He keeps saying you don't belong in the family. That when the funeral is over there will be no reason to stay in contact with you. I don't understand why he's saying these things. Shamus can be…very hurtful." She rubbed her left wrist.

"Bethany, you've got a large bruise on your arm. What happened?"

Bethany's voice faltered. "Shamus got angry."

"He hurt you, didn't he?" Terra said, suddenly feeling sorry for Bethany.

"Shamus is very angry. He doesn't want me to talk to you."

If Shamus didn't want Bethany to talk to her, why was she here? Did Bethany want to go to the police, and needed Terra's support? "Bethany, tell me what's going on. I can help you."

"I…I don't know where Shamus was the night Sean was killed."

"What are you saying?" Terra asked, shocked by Bethany's admission.

"I'm saying that Shawn wasn't home that evening."

"Bethany if you know something about Sean's murder, you have to go to the police."

Bethany shook her head and started for the door. "I've said too much. I didn't mean any of it. I'll go now." She stopped and turned back. "Please forgive Shamus. He's half crazy with grief. Losing a twin is much harder than losing an ordinary sibling. I read somewhere that twins have such a powerful connection. They need each other so much. We all need Sean, don't we?" She pressed her fingers to her lips. "Sorry! I'll go now."

"Bethany, please go to the police."

Without looking back, Bethany went down the walkway to her Mercedes, climbed in and backed onto the street, narrowly missing Carolyn's Honda as her sister pulled up to the curb.

Carolyn got out of her car and walked quickly up the driveway, her carry-on luggage clicking and clacking over the cobblestones behind her. "Was that Bethany?"

"It was."

"What's going on with her? Or does she always drive like that? What did she want?"

"She told me that Shamus wasn't home with her and she didn't know where he was the night Sean was killed."

Carolyn stopped. "Do you believe her?"

"I don't know what to believe. Those two are the strangest people on the planet. But maybe that's why Shamus had put all the top lawyers on retainer. I thought it was to stop me from having a good lawyer, but maybe it was to protect him."

Carolyn's face paled as she looked at Terra. Terra didn't want to worry her sister about Bethany's comments. Carolyn worried about everything; about money, about being in a car accident, being hit by a bus, you name it. Carolyn often remarked about how lucky Terra was to have a husband who earned so well so that she didn't have to worry about money.

"I… Look, the woman is weird. She arrived here out of the blue, telling me she was worried about Shamus, and then saying that she didn't know where he was the night Sean was murdered. Whatever is going on with her isn't up to us to solve. Let's not worry about it. I'll call Derrick and tell him what just happened and let him deal with it."

Carolyn sighed. "Agreed. The only good thing to come out of this is your freedom from the forces of darkness," Carolyn said, curving her fingers into air quotes.

"You sound like Kevin."

"Kevin and I share a lot of the same ideas. How's his relationship with Peter going?"

"How do you know about that?"

Before answering, her sister picked up her carry-on and took it down the hall to the guest bedroom. "You told me once." She disappeared into the bedroom briefly then came back out. "Don't you remember? Right here in this house. We were getting dinner and you told me about Peter and Kevin."

She hadn't told anyone about Peter and Kevin. She was certain of that, but she didn't want to argue. "You're probably right." She followed her sister toward the master suite at the end of the hall, still mulling over in her mind how her sister could have found out about Kevin's secret.

"Okay, let's see. What are you going to do about the carpet?" Carolyn asked, opening the door to the master suite.

The air smelled sweet, musty and warm. "Let's open the windows," Terra said, moving into the room, stopping when she saw the dark blood stain on the carpet. Filled with anguish and a sense of loss so profound she couldn't breathe, Terra backed away until she came up against the door to the bedroom. How could she ever live in this house again, knowing what had happened to her husband in this room? She'd made a mistake, thinking she could stay here, do what needed to be done. She had nothing left to give, no energy to face what lay ahead. "I don't know if I can do this."

Carolyn reached for her, pulling her back out of the room. "That's okay. You don't have to be the strong one all the time. You've lost Sean in the worst way possible. Be kind to yourself. Why don't you go to the kitchen and make coffee while I tidy up the room for you?"

She wanted to run away, as far away as possible. Yet, something stopped her. She looked at her sister for a moment. The two of them could manage here if they both worked at it. Sean would want her to be strong, to take control. "Okay. While you do that, I'll call to have the carpet removed and a new one installed. I'll also call the man who does our…my painting."

"You do that and leave this to me."

Terra headed back to kitchen, picked up her cell phone and made the necessary calls, relieved to have that much over. As she hung up and turned away, the phone rang. She picked it up.

"Terra, it's Derrick, Detective O'Leary."

"Oh, Derrick, I just had a visit from my sister-in-law, Bethany. She had a large bruise on her arm. She told me that she didn't know where Shamus was the night of Sean's death."

"What?"

"That's what she said."

"I'll look into it. In the meantime, would you be willing to come in on Monday afternoon around three o'clock?"

Monday was three days away, three long days, the worst she could imagine. "I haven't buried my husband yet, and you're calling to say you want to see me right after the funeral? I don't understand."

"We need to talk to you. We're hoping that by then you'll remember more about what happened, something new related to the two men who attacked you." He lowered his voice. "Terra I'm really sorry, but I have no choice. Meaghan Wilson will be doing the interview."

At least Derrick was trying to be as gentle as possible, something she appreciated. "I will come if you feel it's really necessary."

"I do. Please don't worry, Terra. It will go okay. This is simply a chance to go over what happened."

Suddenly her hands began to shake so hard the phone nearly slipped from her fingers. She clutched her tummy, fearing that all this stress might harm her baby. Tears filled her eyes, overflowed and ran down her cheeks. How could she go through with the interview? How could she relive those horrible moments?

Terra hung up but was still holding the phone when Carolyn came into the kitchen.

"What's wrong? You look like you've seen a ghost."

"I just had a call from the police. They want to interview me again Monday afternoon. I think I'd better bring my lawyer."

"What for?"

"I don't know what I can tell them that they don't already know, but this just doesn't feel right to me. If I had someone representing me during the interview I'd feel better, more in control. I told Derrick everything I remember, and yet I'm expected to tell my story all over again." She glanced at her sister. "What do you think they want?"

"Would Shamus have that kind of influence with the police? To bring you in for questioning when you're not a suspect? You aren't, are you?"

"Who knows? I haven't even met the lawyer. Oh! No! We were scheduled to sit down yesterday afternoon, and I forgot all about it. How could that have happened?"

"Terra, stop being so hard on yourself. Anyone else wouldn't have scheduled an appointment in the middle of everything that's going on. Under the circumstances forgetting would be easy. Call him and tell him what happened. I'm sure he'll understand," Carolyn suggested.

She called Dennis Sparks, apologized and made another appointment. "Well, that's done. I'm seeing him later today, and maybe he'll be able to help me sort out what's going on here."

"Can you get the police interview postponed?"

"I doubt the funeral will be Monday, and I want this interview to be over with. I'd rather go through the interview and have it behind me, than worry for the next few days about what questions they want to ask."

"So you'll go?"

Terra shrugged. "Yes, I'll be at the police station on Monday afternoon."

"That's settled then. I'm going with you this afternoon. What do you want me to do until your appointment with the lawyer?"

"We need to put Sean's clothes in boxes. They can't stay scattered all over the bedroom. There are boxes down in the basement, the room behind the…I just can't go downstairs." She felt tears flood her eyes, and relived the feeling of the man's hands on her body; her fear for her unborn child.

How would she ever survive in this house without Sean?

Fighting the urge to get in the car and drive somewhere she walked into the bedroom where the clothes lay spread on the floor, a jumbled mess. Sean had a shirt she'd always loved. She'd given it to him as a birthday present, the blue in the shirt matching his eyes. Carefully she checked the floor and the closet for the shirt, wanting to hold it in her hands, breathe in his scent. Not looking at the bloodstain on the carpet, she checked the clothes scattered around the room for the shirt. It wasn't there... Odd. Selena loved to iron. It was probably still in the clean-clothes basket in the laundry room.

"Why don't you leave all of that to me?" Carolyn asked.

"That would be great—"

The phone rang again. She frowned at the caller ID. "Olivia Cameron? She must be calling about the funeral."

"You'd better answer," Carolyn said, a wry expression on her face.

Terra picked up the phone to the sound of Olivia's anxious voice. "I'm sorry about how things ended the last time you were here. I called to see if we could finish up the arrangements for the funeral. We need to talk to Mr. Cox, to finalize things. I've asked him to come to the house tomorrow afternoon." There was an awkward moment of silence. "Would that work for you, Terra?"

Olivia's voice sounded strange, as it were coming from a long distance, a poor connection. Was she on speakerphone? And if so, why?

"The police took Sean's computer, leaving me without the contact information for many of his friends and business associates," Terra said.

A short pause ensued. "Shamus says he can provide the information we need."

Shamus had to be listening in for Olivia to answer without asking him directly. *What was going on?* "That would be good."

"Could you come to the house tomorrow afternoon for an hour or so?"

Uneasy about her suspicion and unsure as to why Shamus would be listening into the conversation without identifying himself, she asked, "Can I get back to you?"

"What about tomorrow evening? Around six? We could have a…visit while we talk. We haven't had a chance to talk about how you're doing, what you're going through. It might help all of us to be together for a few hours."

The last time she'd been in Olivia's home, Shamus had behaved badly. She didn't want to go through that again, but she did respect her mother-in-law, and couldn't deny the fact that the woman had lost her son. "Sure. Okay."

She got off the phone, her mind whirling. Had Shamus been listening in to her call with Olivia? And if Shamus had been listening, why didn't Olivia say so? Why be secretive about it?

She and Sean had kept mostly to themselves after Olivia's husband died, and that was when Sean learned that he'd been chosen CEO over his brother. A furious confrontation led to the brothers not speaking for months, which made working in the same office very difficult for her husband. Olivia stepped in, encouraging her sons to respect their father's wishes. To ease the worry for their mother and for the sake of the company, the brothers agreed to work together. It had been a tenuous peace at first, but in the past year things seemed to have improved.

Terra sat quietly in the open space of her living room looking out over the panoramic view of the back garden sloping down to a stream that meandered through the two acres that made up the property. She wished that Sean were with her to guide her through the next few days. She missed his calm approach to things, his ability to make her feel at ease in any circumstance. If he hadn't died they would be happily planning for their baby.

Yet deep in her heart she knew that without Sean to protect her from his family, she would have to pay close attention to what was going on. She was the beneficiary of Sean's personal holdings, but she had no idea what would happen to his share of Cameron Industries. Sean had mentioned that the business held very large insurance policies on both men should either of them die while still involved in running the company. The insurance money would cover any potential loss due to the sudden shift in management and any perceived injury to the organization.

He'd told her it was sound business practice to insure the executives of the company, should a death occur. He had joked that Cameron Industries would we well off if anything happened to either him or Shamus. Forcing her mind away from all the morbid thoughts, she went into the kitchen and made a pot of coffee, calling out to her sister as she did so.

Carolyn joined her in the kitchen, her face flushed as if she'd been crying. "I'm ready to take Sean's clothing. Is there something you'd like to keep?"

"Are you okay?"

"Yeah. Allergies. So is there anything?"

Terra remembered Sean coming in the door that evening, his suit jacket hung over his arm and a huge grin on his face as he'd enfolded her in his embrace. "Don't take the navy blue suit."

"He has at least four navy suits," Carolyn said.

She couldn't part with the suit he'd been wearing when he came home that evening. Not now, and maybe not for a long time. "Leave all four. I'll look after them."

"I'm sorry you have to go through all this," Carolyn said.

Terra told her sister about her concerns that Shamus had listened in on the call with Olivia. "I hope I'm wrong about him, but after the way he's behaved these past few days, it wouldn't surprise me to learn that he plans to be there when I talk with Olivia. He simply had to be sure that the time chosen worked with his schedule."

Carolyn sat down next to Terra. "You've had enough for one day. I'll finish this later while you're at the lawyer's office. Let's go out for lunch before your appointment. We could go to Pastelli's and then when you get back we can decide whether or not you should stay here tonight."

"Didn't you agree to stay here with me? Have changed your mind?" Terra asked, feeling a level of panic at the thought of being alone.

"I did agree to stay with you. I only wondered if maybe it was too much for you so soon after…after Sean's death."

Terra couldn't seem to decide what she wanted to do—

stay or go. Yet, wanting to reassure her sister, Terra took her hand. "It's not too much for me. And lunch sounds good. Maybe we should take both cars. That way I can leave for the lawyer's office straight from the restaurant," Terra said, relieved to be getting out of the house for a little bit. It was true she wanted to stay here, but she also recognized that it wouldn't be easy. Would she ever be able to come into this house again without remembering the horror of that night?

A little later they left in their separate cars, meeting up at the restaurant. "At least no press. We haven't seen any reporters since yesterday, have we?" Carolyn asked.

"I'm finally yesterday's news," Terra replied, as she glanced around the restaurant. It felt almost disheartening to be doing something so ordinary knowing that she and Sean would never enjoy going to a restaurant together again.

They were escorted to a table near the back of the restaurant and the waiter placed menus in front of them before reciting the specials of the day.

The Italian restaurant had a great lunch menu, which they both enjoyed. Terra didn't have her usual glass of red wine because she needed all her wits about her when she went to the lawyer's office. When they were finished they left the restaurant together. Terra headed out to find Dennis Sparks' office while Carolyn went back to the house to box up Sean's clothing.

Driving slowly along Michigan Avenue she found the narrow building that matched the number she'd written hastily on a piece of paper. She found a parking space a block away from the office. As she entered the building, she spotted his name on the glass door just beyond the elevator. She knocked and the door was immediately opened.

"I'm Terra—"

"I know who you are. Please come in, Mrs. Cameron," Dennis Sparks said, waving her toward an office flooded with sunlight.

Dennis Sparks was a very tall, thin man with anxious

movements, and a sparse moustache that he kept touching. When he sat down in the chair behind his desk his legs stuck out like brown cloth-covered sticks. Slouching in his chair, he motioned for her to sit down. "Mrs. Cameron, you mentioned on the phone that you might need a criminal lawyer. Can you clarify for me?"

"To be honest I'm not sure if I will need you. A friend of mine felt that it might be a good idea to have a lawyer with me at any police interview, given that the police are still investigating my husband's murder."

"Do they have any suspects?" he asked, patting his moustache.

"I don't know. They have asked me to come in. I'd like you to come with me."

He sat straight up in his chair, his gaze locked on her. "When is the appointment?"

"Monday at three."

"Did the police say what they wanted to talk about?"

"I was told they want to go over the events of that night to see if I remember anything more."

Dennis Sparks scratched a few words on a note pad. "Who was the officer?"

"Detective Derrick O'Leary. But he's not conducting the interview," she hastened to add.

"Who is?"

"Detective Meaghan Wilson, I believe."

More scratching on the note pad. "Okay, Mrs. Cameron, I'm going to see what I can find out and prepare myself for this interview. I'll call you this weekend. Will you be around?"

"Yes." She gave him her cell number. "Do you need some sort of retainer?"

"We'll discuss that Monday, after I find out what's going on." He stood up, came around the desk and shook her hand. "I'll be in touch."

Leaving the lawyer's office Terra felt so exhausted and worried she could barely remember where she'd parked her car. Her thoughts were focused on what the lawyer had said. Or hadn't said. He hadn't asked her any questions. He didn't seem very concerned about the upcoming police interview. He didn't seem caring or responsive to anything. Did he really have experience in criminal law? Maybe she should talk to another lawyer or someone who knew this man and see what they said about him.

Andy McIntyre, Sean's friend, was a real estate lawyer. He might know someone who could help her, or at least give her some idea about this guy…

She was so preoccupied she nearly walked past her car.

Feeling a sense of impending doom, she climbed into her car and drove home.

A few hours later and after drinking enough coffee to make her shake, Terra arrived at the Cameron mansion. Driving past the tennis courts, past the pool and around the curved driveway to the side entrance of the house, she noticed Shamus's Audi parked in front of the four-car garage. Another vehicle—she assumed it to be the funeral director's—was parked next to Shamus's.

As she stared up at the imposing façade of the Cameron she regretted not bringing anyone along with her to this meeting. She was afraid of having to face Shamus.

Should she turn around and go home? As much as she wanted to, she couldn't. She needed to complete the funeral arrangements. Besides she and Olivia needed to talk about Sean. He was her son, after all and she was the woman who had given birth to him. She touched her tummy remembering her own child. She was reaching for the bell when the door swung open.

"Terra, I'm so glad to see you," Bethany exclaimed, rushing out the door and hugging her. "How are you doing?" she asked, her eyes bright with determined enthusiasm. "We've all gathered here to talk about the funeral. Mother Cameron is in the living room."

Confronted by the imposing shadows of the foyer she felt as if she were about to be attacked. As she entered the living room her suspicion was heightened when Shamus suddenly appeared along the wall near the window. His appearance there reminded her of the night Sean died and the man who had appeared out of the night, along the wall near the French doors to the patio. She shivered with apprehension.

"Finally you're here." He walked toward her, no hand extended in greeting.

Terra's heart started pounding in her chest when she saw the anger in Shamus's eyes. Staring at his insolent expression, and tired of his behavior over the past days, she stood squarely in front of him. "I came here at your mother's request."

"Well, before you start talking to my mother, I want you to explain this." He clicked the TV remote and the screen showed footage of her and Kevin leaving Kevin's condo a couple of days earlier. "Is this your lover? Were the two of you off having sex only days after my brother was murdered?"

"No! Of course not!"

"Prove it. Prove that you don't have a relationship with this man," Shamus said.

Olivia came toward Terra, an embarrassed look on her face. "It's unfortunate. The press is behaving badly, presenting us all in a bad light."

Terra stared at her mother-in-law in disbelief. Her son was dead and she was worried about the press? "That may be true, but while you have only your grief to deal with, I've been dealing with what actually happened that night, and the police investigation, as well as their demands for more information."

She turned back to Shamus. "That's why I was at a friend's condo. I needed to get away from people looking for a sensational story."

"You expect us to believe that?" Shamus said, his words harsh.

"Olivia, can we talk somewhere private? It would seem that we can't talk about these sensitive things concerning my husband's funeral, here," she said, making her inference clear.

"Certainly." Olivia gave Shamus a warning glance.

He drew in a deep breath, scrubbing his face in frustration. "You owe this family an explanation of how you could be found leaving another man's house days after my brother was killed."

"I owe you no explanations but I will tell you this: Kevin Jackson has been my friend since grade school. We have remained friends throughout our lives. If we were going to be romantically involved it would have happened years ago."

As if on cue, the room went silent. Olivia stared at Terra as if she didn't believe her. Bethany appeared beside Shamus touching his arm and staring up into his face adoringly.

Wanting to escape from all this, and utterly alone in the face of this intimidating family, Terra's head began to pound. Nausea rose through her, making her body tremble. She gripped the corner of the sofa.

"Are you all right?" Olivia asked with genuine concern.

"I'm fine." She couldn't tell anyone in the family about her baby. Not one of them could know until she confirmed it with her doctor and had a plan in place. The trip to the doctor had been second on her "to do" list—right after she told Sean her news. "Can we please complete the funeral arrangements?"

"Absolutely." Olivia dismissed Shamus with a nod. "Mr. Cox is waiting in the den."

They worked out the details of the funeral set for Tuesday morning. The visitation would take place on Monday evening. The funeral home promised to keep the press away. Whether they could manage that remained to be seen.

Yet, overwhelmed by Shamus's cruel words and shocking behavior, Terra could no longer think about the press or anyone else. Her only thought was finding the strength to face those long hours of grief, and the burial of the man she'd loved with all her heart, in front of people she barely knew or recognized.

If she had her way, Sean's ashes would be taken to the coast of Maine and scattered over the broad expanse of gray-green ocean they'd loved.

She was about ready to leave when Shamus came back into the room, Bethany trailing behind him. "I called your friend Kevin. He says you *were* there with him."

"Why? I told you I was there, but as a friend. What right did you have to go behind my back and contact him directly?" Terra demanded, wishing she could walk out the door and never see these people again.

"Because I don't believe that you weren't having an affair with Kevin."

Olivia put her hand on Shamus' arm. "This is your sister-in-law. Stop this now."

Suddenly Terra felt faint. Her head swam. Her stomach churned. "I'm going to be sick—"

Sliding toward the floor she reached out to Olivia.

Olivia gasped as she struggled to hold onto Terra. "Shamus!"

Shamus's fingers bit into Terra's arm as he helped her onto the sofa.

Terra swallowed to ward off the wave of nausea.

"Bethany, get Terra a glass of water. Hurry!" Olivia ordered.

"I'll be right back," Bethany said, racing from the room.

"Terra, what's the matter?" Olivia asked, her voice kind and filled with concern.

Another wave of nausea overtook Terra. Bile rose in her throat. She reached out to her mother-in-law and exchanged a knowing glance.

"Terra, you're expecting a baby, aren't you? My grandbaby," the older woman murmured.

"Yes," Terra whispered.

"You're *what*? How can you be expecting a baby? That's not fair. I'm the one who should be pregnant," Bethany cried out, the glass falling from her hands and shattering on the hardwood floor.

CHAPTER SEVEN

"That can't be true! Sean would have told me," Shamus said, his voice cold and unyielding—his face suddenly pale.

"Sean didn't know," Terra murmured, regretting having said a word. This was not how she wanted them to find out about her baby. She'd wanted to share it with Sean, to experience that first moment of joy with him.

"Why didn't he know?" Olivia asked quietly.

"Because I only found out the afternoon before he died. I planned to tell him that evening. He wanted to tell me something as well, but we didn't get a chance to talk to each other. I wanted to tell him about our...baby." She choked on the words. Tears spilled down her cheeks. "I need to go home," she whispered to Olivia.

Shamus moved closer, his broad shoulders blocking the light from the window. "I don't believe you. I can see what's going on, even if no one else can." His gaze swept past his mother to his wife. "You think that if you claim to be pregnant, that we'll make room in our lives for you, that you'll be able to make a financial claim against the family. Is that it?"

Terra didn't answer him. She took a deep breath and stood up, her knees shaking.

"I have to go now. I'll see you at the funeral," she said to Olivia.

"Why don't I arrange to have my driver take you home?" Olivia asked.

Somehow she would find the strength to get in her car and drive home. "No. Thank you."

Olivia patted her shoulder. "You take care, dear, and we'll talk later."

Terra made her way across the room to the foyer.

"I'll bet you don't know about the woman who sent the yellow roses to Sean last week, do you? I saw him read the card attached to the bouquet. He was going to tell you about her, wasn't he? That's what he was going to tell you the night he died, wasn't it?" Shamus asked, a gloating tone in his voice.

What was he saying? Was he implying that Sean had a mistress?

She turned to face him, the heat of anger rising in her cheeks, her eyes stinging with tears. "If Sean received roses it would be from someone he'd helped. He was always helping people."

"Shamus, don't do this," Bethany said, reaching for her husband's arm.

He shook free of her touch. "You found out Sean was having an affair and was about to leave you for another woman. You couldn't let that happen."

Olivia went over to her son. "Shamus, don't."

He turned on his mother. "Am I the only one in this family who can see what's going on here?"

In the sudden stillness of the room, Olivia stood beside Shamus, the look on her face a mix of worry and sadness as she met Terra's disbelieving stare. "Shamus has been having a really difficult time since Sean died. He blames everyone for what happened, and it would seem he especially blames you. I'm so sorry."

As Terra faced the three of them across the wide expanse of the room, she realized just how much she disliked all of them—so different from the warm and caring man who had been her husband.

Bethany was pathetic. Shamus, a man whose anger ruled his life, was obnoxious. Olivia's compassion for Terra's situation seemed to be reduced to apologizing for her out-of-control son.

Looking at her mother-in-law she saw Olivia's life as

tragic, a life that was beginning to show in her appearance. The expensive makeup no longer disguised the deepening lines around the older woman's eyes and mouth, held at bay with plastic surgery until now. The expensive clothing that told everyone who she was and what she stood for. And surrounding her, this expensive home with all its amenities proved that her life was one of privilege. Yet none of it changed the basic fact that Olivia and this house were filled with unhappiness.

Feeling sorry for Olivia she relented. "It must be terrible to lose a son, especially the way Sean died. I wish I could help you, but I'm barely able to—"

"I understand, dear," Olivia said, coming toward her. "This is a terrible time for you. And to know that you are carrying Sean's baby through all this must be even more difficult." She offered a drawn smile.

"It is and it isn't. Sean shouldn't have died. I should have been able to do something, anything to help him. But carrying his baby is like I have part of him with me all the time, and that's good."

"I know. I know," Olivia said in a soothing tone.

She looked at her mother-in-law, willing the woman to believe her. "When the man tried to rape me, all I could think about was saving my baby, our baby. The anger in the man's eyes, his ugly stare, his strength. I managed to get him off me but not before the other man knifed Sean—"

"Sean would have made a wonderful dad, wouldn't he?" Olivia said, her voice shaking. "And you really loved my son. I know that. I'm worried about you. Are you able to sleep? Have you made an appointment with an obstetrician?"

"I will when the funeral is over, when I can think clearly. I have to protect my baby at all costs. I can't lose…this baby. It's all I have left of Sean."

Olivia slipped her arm around Terra. "I can't imagine how you must have felt when you realized what that horrible man was about to do to you."

She glanced quickly at Olivia, feeling an odd kinship to this aloof woman who had seemed so untouchable. "It's like being caught in a nightmare. At first I was unable to react. My body moved so slowly. I was so scared for my baby that I had to do something. I kicked at him, tried to gouge out his eyes."

Olivia held her away and looked into Terra's eyes. "You're under a lot of stress. You've been through a horrible experience. I'm surprised you're still able to function. I would have gone to bed and not gotten up. You're very brave."

"I hate to bring this up, but Shamus mentioned flowers being delivered to the office. Do you think there's any chance that the flowers and the attack on Sean are connected?" Olivia asked.

"Why would they be connected?" Terra asked, surprised at the suggestion.

Olivia shrugged.

"I'm going to call his secretary, Evelyn Thornton, when I get home. She'll know who sent the flowers," Terra said.

"I'm sorry I upset you. I shouldn't have brought it up. I could have called Evelyn myself," Olivia said.

Was Olivia's show of concern as genuine as it seemed? Or was she only worried about her family and how they would be perceived in all this mess? Maybe she was being kind because she wanted to present a unified front, the perfect family going through a terrible crisis. Knowing Olivia, she probably called her lawyer to see what sort of damage control they should be doing in order to protect the family from any potential scandal.

Terra suddenly needed to get away from the Cameron house, away from the whole Cameron family. She reached for the doorknob. "I'll be in touch."

"Take care, my dear. See you on Monday," Olivia said as if it were a normal day, a day filled with pleasantness.

Terra made her way to her car, her head swimming, her stomach pushing against her diaphragm. Sean didn't have a mistress. He'd loved her with all his heart. They'd been happy...

Everything would be all right once she got home.

Back at the house, and an hour later, Terra still didn't have much information about the flowers sent to Sean. His secretary said the delivery person put the flowers on her desk with a card that was sealed in an envelope. Evelyn assumed that the roses were from Terra, especially after Sean had told her about their plans to spend the evening together.

She'd just hung up from Evelyn when the phone rang again. "Mrs. Cameron, it's your attorney, Dennis Sparks. I think we need to speak before your interview on Monday afternoon. Something has come up."

"What do you mean?"

"I'd rather not say over the phone. Can we agree to meet before the interview at La Costa, the restaurant down the block from the police station?"

La Costa was a high-end restaurant with a bar populated by the newcomers to the world of finance and business. Terra had been there a couple times, but she and Sean both found it too noisy and crowded. "Ah…sure."

"Then that's settled. I'll see you there around two." With that he hung up.

Terra shook her head at the weirdness of it all. Why didn't he ask his questions while they were at his office, or on the phone? Why meet just before the interview? She'd been prepared at their first meeting to tell him what she knew and to get his advice on how to proceed.

What should she do next? She couldn't sit around the house and worry. Carolyn had left a note saying she'd be back after she picked up a few groceries. She couldn't concentrate long enough to watch TV or a movie.

It occurred to her that she hadn't told Derrick about the roses sent to Sean's office. He had said she could call him anytime. She picked up the phone and dialed the number he'd given her, painfully aware that she didn't want Detective Wilson to answer. Derrick answered on the first ring. "Did you find the brown envelope that was on Sean's desk?" she asked.

"No. I went through all the evidence material in the locker, and there is no brown envelope."

"So, who would have taken it?"

"You're absolutely sure it was on his desk?"

"Yes. I met him at the door when he came home. I followed him into his office where he put his computer case on the desk and placed a brown envelope on the top of it. I remember that part very clearly."

"So, sometime between when Sean got home and when you discovered it missing the next day someone was in there and took it. Who knew about the envelope?" he asked.

"Possibly Evelyn Thorton. I assume he brought the envelope home from the office."

"Possibly." She could hear a tapping sound, one she was familiar with. When Derrick was thinking about something he often tapped his pen on the desk. "Where is Sean's cell phone?"

She clutched the phone in surprise. "I assumed the police had taken it, since they took his laptop."

"No. I checked and it wasn't with the evidence we collected. Where would he normally leave it?"

"Where he leaves his keys—in the kitchen. Hold on, I'll check." She went into the kitchen and checked the bowl where his wallet and keys were, a pang of loss blindsiding her. "It's not…here." She gave a half sob, as she tried not to remember that Sean's first action when he got home was to drop his keys, wallet and cell phone off in the kitchen before coming to find her.

"Terra, I'm sorry to be putting you through this. Why don't I come over and we look for Sean's cell phone together?" he asked, his voice gentle.

In that instant she remembered. "Sean's cell phone was on the bedside table that night. I remember seeing it." She hurried down the hall to the bedroom to discover that the carpet had been taken up. Although shocked at the sight, she stepped around the area where Sean had fallen, moving to the bedside table, searching for the phone. "I don't see it," she said, opening the drawer and looking in. "No. Wait. It's here. Shoved in the back of the drawer."

"Don't touch it. I'll be over for it in a few minutes."

She sighed in relief at the thought that Derrick was

coming over. It had been a rough day, and she needed to see a friendly face.

She was sitting in the living room looking out the window when Carolyn arrived, her arms filled with groceries. "I thought we should get enough food in to do the weekend. The men came and pulled up the carpet while you were gone. The painter arrived and covered the blood spots on the wall and baseboard with primer, and said he'd wait for you to decide what color you want in the room."

"Thanks for looking after all that and picking up groceries," Terra said, taking several bags from her sister. She peeked in. "Wow! Doritos? I love them." Putting the grocery bags down on the counter, she started putting things away in the cupboard. "This is the best way I can think of to spend the weekend."

"Yeah. We won't answer the door. We'll order takeout Saturday night, and never let the big screen TV cool down."

"Speaking of answering the door, Derrick is on his way over here."

Carolyn plunked a box of cereal down on the counter. "He is? What does he want?"

"He's coming to pick up Sean's cell phone. I thought the police had taken it that night, but it seems they hadn't. I found it in the bedside table. Derrick told me not to touch it, that he'd be here to pick it up."

A small gasp escaped Carolyn's lips. "Sean's cell phone was in the drawer in your bedroom?"

"Yes," Terra said, hearing the doorbell ring. "That must be him now."

"I'm glad you found the phone," Derrick said as she opened the door. "It will tell us who Sean talked to in the hours before…and we'll be able to determine who might have called him."

She walked with him down to the bedroom. "It would be great if the phone could identify who did this. Do you think those men might have called him?" Terra shivered at the thought.

"We'll know more after the techs have a look," Derrick said, his gloved hand lifting the phone out of the drawer and dropping it into a plastic bag.

"Are you any closer to finding a suspect?"

"We're working on it. Thanks for telling me about Bethany's statement that she didn't know where Shamus was the night of the murder." He tucked the plastic bag in his pocket. "And thanks for this." He indicated the phone. "You've been really helpful, but I've got to go."

He went out the door and down the walkway before Terra had a chance to say anything.

"What was that all about?" Carolyn asked, coming up behind her as they both watched Derrick get in his car and pull away from the curb.

"Sean's phone may help to find his killer," Terra said, relieved at the thought that all the questioning and suspicion might be over soon. "Derrick is having Sean's cell phone checked for calls and messages."

"Sean's phone?" Carolyn asked, a shocked look on her face. "Does he think that Sean's killer called him that night?"

"Possibly. I would imagine that everyone who called Sean will be interviewed to see what they know. Hopefully one of them will be the killer."

Carolyn stared at her for a few minutes, and then gave a shaky smile. "Maybe now we can enjoy the weekend. If the police have Shamus as a suspect you can relax," Carolyn said.

And they did just that. They spent hours eating, watching movies, talking about everything from their childhood to politics. It was the first time since Sean's death that Terra had been able to sleep a little better.

When Monday morning came she felt genuinely sorry the weekend was over. With the funeral arrangements completed, all Terra had to do was decide what she'd wear to the visitation that evening, and the funeral the following day.

She found a short black dress she'd bought in Chicago when she went with Sean on a business trip. Her pearls would go well with that.

Near the back of the closet she discovered a black business suit, one that Sean had bought her, partly in jest and partly as a serious gesture. When they'd first married, Sean had tried to convince her to leave nursing and go into the business with him. She had pleaded ignorance of all business practices, but he'd bought her the suit to prove that he was serious. He told her he'd know she was ready to join the business world when she wore the suit. She lifted the hanger off the rail and looked at it. Fine wool, and the name of an expensive designer told her that he'd spent a lot of money. She'd never worn it and had actually forgotten she had it.

While she put together the clothes she'd wear in the next hours, she tried not to let her mind drift to her lawyer's request to meet ahead of the upcoming interview with the police. She couldn't imagine how they would carry on a conversation in that loud space, but maybe, in the interim, she'd hear from the police that they didn't need to interview her, that they had Shamus in custody. Later, after a calming bath she pulled out the third outfit she thought she might wear. A blue silk jacket and black pants.

"Why are you fussing over what you're going to wear?" Carolyn asked, standing at the door to the closet. "Does it take you this long to dress for work?" she asked, a teasing tone in her voice.

"Getting dressed for work is easy: a pair of scrubs, my name tag and comfortable shoes. Getting dressed for this interview is crazy. You'd think I could pick something and just go with it."

"You'd think."

"Okay, this is it." She took the blue silk jacket and pants off the hanger and got dressed. "There. Finito."

"Do you want me to come with you?"

Terra looked at her for a minute. And after meeting with the lawyer, she wouldn't feel so alone inside the police station if Carolyn came with her. Of course her lawyer would also be with her, but he wasn't family.

"I promise to dress in under two minutes," Carolyn said.

Terra chuckled. "That fast? You're on."

When they reached La Costa there weren't many patrons at the tables or the bar. "The lunch crowd is gone," Terra said.

Carolyn let the door to the restaurant slide closed behind her. "See? One worry down, two worries to go."

"I don't see Dennis Sparks anywhere," Terra said, searching the tables. "Maybe he's at a booth."

"May I help you," a waiter asked as he approached them.

"I'm meeting someone…"

"Mrs. Cameron. Please allow me to extend our sympathies to you and your family during this difficult time."

A little surprised, she looked at the young man. *Did she know him? Did he know Sean?* "Thank you."

"Mr. Sparks is waiting for you. Please follow me."

As they approached the booth, Dennis Sparks stood up to greet them. Terra couldn't believe the change in him. His suit was beautifully tailored, his hair trimmed and his moustache gone.

Carolyn's phone rang, startling Terra.

"I'm sorry, but I need to take this call. I'll just step outside for a minute. I'll be right back," Carolyn said rushing toward the entrance to the restaurant.

Terra nodded, her attention focused on Mr. Sparks. He barely appeared to be the same man at all.

"Mrs. Cameron, please have a seat. We have so much to discuss." He touched his lip as if searching for his missing moustache. "We have to be prepared for questions that might be difficult to manage, given the circumstances."

"What circumstances?" Terra asked as she sat down.

"You realize that the police will want to…to find a resolution to this situation, this horrible crime that has everyone talking?"

What did he want her to say? "I suppose."

"Mrs. Cameron, I need you to walk me through what happened that evening."

"Here? Where anyone can listen in?" she asked, alarmed at the number of people who seemed to be filling tables around where they sat.

"If I'm going to be ready to represent you at the meeting this afternoon, I need to hear your side of the story."

"There is no *my* side. My husband was killed. I am a witness."

"Mrs. Cameron, I must be prepared for whatever line of questioning the police take during the interview."

Out of the corner of her eye, she saw a face she recognized: Tim Martin, the reporter she'd seen outside Kevin's house.

"Mr. Sparks. Is that Tim Martin over there?" She pointed to the table not far from the booth where they sat.

Dennis Sparks squinted in the general direction. "It might be. Why do you ask?"

"Did you tell him you were meeting me here?"

"No!" His voice rose along with two points of color on his cheeks. "Why would you think I'd so such a thing? But come to think of it, maybe it would be a good idea for you to consider giving an interview, getting your story out there, just in case you're put on trial…"

"*On trial?* You believe I could be tried for my husband's murder?"

He shrugged. "As I understand it they don't have a suspect as yet."

"Really?" she said, suddenly very suspicious that this man took her case for the sake of the publicity it would get him. A struggling lawyer in charge of a high profile case— the perfect promotional opportunity, a golden opportunity to attract new clients. It had been Dennis Sparks who wanted to meet here, and somehow Tim Martin had found out about the meeting. Wanting nothing more to do with this man, she glanced around the restaurant looking for her sister.

Where was Carolyn?

She needed to leave, to get as far away from this man as possible. "Mr. Sparks, this meeting is over."

"What?"

"I no longer need your services." With that she got up and walked toward the door. She'd almost made it when Tim Martin caught up with her.

"Mrs. Cameron. I understand you're the only witness to your husband's murder. Would you consider sitting down with me to talk?"

"No. Absolutely not." She kept walking, brushing past him, pushing the door open to the restaurant, nearly knocking her sister over.

"Where were you?" she asked Carolyn, hurrying toward the car.

Carolyn caught up with her. "What's going on?"

"Tim Martin was waiting in there, thanks to Dennis Sparks," she said, her heart pounding so hard she felt as if she might faint. "I'm pretty sure that Tim Martin and Dennis Sparks are acquainted and that's why the reporter showed up today."

"Oh my God. I'm so sorry I left you like that, but I needed to answer that call…about my work…a new writing opportunity. An editor I've been trying to reach for months." Carolyn raised her eyes to meet Terra's questioning gaze. "What happened in there?"

Still shaking with anger Terra told her about the past few minutes; about Tim Martin asking for an interview, and that she had fired her lawyer. "Carolyn, what am I going to do?"

"Take it easy. I don't know who this Tim Martin is, but he was only trying to shake you up, get you to say something he could print."

"What if he follows us to the police station? What if the lawyer told him I was going to the police station?"

"Maybe it's time you talked to Derrick. He might be able to help you," Carolyn said.

"He's the one who said I needed a lawyer." She stopped. "What if this interview is a set up to accuse me of murdering Sean? That's what Shamus thinks and he's powerful in this town."

"But you told Derrick about Bethany's comment, that Shamus wasn't home that night. I imagine he's already following up on it," Carolyn said.

Terra reached for the car door to steady herself. "Maybe I shouldn't have been so hasty. What if I really need a lawyer with me for my own protection?"

"Do you want to postpone the interview? Give Derrick time to do his job?"

She'd never done anything like this before in her life. She'd never been inside a police station, not to mention being questioned in one. She wished she could call Derrick and get his advice after what had happened. But having been a part of his life, and knowing his devotion to his duty she knew that wouldn't work. Derrick had a job to do, a job that meant he couldn't give the impression he was treating her differently from anyone else.

"Terra, I know what you can do. Simply answer any questions that you feel comfortable answering. If you feel threatened, tell them you want a lawyer present," Carolyn said.

"And what lawyer would that be?"

Carolyn shrugged. "A court appointed one?"

"You watch too much television, Carolyn."

When Carolyn and Terra walked into the police station they were put through security checks before being directed upstairs. Derrick met them when they got off the elevator.

"You didn't bring a lawyer?" he asked without preamble.

"Does she need one?" Carolyn countered, stepping closer to her sister.

"No. We simply want to get her statement about the events of that night."

"Can we please get this over with?" Terra asked.

"This way," Derrick said, his eyes meeting Terra's, his expression neutral.

"I'll wait here for you," Carolyn said, pointing to a row of chairs near a desk.

Terra walked with Derrick down the corridor, realizing that she'd never been in his workplace. He's always been adamant that his private life and his work life not intersect. Seeing it now she hadn't expected the place where Derrick worked to be so lackluster and drab.

Why she thought about him or his life in the midst of

her own worry she didn't know. Her throat dry and her palms sweaty, she continued to walk beside him until he stopped in front of an imposing gray door. "Detective Wilson is waiting for you."

He hesitated for a minute, his gaze on Terra's face. "I'm sorry that I can't do this myself, and that you have to go through this interview. But please believe me; we only want to know what you can remember of that night. Don't speculate. Understood?"

What he meant was for her not to say more than the answer to the question. He'd often said that suspects would incriminate themselves more by their casual conversation in an interview than by their answers to the questions. Terra swallowed as fear rushed through her. If this truly was only about the events as she remembered them, why couldn't she tell those to Derrick? He already knew most of them. It would be easier to tell them to someone she knew, rather than a stranger.

Was it possible that Derrick realized that to interview her might be seen as a conflict of interest given their history together?

Once inside the narrow room, seated at a small desk, Terra wasn't sure of anything. The room smelled of stale coffee. The table had a dent along the edge and the woman who strode into the room didn't smile. Not one tiny crinkle of her eyes to indicate that she felt any compassion whatsoever for Terra's plight.

"Mrs. Cameron, I'm Meaghan Wilson. I'd like to ask you a few questions about the night your husband Sean Cameron died." She tossed a half smile Terra's way before continuing. "This is simply a chance for me to be clear on every part of your experience that night. All you need to do is remember and tell me as best you can. Okay?"

"Yes." Terra went through the entire evening from the time Sean got home until he died, the pain of remembering those moments flooding her thoughts, blocking her ability to pull away at times. Through all of it she was vaguely aware of the woman across from her who didn't seem to have anymore questions.

This was going much easier than Terra could have imagined, and for that she was pathetically grateful. She'd just finished when the officer clasped her hands on the table, within touching distance of Terra's fingers.

"Mrs. Cameron, you have self-defense training, correct?"

"Yes."

"Can you tell me why you didn't try to fight off your attacker?"

"I did! I kicked him. I gouged his eyes. I fought back!"

"Then why didn't forensics find anything under your nails? No sign that you scratched him, nothing to go on that proves what you're saying about being attacked."

"But my nails are cut short. As a nurse it's not good practice to have long nails because of the possibility of spreading germs to vulnerable patients."

"Mrs. Cameron, we have video footage of two men at the convenience store about a mile from your home." She passed the photos over. "Do you recognize either of these men?"

Terra looked closely at the grainy photos. "I don't know. They are dressed in dark clothing, the same as the attackers, I guess." She looked again. "The man who grabbed me was tall, at least as tall as my husband...was."

"Is there anything else you can tell me about the two men?"

"I can't remember very much. One of them grabbed me, nearly choked me, and dragged me upstairs. It all happened so quickly. When one of them tried to rape me I was terrified." She swallowed against the memory of the fear and the panic that seized her in those final minutes before Sean died.

"Mrs. Cameron, what were you doing at Mr. Jackson's condo the night after your husband was killed?"

Surprised by the question, Terra fumbled her words. "I...I needed to get away. The press were at my house. Kevin offered me a place to stay."

"What is your relationship with Kevin Jackson?"

She glanced around wondering where Derrick might be. "We've been friends since grade school."

"In what way?"

Terra shrugged, yet felt very uneasy about the question. Did this officer know that Kevin and Peter were lovers? She wasn't supposed to tell anyone, and she would certainly not tell someone who worked for Peter. "We're friends, that's all."

"And your connection to Detective O'Leary?"

"There isn't any. He's investigating my husband's death." Why was this woman asking these questions?

"Did you often go to Kevin's condo?"

"Occasionally, when Sean needed to get away from work for a couple of days. His job is…was very stressful at times. Kevin was kind enough to let us stay there when we needed to."

"Did you husband have life insurance policies?"

"Of course. The company held a large one on his life to protect and maintain the company should Sean pass away."

"Did you know that your husband recently took out a million dollar policy naming you as beneficiary?"

Shocked, she stared at the officer. "No." *Was Sean ill? Why didn't he tell me about the policy?* "I had no idea my husband had taken out a policy like that. I knew the company had an insurance policy on his life, but that's all."

"Surely you must have known that he would have an insurance policy. Come on. Today everyone has insurance."

Terra glanced across the table at the detective. The woman was staring at her, her eyes hard, assessing. Suddenly Terra was frightened. This woman suspected her of killing Sean. A cold shiver ran down her arms. She hugged herself.

"Mrs. Cameron, describe your relationship with your husband."

"My relationship?"

The officer nodded.

"I loved him. He loved me. We were very happy. We were hoping to start a family…" At the words she choked up and began to cry, sobs that shook her body. Struggling for control, she gripped the edge of the table.

Suddenly the door opened, and Derrick charged in. "I think that's enough."

CHAPTER EIGHT

Derrick shouldn't have rushed into the room like that, but he didn't have a choice. He'd told Meaghan to interview Terra, not interrogate her. *What the hell was going on?*

"We have all we need from you for the moment, Mrs. Cameron. Wait here. I'll be back in a minute." He couldn't let his eyes meet Terra's. He'd seen the flash of emotion, the pain and tears the woman had shown during Meaghan's questioning; all genuine, all real.

He turned on Meaghan, holding back the anger pummeling his chest. "Officer Wilson, can I have a word with you?"

Meaghan followed him down to the office without uttering a word of explanation. When they sat down across from each other he began. "What were you doing in there? You can't accuse her like that, and with no attorney present. What were you doing?"

"Getting the witness's story."

"It's not a story. It's the truth. On top of that we now have a conflicting testimony from Bethany Cameron stating that she didn't know where her husband was the night of the murder."

"Hearsay, stated by Terra Cameron who has every reason to plant suspicion on someone other than herself."

He snorted. "Meanwhile Shamus and his lawyer refused to meet with me again to answer a few questions, supposedly because Shamus was grieving."

"Look Derrick. We need to pay attention to the evidence we have. Terra's husband left her a million dollars. Who knows what else she stands to inherit when this is over? You think she's telling the truth, but how do you know?"

"Years of experience and gut instinct."

"Good for you. But from where I'm sitting this woman has a lot to answer for. She is the only witness to the crime. She *says* two men broke into the house, but the door downstairs that goes out into the backyard garden was not only unlocked, but open. Who leaves a door open, and goes upstairs, especially when it's dark outside?"

"Lots of people leave doors open. They were probably down there earlier in the evening, and simply forgot to lock up. It happens all the time."

"And where are the finger prints? We have no fingerprint evidence to prove there was an intruder."

"Are you saying Terra killed her husband? Is this what your behavior in that room was about?"

"I'm saying that we have only her word for what happened in that house. There are no other witnesses and no real evidence to prove that her husband was attacked by unknown assailants."

"So, you're saying that Terra Cameron, who is at least five inches shorter than her husband and at least sixty pounds lighter, managed to knife him in the neck without him fighting back?"

"She was taking self-defense training. They had an intimate relationship, allowing her to get close to him."

"Meaghan, we have no physical evidence that supports your theory."

"We also have no physical evidence to support her version of events. Derrick, think about this. How did two people enter the house, attack Terra and knife Sean, leaving no physical evidence behind?"

He was furious with Meaghan, but he had to get his

emotions under control. "If you're right, what motive did she have?" he asked, struggling to remain calm.

Meaghan rolled her eyes. "Money. Lots of insurance money."

"If we're going with that motive, Shamus would be the first on the list. He stands to gain complete control of Cameron Industries, a powerful motive if you ask me. Besides Terra was hysterical and disoriented when the police got there—hardly the behavior of a woman who murdered her husband."

Seeing the uncertainty on Meaghan's face he pressed on. "And then there's the theory I've been working on involving two known ex-cons." He explained his theory about Lennie Taylor and Buddy Edson and the similarities between the break-in and murder at the Cameron residence and the break-in and murder of Mrs. Pickering.

"Well, anything's possible, I suppose. So if you believe that's the most plausible lead, were you able to find these guys?"

"No. I went to their last known addresses, a few blocks from each other by the way, and both had moved during the past two weeks. A little suspicious, don't you think?"

"Or maybe they decided to leave town for some reason."

"Not likely. Those two were creatures of habit. That's how we caught up with them the last time."

Meaghan glanced at him, thoughtfully. "Derrick, if you ask me, you're reaching for suspects that you can't prove have any connection to Sean Cameron's murder, except maybe a similar MO. I know you don't want to hear this, but you're letting your past relationship with this woman cloud your judgment. Terra Cameron managed in the midst of all this to spend the night at a *friend's* condo, clean up the mess in her house from her husband's death within days of it happening, has not shed a tear that I've seen. To me, she doesn't behave like a woman who lost the man she loved. If you ask me—"

"I'm not asking you. I'm telling you. I want you to focus on the evidence. If you want to chase down possible leads, look into Shamus Cameron's lifestyle. With his brother dead what does he get out of it? Will the insurance money provide him with the funds to keep the company going, or as the

Chief Financial Officer, did he have other plans for that money? Will Sean's shares in the company automatically go to him? If your supposition is correct, that Sean was killed for money, then Shamus would be the number one suspect, wouldn't he?"

Meaghan sighed, glanced away before focusing all her attention on him. "Sorry, Derrick. My mistake. I'm worried about you; that's all. It's clear that you still care about her."

"Not in the way you think. If you're so sure it's her, bring me some evidence. Oh! By the way. Terra says that Sean brought home a large brown envelope that he left by his laptop that night. I can't find it in the evidence locker. Did you see it?"

"No. If it's not in the materials taken from the scene, where is it?"

"Don't know." He shrugged.

"And again we only have Terra's word that it even exists." She arched her eyebrow.

Frustrated with Meaghan he said, "I think we need to put as much effort into investigating the rest of the Cameron family as we have into Terra. That's all I'm saying."

Meaghan looked at him, her face flushed. "Okay. So where do you want to start?"

"What if this all started inside the company?"

"Go on," Meaghan said, looking interested.

"Do we know if Cameron Industries is as financially solid as it seems? What if Shamus and Sean were in financial trouble, and someone went after them?"

"Then, why Sean and not Shamus?"

Derrick rubbed his jaw. "I don't know. But before we put any more pressure on Terra we need to put some time into finding out everything we can about the company. Something may be going on there. We won't know until we look around a little. Besides, if your theory is that Terra stabbed her husband, where's the knife? We searched everywhere on that property. If she stabbed him, where did she hide it? You saw her that night. She wasn't capable of getting off the bedroom floor. How could she have managed to hide the knife?"

"I don't know, but I'm going to keep looking."

He shook his head slowly. "As far as I'm concerned Terra is the victim here."

"Just don't get caught protecting someone because of some sort of guilt trip you're on," Meaghan said, picking up her file of papers, her fingers trembling.

Derrick watched her body language. She seemed suddenly tentative. A woman whose strength and drive often amazed him was showing a vulnerability he'd never seen in her before. "Are you sure you're not letting *your* personal feelings interfere here?"

"What feelings?" she asked, her eyes not meeting his. Her cheeks flamed pink. She pulled a curl down to cover her cheek as she looked away.

Oh…no…Meaghan. Now he understood why this newly minted detective was so eager to work with him. She'd been so willing to please, so enthusiastic. He'd been really impressed with her determination to become a good detective. In the early months he'd been flattered that she seemed to hang on his every word, even took a little ribbing from some of the other detectives about it. Each time, he'd tossed off their comments about Meaghan being infatuated with him. Now he realized that it wasn't just this case, but her determination to focus on Terra that revealed something he hadn't been willing to admit. Meaghan was looking for more from him, a more personal relationship. Did she see Terra Cameron as competition? Was she jealous?

Tread carefully, O'Leary. "I think I'll check in with the ME. He promised a full report today. Why don't you go to Cameron Industries and see what you can find out?"

"You're going to let me go it alone? Seriously?" Meaghan said, disappointment clear in her voice. But she recovered quickly, flipped her curls over her shoulder and left the room.

Derrick came back into the interview room, his expression

one of puzzlement. "Terra, you're free to go. I'm sorry about Detective Wilson's line of questioning."

Terra tried to breathe over the anger and humiliation still rushing through her. All this time she'd expected him to treat her fairly, to look out for her a little, especially since he'd made such a big deal about wanting to help her. Instead he'd left her alone to face Detective Wilson who clearly didn't believe a word Terra said.

"It's all right," she said, lying to him. It wasn't all right. It would never be all right ever again. She hated him. She more despised Detective Wilson who had been so cold and uncaring, so filled with accusation.

"When is the funeral?" he asked.

"Tomorrow."

"Terra, I'm sorry."

She didn't care what he felt. He wasn't living her life. He couldn't imagine the desolation of living without Sean.

"I'll walk you down to the entrance," he offered.

She wanted as far away from this man and this place as possible. "That isn't necessary. Carolyn is waiting for me." She got up and walked out, hoping she'd never have to see him again.

When she reached Carolyn her sister was texting someone. Spotting Terra she snapped her phone closed. "How did it go?"

"They think I killed Sean for his life insurance money."

Carolyn hugged her close. "Never. You couldn't have done anything that awful. Those miserable people." She took Terra's hand. "We're getting out of here and going to my place, just in case the press are waiting for you outside yours. And I'm so sorry; that stupid lawyer! I wish I never I suggested him."

"No. Not to your place. I just want to go home."

Carolyn stopped in mid-stride. "Back to your house? Are you sure?"

"I have to get ready for the visitation this evening. I need a little time to get my head together after the way Detective Wilson behaved."

"I'll come with you. You cannot be alone in that house

after everything that's happened there. My stuff is there anyway."

Thankfully they made it out of the police station and back to her home without seeing any members of the press or media vans or anyone lurking near the house. She'd expected to see Tim Martin after coming across him in the restaurant. The reporter could have made her day worse had he followed her from the restaurant and waited outside the police station. She went into the house, undressed and went in the guest bedroom across the hall from her own room to search the closet for a robe.

She found a blue plaid shirt that Derrick used to wear when he worked in the yard. She took it out, held it close in her arms, and took deep breaths, soaking in his scent, remembering the rose bushes he'd planted in the backyard, the rhododendrum he'd planted just to make her happy. Holding back the tears she wrapped his shirt around her, climbed under the duvet, and snuggled down. Comfy and shielded from the outside world, she sobbed; her face drenched with tears. She clung to Sean's shirt afraid and fearful of what the following days would bring.

How was she going to get through the evening? All those people coming by—more out of curiosity than genuine caring. And if the police saw her as a suspect the whole city would hear the story before the visitation got underway. Why had the detective been so insistent about the money? Was she trying to frighten her into saying something incriminating? And why had Derrick come in when he did, to stop her from asking any more questions about her life with her husband? She had nothing to hide.

Except for watching crime shows on TV, she had no idea how the police conducted an investigation. She tried to focus on something else rather than how difficult her afternoon had been, and she tried to rest for her baby's sake. She patted her tummy. Suddenly she was ferociously hungry. Climbing out of the disheveled mess she'd made of the bed, she went to the kitchen.

"I'm starving," she said to Carolyn who sat at the kitchen counter reading the paper.

"You're eating for two now, remember," Carolyn said, folding the paper and putting it aside. "You'll be pleased to hear that today's paper only has the funeral announcement."

"That's good." Terra looked through the fridge, found a wedge of cheddar cheese and two apples. In the cupboard she found a box of crackers, and took all of it to the counter. "Do you want some?"

"No. While you were resting I made a ham and pickle sandwich."

"Remind me which one of us is pregnant," Terra teased.

Carolyn laughed. "Okay. We have almost two hours before you have to be at the funeral home. Why don't you have a nice long soak in the tub?"

"I don't want to go in my own tub. I'll use the tub in the guest bedroom."

"All this has to be very difficult for you. You can come to live with me for as long as you need to."

"Thanks. I really appreciate the offer." She touched her sister's arm. "I'll have a good soak and see if it helps me relax enough to face this evening."

"I know it will. And while you do, I'll go over to my house and get the clothes I need for tonight and the funeral tomorrow. I won't be long."

"I'll lock the doors and set the alarm system."

Carolyn met her gaze. "Oh, sis, I'm sorry you feel you have to lock up all the time."

She would always lock up; never trust anyone ever again. But her sister didn't need to know that. She forced a smile. "There's nothing wrong with feeling safe in my home."

"I suppose. See you in about an hour."

After a nice long time in the tub, Terra felt a little more like herself. She went into her bedroom, keeping her eyes away from the bed and the floor, found the clothes she wanted to wear, her makeup and went back to the guest room and bathroom.

When she was finished she called to check with the company as to when they'd be coming to paint the walls. She had to get the bedroom back to normal as soon as possible. They promised to be there the day after the funeral.

She was just about to make a cup of coffee when the doorbell rang. Peeking through the side panels she saw her sister-in-law Bethany. *Why was she back here?* Opening the door, she forced herself to smile.

"Oh. Terra. I didn't mean to intrude. I'm headed back home to go to the visitation with Mother Cameron and Shamus, and wondered if you needed a drive to the funeral home."

"No, but thank you."

"You shouldn't be alone. Who is going with you?"

Had Bethany always been a little strange and she hadn't noticed? "My sister and I will be there when it's time."

Bethany scratched her palm, a frown distorting her otherwise pretty features. "You won't upset Shamus, will you? I mean when we get there, it might be better if you…you stay back."

"Bethany, this funeral is for *my* husband. I will not be staying back, as you put it. You and Olivia and Shamus will be behind me. As for Shamus, you stay with him. He's your husband. You support him. I can look after myself."

"You'll be in line first?"

"Yes. Of course."

"Sorry. I didn't know the protocol for something like this, I guess. I thought I was being helpful."

Irritated by this woman Terra moved to close the door. "I'll see you there."

Somehow Terra survived the visitation. As promised, Cox Funeral Home had kept the press away from the building. Yet all the way through the two hours of greeting people, Terra felt she was acting, standing in for someone else. Nothing seemed real. She'd kept a smile on her face until she saw Detective Wilson standing in the hall outside the room. *Why was she there?* It certainly wasn't a show of sympathy for her or for the Cameron family, although she did see her speaking to Bethany. But Bethany was roaming around the room and the hall speaking to anyone who would talk to her.

She and Carolyn were at the back of the building waiting to leave for home when her cell phone rang. When she answered she heard Derrick's voice.

"Terra, where are you?"

"I'm just leaving the funeral home and heading over to my house."

"I need to see you as soon as possible."

"Why? What's going on? Have you found the two men?"

She heard his deep sigh. "I'll explain when I see you."

Because of her treatment during the police interview, Terra wanted to shout at him and hang up. But the insinuations leveled by Detective Wilson made it clear. She was a suspect. As odd as it seemed Derrick was probably her only chance of being treated fairly in the investigation. "Now? I'm...we just held the visitation. Can't this wait until after the funeral?"

"When is that?" Derrick asked, making her feel annoyed that somehow he hadn't paid enough attention to know that tomorrow she would bury her husband.

"Tomorrow morning at eleven," she said, her tone sharp and crisp.

"Can I come to the house after the funeral?"

"I suppose so," she said, wishing that everyone would leave her alone, and allow her to find a little peace.

CHAPTER NINE

At ten-thirty the next morning, Terra faced Sean's family in the anteroom of the church. Shamus didn't look at her, and Bethany clung to his hand, her gaze skidding around the room. Olivia, her hair perfectly arranged, her black suit and pearls perfectly in keeping with occasion, stood stiff and straight next to Shamus.

Wishing that Carolyn hadn't gone into the church to sit with the other mourners, Terra struggled to remain calm by focusing on her breathing as she gazed at the others. Sean's Uncle Jeremy and Aunt Hilda were there. Jeremy had been the black sheep in the family, having left Cameron Industries to pursue a career as a cartoonist for a Chicago newspaper. Terra liked him very much, and had felt a kinship to him, part of their shared feelings as outsiders inside the Cameron family. Hilda was a portrait painter who had carved out a niche market in the Chicago art world.

Bethany approached Terra, her eyes bright. "I envy you so much, Terra," Bethany gushed. "Shamus and I are hoping to get pregnant soon. I would so love to have a baby. It's all I really want now that Shamus and I... But it *will be* God's will not ours." She patted Terra's arm. "And it *is* God's will that you're pregnant, a little bit of Sean, may he rest in peace, is still here with us, don't you think?"

"I...I." Terra felt very uncomfortable around Bethany's hyperactivity.

"I want to help. I could go with you to pick out things for the baby's room. We could go shopping together. I don't have a career like you do, and so I'd be more than willing to be a babysitter for you once the baby is born. I mean we could plan so much together. I want Sean's baby to have everything. Sean would want us all to be there for his baby. A new baby's such a special part of life don't you think?" Bethany asked, a genuine look of excitement on her face.

Terra glanced at her sister-in-law, seeing for the first time how lonely she was. Bethany didn't have any real place in life, other than as Shamus's wife, and Terra could only imagine how emotionally barren her life must be. Feeling sorry for the woman she reached out and touched Bethany's arm. "You and I will talk about this in the next few weeks."

The funeral director, Mr. Cox, came toward Terra. "How are you doing today?" he asked gently.

"I'm okay." Breakfast had consisted of one piece of toast; her stomach had been paining since she'd gotten up.

Mr. Cox motioned to them. "Mrs. Cameron, Terra, I'll escort you into the chapel first, followed by Olivia, then Shamus—"

"I should go first," Shamus said.

The funeral director's glance settled on Shamus's face. "It is normal practice for the immediate family members to go first. Would it work if you took your sister-in-law in, followed by your wife and your mother?"

"No." Shamus said.

Aghast, Mr. Cox glanced at Olivia. Olivia seemed not to notice Shamus's bad behavior.

Terra stared at Shamus, her mind working. Her brother-in-law was not going to embarrass her or make a scene for others to gossip about. Terra straightened her shoulders, turning her attention to the funeral director. "Mr. Cox, Shamus will walk in with me." She turned to Shamus, saw his discomfort and ignored it. "We're doing this for Sean." Not waiting for him to respond she took his arm and moved toward the sanctuary of the church.

Shamus walked close to her, his breathing heavy. Giving him a sidelong glance she was certain she could see tears in his eyes. For a moment she felt sorry for him, and squeezed his arm. He didn't respond. His jaw twitched.

Please may I get through this.

As they moved down the aisle of the church all she could think about was holding it together until she could escape back home. It had been a rough few days, and she didn't know how much more she could take.

As she moved down the center aisle of the church where she and Sean had been married, she felt a rush of longing so strong that it nearly brought her to her knees. She needed to sit down, to block the tears sliding down her cheeks. She couldn't cry now. Not with everyone watching her.

Finally she reached the pew and slid down into the seat, thankful to see that Olivia was beside her, rather than Shamus. As the minister began the service she struggled to hear what was being said about her husband, her grief so overpowering that she could only concentrate on holding back the tears. She stared at the organist, searching for the strength to remain composed while blocking out the words of praise for her husband, words that only added to her grief.

As the service continued she was aware of a pain in her lower abdomen, sometimes sharp, sometimes an ache. She clutched her stomach in dread, she drew in a deep, calming breath. Surely the service would be over soon…

Finally she was ushered out of the church into the bright sunlight. There was to be a private reception at the Cameron mansion, and she had to attend. She didn't want to. She was tired of Shamus and his nastiness, of Bethany's anxiety and Olivia's staunch determination to follow the rules of a society funeral.

Terra didn't care about any of that. She only wanted to sleep.

"The limousine will take us back to the house," Olivia said in a tone that didn't allow for argument. Maybe she was as frustrated with Shamus as Terra was.

Once past the press waiting outside the church, they settled into the leather seats, and the vehicle eased out into the traffic. Shamus tapped his hands on his thighs, and yanked his tie away from his throat. "Look, I'm just going to say it like it is. Terra I think it would be better if you didn't come to the house with us. I'll tell anyone who asks that you weren't feeling well."

There was a shocked silence, followed by embarrassed glances between the occupants of the vehicle.

Terra couldn't believe what she was hearing. At that moment she hated Shamus more than she ever imagined possible. Turning on him, she gritted her teeth and ground out the words. "What are you talking about?"

He ignored Terra. "Mom, she's about to be charged with conspiracy to commit murder. We can't be implicated in that."

"Shamus!" Olivia's eyes widened. "What are you saying? She's Sean's wife."

"And what if she had him killed? What about that?"

"Shamus! Go to hell!" Terra interjected, suddenly feeling perfectly calm. She'd taken all she would ever take off this hateful man.

"That's enough, both of you," Olivia said. "Terra, please don't be angry. We're all under a lot of stress, and you don't want to upset your unborn child."

Terra closed her eyes, remembering the day she'd met this family, the day Sean had taken her to the mansion. Everyone had seemed so courteous. And as the years passed, she'd come to realize that being courteous was their way of snubbing someone. The family's secret handshake. But with Sean's death she was finally free of all of them.

"It's okay. I don't want any more trouble with any of you. Take me to my sister's. She's waiting for me."

"Oh!" Bethany slid her hand into Terra's. "Please don't go."

Terra couldn't bear to look at her sister-in-law. "Bethany, it's okay."

A few minutes later the limousine pulled up in front of Carolyn's house. Bethany began to cry. "Please don't go, Terra, please." She touched Terra's arm. "I'll call you, okay?" Bethany squeezed her hand. "We can go looking at baby things, please?"

Terra didn't answer. Instead she got out and walked to the door, not turning to look back. She had never really ever fit into the Cameron family's plan. Sean had married her out of love, not a sense of duty.

Whatever happened in her life, she would make it on her own—she and her baby. At the thought of her child, her heart warmed, her equilibrium returned. She couldn't waste energy on these people when she had to care for her baby.

Having arrived home from the funeral ahead of her, Carolyn was talking on the phone when Terra arrived at her house. She put the phone down, coming down the narrow entrance hall toward her, her arms wide in a hug.

"I thought I'd get us something to eat. Are you hungry? How are things with the clan?"

"I had another round with Shamus. There was simply no way I could stand to be near him after the way he behaved."

While they sat across the table from each other Terra told her about after the funeral, what happened with Shamus, and how upsetting it was. When she finished Carolyn said, "You need a distraction from your crazy outlaw family. Let's have a pot of tea. Kevin and I sat together at the funeral. He wants to talk to you."

"Oh, yeah, I forgot. Shamus called him. He probably wants to tell me what was said."

"Nothing good would be my guess."

They were finishing their first cup of tea when Kevin pulled into the narrow driveway. Terra met him at the door. "How's it going?" he asked, hugging her close.

"What's another word for disastrous?"

"Got it. The goons from the mansion were out in force."

She looked up into his face, saw the concern and felt better than she had all day. Kevin wasn't a person who wore his emotions on his sleeve, but she knew how deeply he felt things. "So you and Shamus had a cozy chat," she said, hugging him.

"What an arrogant SOB. He accused me of having an affair with you. Can you believe that?"

"I can. After the day I've had, I'm surprised that's all he said." She walked with him to the kitchen.

"Well, that's not quite all." Kevin sat down across from Carolyn, took the tea cozy off the teapot, poured himself a cup and settled in. "He sort of threatened to look into my life, see what he could dig up... Or at least I think that's what he said. He was talking so loud I put the phone on the counter and let him yell, get it out of his system."

"So, you're not worried?" Terra asked.

"Not in the slightest." He patted her head playfully. "I can handle Mr. Cameron with one arm tied behind my back."

They talked a little while longer, mostly about Kevin's latest project and how hard he was working, avoiding any mention of the funeral. During the conversation Terra couldn't help but notice how often her sister checked her cell phone.

Kevin finished his second cup of tea then placed his hand over Terra's. "Will you promise to call me if you need me for anything? I know you want to get back to your house, and try to get your life straightened out a little, but please don't rush it. Hear me?"

"I hear you," she said.

"Okay, then, I'm out of here. My illustrious career is calling. Talk tomorrow?"

"For sure."

After she walked him to the door, she came back to find Carolyn texting on her cell phone. "Do you have a secret lover or something?"

Startled, Carolyn put the phone down. "I'm waiting to hear about my book proposal. A friend is supposed to get me the name of an editor he's worked with."

"My sister, the author. That's awesome. Can I read it sometime?"

"You sure can."

They talked about writing, about their mother's great recipes that Carolyn planned to turn into a book and never got around to. Their talk about happier times soothed Terra. "Can I stay here tonight?"

"There was never any question about that," Carolyn said.

She slept at her sister's house that night, and went back to her own house the next morning, determined to start her new life in the home she loved. Both Carolyn and Kevin offered to stay with her, but she wanted to get moving on all the changes she had to make in her life, but most of all she wanted to be in the house with her memories of Sean.

She also had a meeting with Derrick, one that she wasn't looking forward to. She'd agreed to meet him at her home, not only to let him see that she was in charge but also to reassert her feeling that being in her home, the one place she loved, was a natural thing for her. Besides she owed it to Sean's memory not to give up, or hand over control of her life to anyone. And that included the police.

She saw Derrick pull up, and took a deep reassuring breath as she opened the door.

"Terra, thanks for seeing me. And again I'm sorry for the questions the other day, and my partner's brusqueness. She can be a little overzealous at times."

She nodded and led the way into the living room. "What do you need from me?" she asked over her shoulder.

"Terra, believe me when I say, I'm sorry for your loss."

She didn't care, couldn't care about what he felt, or how he felt. She just wanted him to ask his questions and leave her alone. "Thank you."

"And I wouldn't be here except we need to find the men who killed your husband."

"Yes, and maybe the brown envelope that Sean had with him that night." She sat down on the sofa. "Do you have any idea where it disappeared to?"

"As I said, the envelope was not among the evidence taken from the scene." Derrick's gaze followed her as she adjusted a pillow on the sofa. "Which means that either someone took it during our investigation, or the killers took it when they left the house. But if they took it, they had to have been looking for it, and have had the presence of mind to take it with them when they left. Since they forced you upstairs and straight to your bedroom, they didn't have an opportunity to pick it up before the stabbing. They must have picked it up on the way out. Or someone else took it…"

"Why would Sean have an envelope that would be of interest to those murderers?" she asked.

"Good question. One I can't answer until I see what was inside."

As her eyes met his, she remembered what they once had—the love, the caring. As Derrick used to say, they had each other's back. He seemed to care now, in that moment, but he was a cop, and she knew a cop's first loyalty had to be to the case. "Sean was very excited that evening…before the attack. He said he wanted to talk to me about something important. I assume it was about business, and that the envelope he'd had in his hands when he came home had something to do with what he had to tell me."

"The medical examiner's report backs up what you said about the attack, except for there being no unexpected fingerprints on the scene, and no DNA."

"But I gouged the eyes of the man who attacked me. The detective who interviewed me said there was nothing on my hands or my nails. How can that be?"

His expression was apologetic. "From the investigation so far we have no forensic evidence to prove that there were two assailants."

"What? You've got to be kidding me! Is my testimony not good enough? There were two men… Oh, I see. The police don't think there were two men. They believe I made up the story about there being two men. If there was only one assailant someone could suggest that as a person trained in martial arts I should have been able to overpower him, stop him." She pointed her finger at him. "You people are incredible. My husband is killed in front of my eyes. I'm nearly raped, but I'm not a believable witness, is that it?"

"No!" He shook his head in disgust. "No, not at all. I hate this, Terra."

"Hate what?"

"Asking you questions like this. But I…the police need to be sure your story is solid."

"Did you look into Shamus's alibi after I told you what Bethany said?"

"I interviewed both of them separately and they both stated that he was home that evening."

So Bethany had caved. She should have expected that Shamus would ensure she stuck by his alibi. She wanted to run screaming from the room and never speak to Derrick ever again. But she also knew that he was doing his best to protect her from others, like Detective Wilson who wouldn't be as kind. "I'm telling you the truth. I would never have harmed my husband. I loved him with all my heart."

He looked like she had struck him. He recovered and continued. "I'd like to have a look around Cameron Industries, but I need a warrant, something I won't get without probable cause."

"And you think I can help you?"

"Can you?" he asked coming to sit in the chair near her, and as he approached she caught the naked interest evident in his eyes. She looked away. Uncomfortable, feeling disloyal to Sean for how Derrick made her feel—protected, and cared for—she focused her attention on the mirror over the fireplace.

"I have nothing to do with Cameron Industries. It's a family business." She didn't tell him she had no intention of seeing anyone from the Cameron family again.

Derrick hesitated for a moment. "Terra, we need to find out if there is something in Sean's will, anything that would lead someone to take action against him, or to have cause to kill him."

"Are you telling me you still have no idea who killed him? No suspects at all?" She saw the shift in his gaze. "Other than me. Is that it? You think I hired someone to kill the man I loved because he took out life insurance? Or maybe you believe that I killed Sean because I wanted shares in Cameron Industries?" She gave a harsh laugh. "You, of all people, the one person other than my husband who knew how much I wanted a child, you think that I killed Sean, the father of my baby?"

Startled by her disclosure, Derrick leaned back in his chair. "I had no idea."

"Most people don't. But you see I had every reason to want my husband alive, and no reason to want my husband dead. Is that clear?"

Derrick looked away, his gaze swinging back to her, a look of utter determination in his eyes. "Terra, do you know when the reading of the will is?"

"That won't be necessary. Sean and I made each other the beneficiaries of our estates. We revised our wills less than a year ago."

Derrick rubbed his jaw in thought. "Your husband's will should be among his personal papers. Do you know where they are? Would they be in his office or here somewhere?"

Terra was sick and tired of constantly feeling under siege. She was the one who had lost her husband. She was the one faced with raising her child alone. She gave a heavy sigh, crossed the hall to the den, went to the bookcase, moved a couple of books, opened the safe recessed into the wall and pulled out an envelope.

He followed close behind her, so close she could feel the heat of his body. Trapped by the intimacy of his action, she stepped away from him, opened the envelope and passed him the will.

He glanced at her; then took the will from her hand. He read quickly for a few minutes, ignoring her completely as his eyes scanned the pages. He put the document on the desk. "Terra, according to this document your husband left you everything including his shares in Cameron Industries."

Her breath stopped. "No. He couldn't have. His shares revert back to the company. That's what Shamus told me."

"When did he tell you that?"

"It had to be during one of his hateful rants. He's been pretty awful with me these past few days."

He looked at her, sympathy evident in his eyes. "I'm not

surprised, but I am sorry you have to endure his bad behavior."

She shrugged and looked away.

Derrick glanced at the will again. "This will was only drawn up a little over a month ago. Maybe Shamus doesn't know that Derrick changed his will."

"A month ago?" She picked up the will and checked the date. "Sean redid his will and didn't tell me? Why would he do that?"

"Maybe you're not the only one who doesn't like Shamus." He looked at her, his eyebrows arched in question.

"Care to share?" she asked, then realized she'd used a question she'd so often posed to him when they were together.

"Maybe what your husband had to tell you that evening had to do with something going on inside Cameron Industries." He glanced at the will. "With this, I may have just found Shamus's motive for murder. If your husband changed his will, he had to have a good reason. I need to get a good look inside Cameron Industries."

"I wish I could help."

"You realize that Shamus will contest this will? I mean the part about you getting shares in the company," Derrick said.

"He wouldn't be Shamus if he didn't," she said, ruefully.

Derrick rolled his shoulders, something else that reminded her of their time together. She always knew when he moved that way that he was exhausted and worried.

"Since I now hold a substantial number of shares in Cameron Industries, I'm going to call the company lawyer tomorrow, and find out just exactly what that means."

"Who's going to break the news to Shamus?" Derrick asked, a familiar smile lighting up his face. "I'd love to be around for that."

"I would too," she said.

"Would you let me know how it goes?"

"You're thinking that with my new standing at Cameron Industries I'll be able to give you access to the inner workings of the company."

"I'd appreciate any opportunity to get a look at the company."

If Sean left her his shares he had a good reason. He had plans for his legacy that didn't include leaving the business solely in the hands of his brother. Whatever had convinced Sean to change his will, she would follow through and see that his wishes were carried out. She looked across the narrow space separating her from Derrick, seeing an expression she recognized. Derrick would not stop until he found the truth. On that much they agreed.

"I'll let you know what I find out when I visit the office," she said in a light tone, but deep inside she felt sad and confused. None of this, not the money or the company shares would bring her husband back.

After Derrick left, she went from room to room, at one moment crying uncontrollably, at another moment smiling at a memory. Yet at times she felt reassured. She had faced down Shamus, endured Bethany's weird behavior and convinced the police to look elsewhere for a suspect. With those thoughts uppermost in her mind, she called her sister to invite her over for supper.

Carolyn arrived a half hour later, her arms filled with grocery bags, and a smile on her face. "Well, sis, so glad you kicked a little butt today." She put the bags on the counter. "I brought a cheese tray, a fruit tray, two salmon steaks, asparagus, a rice pilaf from the deli section and chocolate mousse for dessert."

"We aren't feeding an army, are we?" Terra teased.

"No, but between us we're eating for three."

They took the containers and dishes to the table, filled their plates and began to eat. "This is so good," Terra said, appreciatively. "I'm so hungry."

"So, tell me all about Derrick's visit today."

Terra went over all the details, including the will.

"You've inherited shares in Cameron Industries? Wow! My sister the millionaire."

"But why did Sean change his will and not tell me? What was going on with him? What was going on in the company that would make him leave his shares to me?"

"And he must have checked with his lawyer to be sure he could leave the shares to you. Are you sure Sean didn't have any idea you were pregnant?"

"Why do you ask?"

"Could he simply have been guaranteeing that, if necessary, you would be able to pass on his hard work in the company to his child?"

"No. He didn't know. I took the home test a day before he died. I did it twice actually. I couldn't believe that we were going to be parents. I hadn't made an appointment with the doctor…which reminds me." She got up and went to her cell phone on the counter. "I'm putting in a reminder to call Dr. McIntyre in the morning—"

The sound of breaking glass and stone smashing onto tile floor shattered the air around her. "Carolyn!" she screamed.

"Get down, Terra," Carolyn raced to her, pulling her back from the windows that looked out on the backyard and the jagged opening in the long expanse of glass. "Where's the phone?" She glanced around, her arms encircling Terra.

They huddled on the floor together, hearts pounding as they stared at the large rock surrounded by broken glass, afraid to get up off the floor.

"Who would have done this?" Carolyn asked as she left Terra, found the phone and dialed 911. "I don't get it. What is going on?"

Terra's body began to tremble, her hands started to shake. A sudden pain tore at her side, down into her groin. She felt sick, shaky and panicky. She clutched at her abdomen as another sharp pain wrenched the air from her lungs. Pulling her knees to her chest she lay on the floor waiting for the pain to ease. Seconds later she wanted to throw up, the pain was so bad. "Carolyn, help me."

In the distance she could hear her sister's voice, anxious but calm, talking to the 911 operator.

A sensation of warmth flooded her lower body, a soft

gush of something wet seeped through her underwear. She needed to get to the bathroom...

"Carolyn, help me. I can't seem to get up," she said, her fingers edging along the floor.

Clinging to her last moment of awareness she heard her sister's voice in the distance, but couldn't seem to focus on what she was saying. Her last thought before she passed out was of Sean.

CHAPTER TEN

When she woke up a woman was standing over her, her eyes intent on the blood pressure cuff on Terra's arm. "Mrs. Cameron, please remain calm. You're in Emergency. You're bleeding."

"Where's my husband? Where's Sean?"

"I'm sorry?" The nurse's eyes were kind. She took the blood pressure cuff off her arm. "Mrs. Cameron, your husband passed away—"

"Oh! God!" Pain stabbed her abdomen. "I can't lose my baby." She clutched the nurse's arm. "Promise me I won't lose the baby."

"We're taking you to surgery," the nurse said, her tone soothing.

In the distance Terra heard people moving around her. The stretcher she was on began to move out of the room, the ceiling above her swirling as the stretcher moved faster. Closing her eyes, she prayed with all her heart, promised God anything and everything to save her child. She couldn't lose her baby, the only thing in the world that mattered to her...

Some time later she woke up in a hospital bed, the sun streaming across the room.

"Terra?" her sister whispered. "You're awake."

She turned her head to see her sister's face awash in tears. "Is my baby okay?"

Carolyn didn't answer. "Carolyn, tell me. Is he okay?"

"No," she sobbed, reaching for Terra and putting her arms around her. "No."

They held each other as they cried, gulping gasps of pain and agony. The baby she'd waited for, dreamed of, her last connection to Sean, was gone. "Carolyn, I need to go home."

Carolyn sat down next to the bed, her fingers holding Terra's hand. "The doctor is supposed to discharge you today." She wiped her sister's cheeks, gently and calmly. "I'm so sorry. I wish I knew what to say, how to ease your loss."

"Carolyn, I have to go home," she repeated, feeling the anxiety rising to panic. Her fingers fumbled along the side rail of the bed until she found the nurse call button and pressed with all her strength.

"Good morning, Mrs. Cameron. How are you feeling?" the nurse said as she entered the room, a look of concern on her face.

She couldn't think, couldn't seem to get her breath. "I...I want to leave now," Terra said, sitting up on the edge of the bed, her head swimming, her stomach threatening to explode.

"Terra!" Carolyn reached to steady her. "You're not well enough to go just yet."

"I'm fine. I want to go home," she said, feeling as if her words were not getting through to anyone. *Was she dreaming?* She glanced from her sister to the nurse. "I'm going home. Where are my clothes?"

"Terra, your clothes were...soiled. I brought a clean change for you. I'll get them." Carolyn went to the small closet in the corner of the room.

Terra focused her attention on the nurse. "Please call the doctor and tell him I want to go home. Now."

The nurse nodded and left. In a few minutes, Dr. McIntyre came and did a cursory examination. "Mrs. Cameron, I don't advise it, but you are free to go if you choose. You've been through so much these past few weeks.

If you have any problems, anything at all, I want you to call me," he said, sincerity in his eyes as he passed her a card with his name and phone number on it.

She took the card. "Thank you."

Once the doctor left the room she dressed quickly, and with her sister's help, used a wheelchair to get to the car. Carolyn drove through the residential streets near the hospital making her way to the crosstown parkway. "I'm going to stay with you at the house. You'll need someone with you."

Terra didn't say anything. There was nothing to say, nothing to do but go home.

When they pulled into the driveway, Bethany was standing there. "What's she doing here?" Carolyn demanded.

"Who cares?" Terra got out of the car.

"Terra!" Bethany rushed to her. "I heard that you lost the baby. I'm so sorry. What can I do? I've sent flowers. Mother Cameron has sent flowers. Are you going to be okay?"

The last person Terra wanted to see at that moment was Bethany.

Carolyn came around the car. "Bethany, I think it would be better if you left. Terra is exhausted."

"What happened?" Bethany asked, her hand fluttering around her face, tears streaming down her cheeks.

"Someone threw a rock into the kitchen, breaking glass and terrifying us. That's what happened." Her words sounded harsh, even to her, as she approached Bethany.

Bethany backed away. "I'm so sorry this happened to you. I know you probably think that Shamus had something to do with it, but he didn't. He was with me all evening. Shamus wouldn't do something like that. He's grieving and he's upset, and he's said some pretty mean things. But you have to believe me. He wouldn't do something so mean."

Neither Carolyn nor Terra answered her. Instead they went straight into the house, locking the door behind them.

"I'm going to get you into bed, and then I'll make you something to eat," Carolyn said.

"I'm not hungry," Terra said.

"You have to eat to keep up your strength. The police were here and took my statement but they want to interview you as well."

"I don't care. I don't care about any of it."

"Well, I'm here and I care." She took Terra's arm and led her to the guest bedroom. "You're going to lie down. I'll bring a tray to you. The painter was here and we chose a color. Your bedroom looks like new, but it's not the place for you for a while." She pulled back the duvet and turned to Terra. "I'll be here for as long as you need me."

"But your job. What about that?"

"My boss understands. I'm taking time off to be here with you."

In her blur of emotion, Terra met her sister's concerned expression. Carolyn was doing everything to help her, everything she needed right now. She couldn't remember ever feeling as much love for her sister as she did at that moment.

But it wasn't enough. It would never be enough to stop the overwhelming sense of loss, of abandonment and grief. Her life felt like it was over.

Terra was staring out the window when her sister came back with a tray. She sat up, resting against the headboard of the bed, feeling empty and so sad she could hardly draw a breath. "Thank you for this."

Carolyn placed a napkin on Terra's lap. "I've always wanted a chance to look after my little sister. Now I have it. All you have to do it get used to it," she said.

Terra felt empty…lost. "I'm so glad you're here."

While Carolyn sat on a chair next to the bed, Terra tried her best to eat the food her sister had prepared. "You remembered that I like tomato soup and grilled cheese sandwich," she said, taking a small sip of the soup, the liquid warm but tasteless. She took a bite of the sandwich, and it too seemed to lack flavor. Not wanting to disappoint or hurt her sister's feelings she ate several more bites before giving up.

"You don't feel like eating," Carolyn said soothingly.

"I don't. I'm sorry."

"No need to be." Carolyn picked up the tray. "Why don't you rest, and I'll clean up. The glass company came and replaced the window in the kitchen. Everything is under control."

After her sister left Terra fell into an exhausted sleep fuelled by fragments of a dream about running toward a dark forest, people following her, yelling unintelligible words at her. She didn't know how long she'd been asleep, but when she woke Carolyn stood over her, a perplexed expression on her face. "Hi Terra. How are you feeling?"

"I…I guess okay." She eased onto one elbow, picked up the water glass from the bedside table and taking a sip. "I'm a little dry and my head is groggy. How long was I asleep?"

"Just a couple of hours. But you're looking a little better than you did earlier."

Her mouth felt dry, her lips sticky. She leaned back down on the pillow. "The way I feel right now I could sleep for the rest of my life."

"Derrick called. He needs to see you as soon as possible. I said you'd call back."

Terra didn't care about Derrick or anything. "I don't feel like calling him."

"It seems they've had a break in the case."

She didn't want to hear what Derrick or anybody else wanted. Pulling the duvet over her shoulders, she curled up, pulling her legs up to her chest. If only she could fall back to sleep…

Carolyn sighed and left the bedroom.

Sometime later Carolyn was back at the door of the bedroom. "I'm sorry to bother you. I tried to put him off, but Detective O'Leary is here. He says he needs to talk to you."

Terra stared at the window, noting that the light had shifted away to the west of the house; another day was ending. "Did you tell him about my baby?"

"No. I didn't." Carolyn sniffed and swallowed. "I couldn't talk about it."

Her sister's face was drawn, exhaustion clearly evident in her features. Carolyn had to have been under a lot of pressure from Derrick for her to come in here, encouraging her to see him. "Okay, I'll get dressed. Tell him I'll be out in a few minutes."

When she reached the entranceway, Derrick was waiting, a look of concern on his face. "Terra, can we talk?"

She shrugged. "You're here," she said, not caring what he had to say, only that she wanted him to leave.

"Let's sit in the living room," he offered.

They sat across from each other, Derrick glancing around as if he didn't know where to start. "There is an eye witness who saw a car leaving the scene after the rock-throwing incident. We have a partial plate, and our first decent lead in the case."

"Why is that?"

His gaze focused on her and Derrick leaned forward. "Because so far we've turned up no prints, no weapon, no DNA in the bedroom other than yours and your husband's."

This was old news. When she'd first heard it days ago, she had been been upset, asking questions about how this could be, fearful that she was the only suspect. Today none of it mattered. "What do you want from me?"

"I want to have someone with you at all times until we know more."

"Why?"

"There is reason…I believe that the death of your husband, the home invasion and the rock throwing may be connected…to you."

She felt confused, a headache forming behind her eyes. If only he'd leave. "I don't understand."

Derrick leaned toward her, his expression grim, a solemn look in his eyes she'd seen many times before when they lived together. "What if Sean isn't the only person the killer is after? What if Sean's death is not related to something in his life, but to yours?"

Trying to concentrate on what he was saying, she asked,

"You're saying that someone is after me? Why would that be? Why would anyone want to hurt me?" She couldn't take any more. She had to lie down. She rose, her knees trembling, tears splashing down her cheeks. "I want you to leave. You don't have anything to go on, after a week of looking for my husband's killer, and now you want to have me followed everywhere I go."

"No. Not followed. Protected."

She reached the doorway leading to the hall. "I don't believe you. What better way to keep an eye on your only suspect than to pretend to protect her." She pushed the hair from her face. "I can't do this anymore. I can't. I've lost my husband and my baby. There's nothing more any one can take from me."

Oh God. He'd had no idea she'd lost her baby. Terra's dream was to have children, and now her baby had been taken from her. "Oh, Terra…" Seeing the searing pain in her eyes, the desperation on her face, Derrick went to her and folded her ever so gently into his arms, inhaling her familiar scent, remembering the way she'd felt in his arms all those years ago when they'd loved each other. A love he'd tossed in the garbage. "I didn't mean to upset you. And I'm so sorry you lost your baby," he said, knowing the inadequacy of his words but unable to stop saying them.

She trembled beneath his touch, her breath coming in harsh gasps. Her racking sobs shook him to his core. Her pain was his. The way she clung to him severed his objectivity.

It was as if time stood suspended and the air couldn't reach his lungs. He'd never stopped loving her. He had made a horrible mistake in marrying someone else, a mistake he couldn't retract. Now his future seemed so overwhelmingly bleak without Terra. He held her cautiously, fearing the moment when she would pull away from him, and he would once more be alone in the world, denied the one person he had ever truly loved. Yet, as he held her close, a strange feeling came over him. He was content, somehow open, to the shame of what he'd done to her. He had betrayed her, hurt her immeasurably and left her to face all of it alone.

As he waited for her tears to subside, for her to become aware of his arms and push him away, he vowed that he would protect her no matter what happened to him. And, as much as he loved her, he vowed not to allow his feelings to intrude on her life. His feelings meant nothing if she didn't return them. And she most certainly wouldn't feel anything for him in the midst of her grief and because of their past.

Respecting her pain, her need for privacy he would remain silent, do whatever it took to help her, and give her back what remained of her life and her world.

As she eased away from him, she looked up into his eyes. This moment, this connection, was all he had.

"Terra, whatever it takes, I will find the people who killed Sean. I will find the people responsible for invading your home. I will do everything in my power to help you, but I will not impose a police presence in your life if you feel I have other motives than your protection. But I will watch out for you, and have the police patrols stepped up in your neighborhood. Will you do just one thing for me?"

She nodded, her eyes still fixed on his.

"Will you memorize my cell phone number in case you need me in a hurry, and put my number on your contacts list? I want you to call me whenever you need help, whenever you feel frightened, or for any reason at all. I'm here for you. We will get these bastards. It may take a little time, but we will find them and you will be safe."

"Why does it matter, if you still believe I killed Sean?"

His hand reached for hers, entwining his fingers with hers. She let him touch her, and he was filled with joy, hope even, that somehow they might one day reconnect, that she would find it in her heart to forgive him.

"There is only one thing I'm sure of when it comes to

this case. You didn't kill your husband. You're not capable of murder."

As he left the room and went out the front door she stood perfectly still, her legs refusing to answer her need to walk back to her bed. Watching him as he moved down the walkway to his vehicle, his long legs covering the distance in seconds, a rush of memories seized her mind.

Memories of the day they'd moved in together and he'd banged his thumb with the hammer trying to hang a painting she'd bought on a whim at an auction. The day he'd brought home a straggly bouquet of daisies he'd picked when he was out hiking with his buddies and she was home nursing a cold. The day they'd bought their first piece of furniture together—a huge king-sized bed that they covered in pillows for reading and spending long nights in each other's arms. The day he'd told her he loved her…would always love her…

"Terra, are you okay?" Carolyn asked.

She turned to face her sister. "Not really." She smoothed the moisture from her cheeks, her body still remembering Derrick's arms, his closeness, all of it flooding her heart with memories of the past.

"Well, I don't mean to add more distress to your day, but Kevin is on the phone and he needs to talk to you." She held out the phone.

"Hi, Kevin."

"I'm so sorry you lost your baby. So sorry," Kevin said, his words consoling. "I would have been there when you got home, but the police called me in for questioning. A Detective Meaghan Wilson was going to interview me. And Peter didn't warn me. He claims he didn't know," Kevin said. "I was so anxious, and so hurt that Peter didn't tell me what was going on that I messed up answering their questions and now they think I'm somehow involved in Sean's death." He paused. "Just wanted to let you know how much I wish I'd been there for you."

"It's okay, Kevin. There was nothing you could have done. It all happened so fast. When someone threw a rock in the kitchen window, I guess the shock was too much, or maybe my baby wasn't going to live, regardless." She felt the tears forming again and was helpless to stop them.

"I'm coming over to be with you. You can't be alone. I know Carolyn's there, but I'll come and stay for a while and she can go grocery shopping or run errands."

She needed her best friend with her. She needed to feel his love and caring. "I'll be waiting."

Carolyn had gone to her room for a few minutes, leaving Terra alone. Terra was staring at the phone in her hand when it rang. *Cameron Industries?* She picked up the phone.

"The lawyers just brought me a copy of Sean's will. I don't know what you did to my brother to make him think he could leave his shares of Cameron Industries to you. He was my brother, my twin. We knew each other better than anyone. How did you get Sean to change his mind? It was only done a month ago. Was that your plan? Get Sean to change his will, leaving everything to you, and then have him murdered?"

His shocking words ricocheted though her, forcing the air from her lungs. She collapsed onto the sofa. "Shamus, I can't talk to you," she said feeling a deep weariness, a sense of foreboding that claimed even her voice.

"You will too. You have destroyed my life. You've made me look stupid because I didn't know that my only brother had betrayed me, left me unable to run the company without your interference. I will stop you no matter what it takes," he threatened.

Her head ached from the fury of his words. There was nothing she could do or say that would change anything. It was all so hopeless.

"Are you still there?" he said, his voice filled with anger.

There was nothing left of her life. All that mattered had been taken from her.

She clicked the phone off and searched the hall table for her keys. Her hands trembling she headed out to her car. *Was it in the garage or in the driveway?* She found it in the driveway, opened the door, and started the engine. With the seatbelt warning blaring in her ears she pulled out of the driveway and headed down the street.

She had to get away. She couldn't live like this anymore. The pressure, the darkness, the anger and hurt and helplessness. There was nothing she could do to ease the pain, to find a way out.

If only it could all be over.

CHAPTER ELEVEN

With no memory of how she'd gotten out of her subdivision and out of town, she found herself on the two-lane highway that ran across open countryside, climbing toward a ridge of hills shimmering in the sunlight.

There was nothing left except the feeling of inevitability, of a loss so profound, so despairing she wanted to curl up, end it all, finally release her soul from the agony that claimed her.

She clung to the wheel, the seatbelt warning fading from her mind as she drove faster and faster along the narrow road. Up ahead an oncoming eighteen-wheeler, its load of wood strapped to the flat bed, the truck cab rising high over the road, lumbered toward her.

The slow thump of her heart was all she heard as the truck drew nearer, its large insect-like windows beckoning her. Easing her body forward in the seat, her eyes focused on the narrow line separating her lane from that of the oncoming truck, she braced herself for what was to come. One slight movement of her hands on the wheel and it would all be over. All that was needed to escape…to be with Sean and her baby.

Hypnotized by the undulating ribbon of road separating her from the truck, she lifted her foot off the gas. The speedometer counted off the drop in speed. Her body tensed as her hands gripped the wheel. The dark sedan ahead of her sped up, widening the space between the two vehicles.

Her breath came easier as she relaxed a little… It would all be over soon.

Tears streaming down her face, she clung to the wheel.

The car in front of her moved faster, clearing the way for her.

In just a few minutes she'd be free of these horrible feelings of nothingness, the pain of knowing that everything was hopeless. All she had to do was turn the wheel to the left and into the oncoming lane. She closed her eyes, her fingers edging the wheel ever so gently to the left.

Terra! Watch out! Sean's voice boomed in her head.

It was as if he were there with her, beside her. She opened her eyes. The car ahead of her had moved and was going the wrong way on the highway—right into the oncoming traffic—headed straight for the truck. Suddenly the ground shook. The sound of screeching tires, the smash of metal on metal, the whack of an exploding truck tire filled the car.

Terra swung the wheel to the right. The truck careened toward her, horn blaring, air brakes wailing, coming to a halt along the edge of the road in a hail of dirt and gravel, a few feet ahead of her.

Terra slammed on her brakes. Her hands quivering as she stared in disbelief. The truck teetered for a few seconds before settling back on its wheels. Farther ahead she saw the dark sedan splayed out across her lane, the driver's door smashed, the side of the car crumpled like paper, smoke billowing from under the hood.

"No!" Shock skittered through her as Terra shut off the engine, scrambled out of the car and ran toward the other car. As she got near the truck, the driver climbed out of the cab.

"Oh! God! I hit her. I've killed her. I saw her coming toward me. She was too close to the inside of the lane. Then she crossed over the line. I didn't mean to hurt her!" the driver cried.

Terra kept walking, her heart pounding so hard she could barely breathe. "I'm a nurse. Help me see if she's still alive." She ran the last few feet, coming up to the door of the car. The woman's head was twisted at an odd angle. The driver's side window held only fragments of glass, leaving a gaping hole through which she saw the woman. As she approached, the only sound she could hear was the hissing of something under the hood. Terra reached in, past the airbag, searching for the woman's carotid artery.

"Is she alive?" the driver asked.

"I can't find a pulse."

"Are you sure?"

Not wanting to make a mistake, she pressed the soft skin of the woman's neck, but no pulse, no movement in the skin under her searching fingers. "Yes, I'm sure."

"No!" The truck driver pushed his fist against his teeth, his shoulders shaking.

As if moving in a trance, Terra dialed 911. When the operator answered she gave the details of what had happened. After what seemed like hours the dispatcher told her that help was on the way. She put her phone in the pocket of her jeans, feeling a strange sensation pulsing through her. An unreal feeling, as if she were sleep walking.

"How do you do that? How can you be so calm? The woman is dead!" the driver demanded.

"I was an Emergency Room nurse. You get used to it," she said, her words sounding in her ears as if they were coming from the bottom of a well.

The driver collapsed against the rear wheel, his groan of agony cutting through Terra. Crouching beside him, she tried to comfort him, but no words would come. She hadn't thought what it might mean to the driver of the truck. She hadn't. She'd only been thinking about how to end it all; how to escape the pain. Looking at him now, remorse settled around her heart, making it pound in her throat.

What if she had run into this man's truck? What sort of pain would she have inflicted on him for the rest of his life?

"You didn't do anything wrong. This woman did this to herself. She wanted it this way. But we need to move away from the car. There's smoke or something coming from the engine."

The driver glanced at her, his cheeks coated in tears. "Why me? Melanie and me, we just had our first baby. I was on my way home… Taking a couple weeks' vacation."

His sobs were interrupted by the blare of sirens. Several cars had stopped on the other side of the road not far from the truck. "Come on. Get up. We'd better step back and give the emergency vehicles room," she said, taking his hand. They moved together off to the side of the road and watched as the police and ambulance pulled up and a scramble of police and emergency personnel converged on the wreckage.

Terra watched as if from behind glass, slightly removed and disconnected, as the police got the woman's purse, found her cell phone and called someone. Terra couldn't imagine how it must feel to learn that a loved one died in such awful circumstances. Yet it so easily could have been her, would have been her sister receiving the call, but for Sean's voice in her head.

What had gotten into her only a few minutes ago? Had she been so desperate, so out of control that she considered taking her life? But deep in her heart she knew that she wasn't thinking rationally, that she'd lost hope for a few critical seconds that could have been her last.

She was still standing next to the driver of the truck, her body shaking uncontrollably, when the police officer approached them. Listening, she heard the anxiety in the driver's voice as he recounted what he could remember of the accident. When it was Terra's turn she said only that she hadn't seen the woman move into the oncoming lane.

She could not and would not speak about her own feelings. She was ashamed of how she had felt only a short time ago, how selfish she had nearly been.

They stood to the side as the crew used the Jaws of Life to remove the body. To one side she could see a man approaching, forcing his way through to the crash site, his hair disheveled, his eyes wild.

"My wife! Please God!"

The officer stepped into his path, pulling him away from the car. "Do you not have family you can go to?"

"No one. It was just my wife and me and our son. We moved here to start a new ministry. She was lonesome after the baby arrived. Mrs. Bradley was babysitting Jeremy. When Melanie didn't come back to the house she called me. I couldn't reach Melanie on her cell phone. I didn't know where to look for her…" His voice trailed off.

Instinctively Terra reached out to him. "Come stand over here with me. I can only imagine how you're feeling," she said soothingly as she walked with him a short distance away from the scene.

"Jeremy is only two months old, and now his mommy is gone."

"Was she not doing well after Jeremy was born?" Terra asked, trying to stop the shaking in her body, focusing instead on the man and what he must be going through.

The minister's expression was riddled with anxiety. "Have the police said anything about what happened? Why she ran into the truck? Did she have a flat tire, or something? Maybe she fell asleep at the wheel."

"They haven't said anything to either of us."

He stared hard at Terra. "I know what you're thinking: That my wife committed suicide. But that's not true. The doctor told Melanie that she had the baby blues, but it would all be better when she got a little rest. Melanie couldn't have committed suicide. It's against God's will. She wouldn't have done such a terrible thing."

"We don't know how people will respond to things. Maybe your wife didn't see any way out of her agony, her depression. Maybe she was simply overpowered by the need to end it all."

His eyes questioned her. "What would you know about it?"

She couldn't answer him. She'd seen the woman driving toward oncoming traffic, and knew that the woman hadn't slowed down or attempted to return to her own lane.

Regardless of the minister's assertion that his wife didn't commit suicide, the events of the last hour had shown her that life was precious, that life was worth living…for most people, no matter their pain or feeling of hopelessness. The fact that his wife had ended her life, a life with so much promise, could not be denied or diminished.

"I know what it feels like to be in a shadowy place, a space so dark and painful there seems no way out. I know that when it first starts you feel only pain, then the pain moves to a sense of loss so profound that it blocks reasonable thought and leads to a space where everything seems completely pointless, misguided and so overwhelmingly exhausting that it's not worth the effort to try to get beyond it."

"I don't believe my wife took her own life. She loved Jeremy and me. We were happy—" He sobbed into his hands.

The words "you're not to blame" were on her lips, but it went deeper, a lot deeper than that. She understood the hopelessness of loss, of disbelief that life could be so cruel, leave no choice but one.

"You had no part in what she did. She wasn't doing it for any other reason than that she couldn't help herself. In her mind it was her only way out of the pain and agony."

She couldn't tell the stranger why she'd been on this road. She hadn't known the reason, herself, until that moment just before the accident. She couldn't tell anyone about it ever. It was her secret. Her shameful secret. Her entire nursing career had been spent caring for others, believing in the sanctity of life. And yet in one awful moment she'd nearly destroyed her own life.

But she no longer felt the way she had. Whether it was the trauma of the accident she'd just witnessed, or the fact that hearing that Melanie's pain hit a nerve—she didn't know. The only certainty in all of it was that her life would start from this moment and move forward.

If she had inflicted that kind of pain on Carolyn or Kevin or others who loved her, it would have changed their lives forever. It would not have changed the fact that Sean had been murdered, or that her baby hadn't lived to grow into a beautiful human being. Her suicide would have taken much more than her life. It would have left a pain-filled void for those who cared about her.

She had been saved from her grief and pain by the death of another. For that moment of mercy she would always be grateful. "I think it's time we left. They have my statement and my contact information. You shouldn't stay here. You have Jeremy to care for."

"Do you have family?" he asked.

"I did have. I had a husband and was expecting a baby, so you'll understand when I say that I don't feel any connection to God at the moment."

"You can't turn away from God. He's knows our every thought, our sins and our prayers."

"I'm sorry to disagree with you, but God and I aren't on speaking terms." She gave him a wry smile as a thought formed in her mind.

She was on her own now; that was an irrevocable fact. She'd loved Sean with her whole heart. If she was going to make any sense of what had happened to her she needed to take back control of her life and move forward.

She would find her husband's killer. She would stay in her home and make a new life for herself. She would honor Sean's memory and their life together. With startling clarity she knew what she had to do.

She would be available if the officers at the scene wanted to talk to her. But for now all she wanted to do was go home and start her life over. It wouldn't be easy. She would have bad days, be overwhelmed at times. But she owed it to Sean and herself to move forward with her life. She would never forget Sean, would spend years getting over the past few weeks, but it would all be worth it in the end.

"I really have to go. I have a dear friend I need to talk to."

Chapter Twelve

The police offered to drive her home, but Terra needed to feel in control, to know that she was okay. As she drove slowly, methodically, feelings of disbelief and sorrow swept through her, leaving her crying one minute and calm the next. In that moment she realized that what she had nearly done would leave the people she loved to live the rest of their lives wondering if somehow they could have stopped her from such a desperate act. Yet as she drove toward home she couldn't seem to remember what she'd been feeling as she saw the truck coming toward her on the highway. So much of it seemed a blur that was fast disappearing from her present reality.

Now all she could feel was a profound sense of relief, mixed with sadness that someone she'd never known had done something she came so close to doing herself. She felt an eerie sense of connection to the woman whose life had been lost on that narrow stretch of highway. At the same time she felt a strange sense of elation. She was so glad she hadn't done it, so thankful to be alive. She had a new chance to face her life, to find peace and eventually to accept Sean's death,

She continued on home as if on autopilot. As she reached her house she saw Kevin's and Derrick's cars in the driveway. *What were they doing here?* She slowed to a stop at the curb. *Was she ready to face her friend? Her sister?* Whatever she did she couldn't tell them how close she'd come to ending her life, and leaving her family and friends to mourn.

She entered the kitchen to Kevin's words of concern. "Where were you? You scared us half to death. You said you'd be waiting for me. I get over here and you're gone. What's going on?"

"Kevin, I'm sorry." She hugged him close.

"I even called in the cavalry." He tapped her nose, a smile wreathing his face. "Derrick rode in on his trusty steed and has been here waiting. He's the one who told us you were at the scene of an accident."

"How did he know?"

Derrick came toward her. "Because I checked all over the county wondering if something had happened to you. One of my police academy buddies who works for the sheriff's office told me you were a witness to a highway crash in which a woman died. I was just about to head out there."

Carolyn rushed into the kitchen past Kevin and taking Terra into her arms. "Oh, sis, you had me so scared."

"I'm sorry. Truly I am. I had a really nasty call from Shamus and I had to get out of the house for a little break. I didn't mean to worry you." She kissed her sister's cheek.

"You're here now, and that's all that matters," Carolyn said. "I'm going to put coffee on, and then you're going to tell us everything."

Terra looked expectantly at Derrick, suddenly aware that he might have sent people out looking for her. Had he realized that she was in crisis? Of all the people in her life he would know how she responded to stress.

Derrick met her gaze, his eyes filled with concern, but he said nothing.

"Derrick, you don't have to leave now that Terra's back. Please stay for coffee," Carolyn said.

Terra couldn't take her eyes off Derrick, her heart pounding, remembering how good they'd been together, how much in love they'd been. That was all in the past, but his concern touched her in a way she'd never imagined possible.

"Have a coffee with us. I do have something I need to talk to you about," Terra offered.

"I also came here for another reason," Derrick said.

"What's that?" all three asked in unison.

"The rock that was thrown through the kitchen window had a smooth area that forensics found a print on, and the boot print found outside the house the evening the rock was tossed into your kitchen matches the boot print we found just off the patio the night of Sean's death."

"That's great!" Kevin said. "Finally something that might produce a real suspect." He gave Derrick a look. "Unless of course you want me to turn over my boots."

"No one could suspect you of such a crime," Carolyn said, giving him a quick smile.

They sat down around the coffee table in the main living area while Carolyn made coffee, each chatting in turn about the possibilities. Then the talk turned to the accident.

"So the drive helped clear you head?" Kevin asked.

"Yes it did. I feel I can face things a little better now," Terra said as Carolyn brought the coffee things to the table. "Now I appreciate all that I have, even without Sean. I'm so glad to be home in my own kitchen."

"Amen to that," Kevin said, raising his coffee mug in salute.

Derrick watched Terra, the frantic beating of his heart finally slowing in his chest. He'd received a call from Kevin Jackson, so excited and garbled he could hardly understand him.

Once he had Carolyn on the phone, and she explained about Shamus's call, he realized that Terra, true to form, was running away. During their life together whenever she'd had a particularly difficult time on shift in emergency, she'd come home too stressed to talk, and too wired to rest. Her usual thing was to get in the car and go down to Starbucks where she'd sit and sip a coffee for an hour or two before she returned home.

He'd checked the coffee shops in the area, and then called in a few favors from some of his police friends. When he'd first talked to his buddy in the sheriff's office, he was certain that Terra was the woman who had died. In his mind's eye he could see how she might have left the house upset and distracted, driven dangerously and been killed. He'd never been so afraid in his life as in those moments before his friend identified the woman who had died.

"While I was out driving around," Terra said, pushing her cup aside, "I decided that since I now own Sean's shares in Cameron Industries, I'm going into the office. I want to spend a little time in Sean's office, become familiar with the space. It has always been his office, a place I visited once in awhile. As part owner I'll have a role to play in the company and I intend to make his office mine." She glanced around, gauging their reaction.

"I don't think that's a good idea," Carolyn said. "Just because you own a bunch of shares, doesn't mean you have to take on a job there, does it?"

"It doesn't." Terra clasped her hands, lifted her chin and looked across at Derrick, indicating she was ready to take on Shamus and the Cameron family if necessary.

He was so damned delighted. "What do you plan to do?" he asked.

"The night Sean died he told me he wanted to talk to me about something. I think it had to do with the brown envelope that went missing off his desk in the den, that there was something going on at work that he needed to share with me. I didn't know he changed his will, but the only reason I can think of for him doing that is that he didn't want to turn over control of Cameron Industries to Shamus."

"That reminds me," Carolyn said, "That Neill Baxter left another message. He says he wants to see you."

"Neill Baxter? He's a PI," Derrick said. "Why would he want to see you?"

"He's been leaving messages for a week. I don't know him, and just didn't feel like returning his calls," Terra said.

"Now might be a good time to find out what's going on," Derrick said, offering her an encouraging smile.

"Is it too late to call him?" She looked at her watch and made up her mind. "I'm calling him right this minute." She scrolled through the caller ID list on the home phone, looking for one of his earlier calls, clicked the button, tossed her hair off her face and pursed her lips.

Each movement, each gesture brought forward fond memories for Derrick. As he studied her, his heart shifted in his chest.

"Yes, please come over now," Terra said, her expression one of puzzlement as she hung up. "He says that Sean hired him to look into problems at Cameron Industries."

Derrick couldn't keep the grin off his face. He'd bet a year's pay that Shamus was involved. If he was, that made him the number one suspect in Sean's murder. He had no intention of leaving until he talked to Neill Baxter. The PI's information might break the case wide open. Whatever was going on inside Cameron Industries would almost certainly lead to Sean's killer.

When Neill Baxter arrived in her kitchen, Terra introduced Derrick, Kevin and Carolyn while holding her curiosity in check. If Sean hired this man it had to be for a good reason, and she intended to find out what it was.

"Mrs. Cameron, I'm sorry for your loss. Your husband was a good man, and he wanted to do the right thing."

"What do you mean by that?" Terra asked after inviting him to sit around the coffee table with them.

"I sent him a report on what he asked me to look into. I met him away from the office the afternoon he was killed and gave him the report. He said he was taking it home with him. Do you have it?"

"No. Was it in a brown envelope? He had a brown envelope when he got home."

"Yes, it was. When you didn't return my calls, I began to wonder if somehow you hadn't found it." The PI pulled an envelope out of his jacket pocket. "This is a copy of the report," he said, passing it to her.

She hesitated to open it, realizing that what she found could point the finger at problems in the company, problems someone in the company had perhaps tried to keep hidden, problems that could offer motive for the murder of her husband. Reluctantly she pulled the report out of the envelope. She read carefully and passed each page over to Derrick as she finished reading it, an action so automatic, so much a part of her past, she was only vaguely aware she did it.

"Basically what it says," Neill Baxter began, "is that Cameron Industries is in serious financial trouble. Someone inside the company, almost certainly in the accounting department, has been skimming money for years. Sean intended to take this report to the police."

"Shamus is Chief Financial Officer for Cameron Industries," she said to no one in particular.

"But that doesn't mean Shamus knew the extent of the deception and the loss. As far as I could determine, neither Shamus nor Sean had visited the four plants in the Midwest in recent years," Neill said. "They left the plant operations to the plant managers. Those managers might be involved in this as well."

"Did Sean talk to Shamus about this?" Derrick asked.

"He said he wasn't going to until he had the report. He wanted to go over the report before he talked to his brother."

"Sean must have suspected his brother was behind this, or possibly knew who was," Derrick said.

"I agree," Neill Baxter replied.

Derrick glanced across the table at Terra, trying to catch her eye. "With this report we can get a warrant for Cameron Industries' financial records. We now have a viable suspect."

"Thank God!" Kevin yelped and clapped his hands. "I'm free!" Kevin hopped up, kissed Terra's cheek and headed for the door. "I've got things I need to do, people I need to see. Talk later." The door closed behind him, leaving the room very quiet.

"Despite his bad behavior I can't believe that Shamus would be ripping off the company. He doesn't like me, never did… But to take down the company his father founded and that he and his brother ran together… It doesn't make any sense," Terra said.

"Shamus has an expensive lifestyle," Neill Baxter offered. "You don't have a house off Bridle Pathway without a good cash flow."

"If Sean wanted me to have a position in the company, to hold shares, he had to have a reason. Maybe it was simply him wanting to leave something special for our children."

"Or maybe it was something else. He left you his personal wealth, an insurance policy worth a million and his shares in the company. If Sean's murder was motivated by greed, that makes you the next target," Derrick said, his words focusing the attention of the others on him.

Fear rushed down her spine. "Will you stop that? No one would want to harm me."

"Then why did someone break into your house and go through everything, even scatter Sean's clothes around? And why throw a rock at your window? Sean isn't here. If we believe that Sean was the target, the clothes, and the rock incidents shouldn't have happened." He tilted his head to the side. "I think it would be better if you didn't stay here."

"For the final time, I am not leaving my home. I'm tired of feeling pushed around, people being angry at me, other people offering me advice. I need to think things through."

Derrick gave her an assessing glance, shrugged and stood up. "Okay. I'll leave you for now. If you want me to go to Cameron Industries with you, let me know."

She walked him to the door. "Thank you."

"Anytime," he said, his eyes on her, his broad shoulders offering her protection. As she watched him leave she wished that someday they might be friends. She'd like that very much.

Terra returned to the kitchen to hear Carolyn telling Neill Baxter about the rock throwing and Sean's clothes being strewn all around the bedroom.

They both looked at her. Neill Baxter put his business

card on the table. "Mrs. Cameron, your husband hired me to help him find the truth behind the loss of money at his company. If you're going in there to see what is going on, you may need an outside person to help you. I'm pretty good at what I do. I'd be willing to go into the office with you."

"That's very kind." She tapped the card with her finger, her mind going over the past few hours. "I think what I'm going to do is make an appointment with the company lawyer, find out what exactly it means for me to own Sean's shares, what rights I have and what my role could be in the company."

"That sounds like a really good idea. And as I say, if I can help you, please get in touch. Should I send my bill directly to you?"

"Please." Moving with him toward the door, she wondered what the next few weeks would mean to her, to her life and her future. Terra knew that if she was to get her life back she had to take action, to set her own course.

She would begin by going into Cameron Industries. Sean had left her his shares in the business.

Sean would have wanted her to take over for him.

CHAPTER THIRTEEN

The following Monday, Terra put on the black suit Sean had purchased for her, and her one pair of dressy black Manolo Blahnik shoes and headed downtown to the corporate offices of Cameron Industries. She hadn't mentioned to anyone that she was going into the offices that morning, and she wanted her arrival to remain unexpected. She was well aware that Derrick, Kevin and Carolyn had wanted her to take one of them with her. But in her mind, the only way she could start fresh with her life was to stand on her own two feet. She had Derrick's private cell phone number on speed dial if she ran into any trouble.

At some point she would have to take Sean's personal things out of his office, but that would come later when she was ready. The legal offices of the company were on the first floor while the main administrative offices were on the third floor.

If the shares she inherited gave her the right to take a position in the company, she would need Sean's office. If she decided she didn't want to have anything to do with running the company then she would simply remove Sean's things and take them home with her.

She parked in the visitor parking area and walked through the main doors. The legal department offices were off to the left. David Franks, one of the company attorneys, said he'd be waiting for her. And in fact, he met her as she walked into the reception area.

"It's good to see you, Mrs. Cameron. I only wish it were under different circumstances. I'm sorry for your loss."

"Thank you." She reached toward him, giving him a firm handshake. "By the way, it's Terra."

He smiled and his whole face lit up. "Understood. Please call me David. Come this way and we'll get started. You said on the phone you wanted to know what was involved in being a shareholder in Cameron Industries."

"That's correct."

"Well, for most people it would be collecting dividends and attending the occasional board meeting. But in your case, since Sean left you his shares, which is just a little bit over 50%, you basically can run this company, if you choose to do so."

Shocked and feeling a little intimidated, she asked, "What are my other options?"

"You could sell your shares to a family member. Shamus would certainly be interested, although I understand he's retained a lawyer to look into breaking Sean's will."

"Could he succeed?"

"Highly unlikely, but that won't stop him from trying. You realize that there was quite a scene here the day he learned that Sean had changed his will. Shamus believed that Sean's shares went to him, not you."

"Yes, I had thought so, too. When I read the will I couldn't believe it, but I respect my husband's business sense and know it was done after careful consideration. Not a frivolous gesture. Shamus's call to me made his displeasure more than clear. I think his anger related to the fact that because he wasn't a beneficiary he didn't have access to the will. He had to find out the provisions of the will from Sean's estate lawyer."

David Franks focused his full attention on her. "I'm probably about to say something I shouldn't but I have been a part of this company for thirty years. Despite how well your husband managed the operational side, there have been rumors floating around about money issues in the organization for quite some time."

"Yes, I understand that."

The lawyer leaned forward in his chair. "Who told you?"

"Sean hired a PI whose report recommended a full audit of the company."

"Do you really want to be involved in all that? I mean with the stress you've already experienced, wouldn't it be better if you simply sold your shares to Shamus? After all, he is the only one left in the Cameron family who can run the business."

She'd never told anyone except Sean about her fear of being penniless, what the lack of money had done to her childhood, her father's drinking and fighting, the police visits to the house, all the sorts of things that made her childhood difficult.

As she stared at the lawyer, it was as if Sean were standing next to her, encouraging her. It was almost as if she could feel him, his aura, giving her strength and comforting her. Her mind jumped back to that moment on the highway, and Sean's voice inside her head, warning her. Drawing comfort from the realization that Sean might be with her at this moment, she said, "Mr. Franks, I am considering taking over my husband's position in the company. I have a lot to learn, but it is mine to learn. If Shamus doesn't like that, he can take it up at the next board meeting."

"I've already initiated the procedures to have the shares transferred into your name."

She wasn't clear on what all the lawyers at Cameron Industries did, but she was certain she'd find out over the coming months. She stood up and extended her hand. "I look forward to working together."

He stood up, taking her hand in his. "I do too."

She turned to leave and then remembered something. "By the way, I want Cameron Industries to remove all their claims for the services of outside counsel. In other words, if I need to hire a lawyer I won't be blocked by whoever it was that put all the criminal lawyers in the city on retainer."

"I certainly didn't do it!" David Franks said, shocked at her words.

"I didn't say you did. But I am requesting that you undo whatever Shamus has done so that if I need a criminal lawyer in this town I can hire one."

"Why would you need a criminal lawyer?"

"Because when Shamus learns that I intend to occupy my place in the boardroom and in the administrative suite, he will do everything in his power to turn me into a suspect in my husband's murder. Not that he hasn't tried already, but now he'll have even more reason to exert his influence. Having access to the best criminal lawyers in town will ensure that I get fair representation."

The lawyer gave her a wide grin. "Terra Cameron, I like your style."

Flushed with adrenaline she rode the elevator to the third floor, through the lobby and into Sean's office before she stopped to take a breath. The first thing she noticed was that the photo of her and Sean on their wedding day was missing from his credenza. She turned to the opposite wall. All of Sean's sailing trophies were missing.

"I'm sorry. I wish you had called to say you were coming. I would have been waiting," Evelyn Thornton said, following her into the office. "I'm so sorry about Sean. He was a wonderful boss, so easy to work with. He will be missed."

"Thank you, Mrs. Thornton."

"It's Evelyn, and what can I do for you?"

"Where are all Sean's things?"

"Oh. Shamus came in a couple of days ago, gathered everything up, and said he was delivering them to your house. I think he said he was sending them by courier."

"If that's the case they should have been delivered by now."

Evelyn's expression showed surprise. "They weren't?"

"No. Would you check to see if Shamus is available? I'm

sure he knows all about Sean's things, and what he did with them," Terra said.

Evelyn's expression once again registered surprise. "I don't understand. What has Shamus done?"

Terra bit back the words she was about to say. Now was not the time to talk about Shamus. She had more important things to work on. "I shouldn't have said anything. What's important is that I am taking over this office."

"So, it's true. You inherited Sean's share of Cameron Industries."

"It is. I'm starting today. I'll bring my own things in tomorrow, and please clear your schedule for the next few days. You are going to bring me up to speed on everything Sean was doing here, all his files and business activities."

"I can do that, certainly. Does Shamus know?"

"He knows the contents of Sean's will. He does not know that I intend to work here. I'm sure the minute he learns I'm here with you he'll have something to say. The fact that Sean's will didn't give him complete control of the company has probably made Shamus very angry."

Reason enough for murder, maybe?

Whoops! She hadn't said that out loud, had she?

"Well, in that case we can start right away. Let me get a few things organized."

Evelyn left the office, leaving Terra to settle into Sean's chair. The smooth leather carried his scent and her throat constricted with unshed tears. She reached for a tissue in his desk drawer. Her fingers came to rest on a flash drive, wedged in behind the box of tissue. Terra took it out, turning it over in her fingers. So Shamus hadn't been as careful cleaning out Sean's office as she'd expected.

If Sean put the flash drive into the top drawer of his desk, it had to be important to him. Whatever was on this flash drive would be viewed in the privacy of her home, away from prying eyes. She slipped it into a zippered pocket of her bag just as Shamus strode into the room.

"Why are you here?" he demanded.

"I'm here because I wanted Sean's things—"

"I sent them to your house. They will arrive sometime today."

She got up and came around the desk. "I think it only fair to tell you, I'm going to be working here."

"What! You don't know the first damned thing about this business. You'll just meddle in things and leave when you're bored. Besides you have a nursing job. Go nurse someone."

Terra sighed as she stared directly at him. "Whether we like it or not, you and I now own this company together. So why don't we see if we can get along? I understand there's a lot to be done."

"What do you mean by that?"

"Did you know that Sean had hired a private investigator to look into the company?"

"No! Sean would have told me."

"Well, obviously he didn't."

"What does that mean?" Shamus glowered.

"It means that we have work to do, a lot of it, if we're going to save this company. We need to find out what is going on, what our financial position is, and what action needs to be taken."

"This company doesn't need saving, and certainly not by someone like you. And we sure as hell don't need another woman hanging around here."

What did he mean by that? She wanted to ask him, but decided against it. She'd find out soon enough, once she settled in to work here. "Shamus, I know you're grieving. So am I. Can we try to be civil with each other for a little while at least?"

Shamus scrubbed his face, his eyes glistened with unshed tears. He gulped air; turned away from her for a few minutes. When he turned back his voice held a rasping, pained tone. "I loved my brother. We were more than blood. We were twins, special, inseparable. I would never do anything to hurt him. We grew up knowing we had each other's backs. Sure I'm furious with him for leaving his shares to you, and even angrier that he didn't tell me. I can't believe he didn't trust me enough to tell me that he changed his will. But I loved him. He was my brother, my only brother, and I loved him. Regardless of what happens between you and me, don't ever suggest that I would do anything to hurt Sean in any way."

Terra was dumbstruck by Shamus's words and the emotion behind them. Both had the ring of truth. In her experience men didn't fake tears. Besides, she was pretty sure that Shamus didn't care what she thought of him, certainly not enough to lie to her about how he felt. Maybe it was time for her to go back to the house, plug in the flash drive and see what was on it. Hopefully it would explain what was really going on the last days of Sean's life, and reveal who had reason to murder her husband.

"Shamus, I'm going home for now. We'll talk about all of this later."

The surprised look on his face told her he hadn't expected her to leave without putting up a fight.

When she got back to the house, there was a courier in her driveway. "Are you waiting for me?" she asked the tall man.

"Are you Terra Cameron?"

She assured him she was. Once she showed him her ID, he leaned into the open trunk to retrieve a large box and carried it to the door for her.

"There are two large boxes. This is the smaller of the two." He walked back to the truck. "I will carry them in for you, if you like," the man offered, struggling with the larger box.

"Thank you," she said, opening the front door and stepping aside. Once both were safely deposited in the entryway he pulled a device from his pocket and held out the mobile unit for her signature. She signed the slippery surface. Then he wished her a good day and drove off down the driveway.

Once he'd gone, she put her bag on the front hall table and knelt to open the first box. Inside were all the contents of Sean's desk, which mostly consisted of boxes of Sean's favorite treat, M&M's. She laughed and cried when she saw them. She remembered teasing him about being her very own sweetaholic. Every year she filled his Christmas stocking with more boxes, and laughed at his delight when he opened them.

Suddenly a wave of acute grief overwhelmed her, filling her with loneliness and dread that somehow her life would never be good again. She and Sean had been perfect together. They loved each other so much. She felt incredibly angry and cheated by what had happened. Why did she have to lose Sean? And her baby…. Oh God, her baby.

She pushed the boxes aside, and stood up, anger settling around her heart. Life was not fair. Not fair at all. She brushed strands of hair off her face and picked up her bag from the table.

The first thing she wanted to do was to see what Sean had placed on the memory stick she'd found in the back of his desk drawer. She needed to concentrate on the present, to focus on her plan to be part of the company Sean had loved so much. Swiping the tears off her cheeks she plugged the memory stick into the USB port and waited.

She clicked on the icon, and saw a long list of what looked like…emails. *Why would Sean have gone to the bother of preserving a bunch of emails?* Were they proof of what he suspected was going on at Cameron Industries? Was he saving them in the event of an investigation? Did she want to look at these emails alone?

Reading his emails didn't feel right to her, somehow. Sean would never have read hers. But what if they contained something important to the investigation of his murder? Or maybe he saved emails from people he suspected of being involved in whatever was going on in the company.

Taking a deep breath, she clicked on the first one, an email from sender "BBTAY" dated the day he died. The words shouted at her: *If you don't agree to meet me in person, you won't be happy…ever again. I'll make sure you live to regret it.*

Terra jumped back from the computer as if she'd been scalded. Scrambling through the contents of her purse she found her cell phone and dialed Derrick's number.

He answered on the first ring. "Terra, are you okay?"

"I'm home. You need to come over here now."

She heard a rustling sound, then Derrick's reassuring voice. "I'm on my way. Are you alone?"

She glanced around the quiet, and now strangely sinister space. "Yes. Hurry. I've found something."

She hung up and sat shaking in the desk chair, the cursor on the screen beckoning her to open more of the emails. She couldn't. She didn't want to feel what she was feeling, this sudden sense of fear and betrayal. Who was Sean emailing with? Who wanted him? Was it a woman?

And if so, everything she'd ever believed about her marriage was in danger of disappearing before her eyes.

CHAPTER FOURTEEN

Worried about Terra Derrick roared through the downtown traffic. When she'd called he'd been in an argument with Meaghan about whose approach to the investigation was best, something that had never happened before. In the past few days Meaghan had argued twice with him that his judgment was flawed because of his prior relationship with Terra, a totally unsubstantiated argument, and something Meaghan had never insinuated about him at any other time.

She'd ended the argument by swearing at him, and then bursting into tears—so out of character for her. After her earlier objections he thought they were on the same page until he learned that she'd taken a call from Mike Fenton and then said she somehow forgot to tell him.

As a result he'd found himself questioning her judgment, the judgment of a partner he needed to depend on. She'd basically attacked Terra in the interview. She'd been pursuing suspects such as Kevin Jackson with no real proof that Kevin was involved, except that he'd been with Terra the second night after Sean's death. Then she announced that she wanted to bring Carolyn in for questioning based on the fact that she might know something about her sister that would be worth investigating. It was clear to Derrick that Meaghan was determined to investigate anyone connected to Terra, an ill-advised strategy in his mind.

He had to admit it had taken him a while to figure out that Meaghan saw him as more than a partner, and that was something he had to deal with, sooner rather than later. They could not have anything other than a working relationship, and he'd never considered her in a romantic way.

Yet in the back of his mind he couldn't help wondering if something else was going on with Meaghan. After all, being infatuated with him should have meant that she would be more willing to follow his lead rather than go off chasing questionable avenues of investigation such as Terra's sister and her friends.

Earlier, he'd put a call in to Mike, his retired partner, but there hadn't been any answer, which probably meant that Mike was at the local pub about a block from his house. Derrick had been on his way to find Mike when he got the call from Terra.

He'd wasted no time in getting off the parkway onto the boulevard leading to Terra's subdivision. When he reached her house she was waiting at the front door.

"I'm glad you're here. I think I've found something. When I was in Sean's office today, I found a flash drive tucked away in his desk drawer." She stepped around the boxes still in the hall. "I brought it home, plugged it in. Come and see what I found." She led the way into the den, and pointed at the laptop open on the desk.

"What is all this?" Derrick asked sitting down in front of the computer.

"Well, I opened the first email at the top, sent to Sean the day he died." She moved the mouse and the screen brightened. "See, here. It's an email threatening Sean and written by someone named BBTAY."

Derrick read the email, opened the next one containing words of pleading, declarations of wanting to see him, waiting for him, the further down he went into older emails, the more hopeful the emails sounded. He scrolled down the list, determining that the emails covered a period of four weeks. He turned to Terra, "Did anything happen about four weeks ago? Did Sean seem different? Did he say anything?"

"No. He was preoccupied, busy and out a lot, but there was a lot going on at work. What are you suggesting?" she asked, her voice sounding as if she were about to cry.

Derrick looked up at her as she stood beside him, her fists at her side, her eyes dark with defiance. He wanted to take her in his arms, tell her that it was okay, but that wouldn't be the truth. And right now the truth was what she needed. "Someone, using the name BBTAY, has been emailing your husband. There is no way to know the motive, only that a threat was issued. It could be that someone was trying to put Sean in an embarrassing position. If he was saving those emails, he had a reason. The earlier emails started out relatively benign, but over the past month they escalated into a threat. Sean may have been saving them to take to the police."

Terra didn't answer.

Derrick turned back to the computer screen, while his hands ached to reach out, take her hands in his and pull her into his lap the way they'd done so many times before—back when his life had been perfect. He settled for something much less. "Why don't you pull up a chair and we'll go through these emails and see what we can learn about the person who sent them?"

Once she was seated next to him, he scrolled down to the earliest entry and read it aloud carefully, searching for any hint of who this person was and their relationship to Sean... All the while Terra's scent played with his concentration, reminding him of when they'd been together.

"Look, what's that?" Terra pointed leaning closer. "She's saying something about watching him work."

Derrick stared at the screen. "That would mean that she was either able to watch him in his office at Cameron Industries, or here at the house, right?"

"Yeah... But when Sean worked at home he was always alone in his office. He didn't bring anyone here. Normally, the only person in the house when I wasn't here would be our housekeeper Selena Shepherd."

"Sean didn't have another office? On another floor in his office building or something like that, did he?" Derrick asked.

"Not that I know of," Terra said, chewing her lip. "The only person that could watch his office would be Evelyn Thornton, his secretary. But Evelyn wouldn't do something like this. And if this person was the same one who killed Sean I know for certain that Evelyn wouldn't harm so much as a hair on his head. Evelyn was Sean's right hand. I'm spending the day with her tomorrow to go over all the files Sean was working on, and to familiarize myself with the office."

"Are you sure that going in to work in his office is a good idea when we still don't know who killed Sean?" he asked.

"I'm not sure of anything. All I know is that Sean left those shares to me. He wanted me to take over from him."

"But you could wait and start after we catch Sean's killer," he said.

"You mean stay home out of sight and wait for whoever killed Sean to do something more dangerous than throwing a rock through the window?" she asked.

He knew Terra well enough to know that she could be very stubborn once she'd made up her mind about something. He'd arrange to have the patrols around Terra's neighborhood stepped up until they had a suspect in custody, something he was feeling more confident about given these emails. The techs would be very helpful in finding who wrote them, and the sooner he got them back to the police station, the better. "Okay. Point taken."

But the fact remained that whoever wrote those emails must have been able to see Sean working in his office. In his mind Evelyn Thorton was the most likely person to have sent the emails. "What if Evelyn wanted to be more than his secretary? Maybe this isn't about love, but about wanting more power, more authority within the company? Is that possible?" he asked as an illusive thought floated just out of reach of his tired mind. His argument with Meaghan was affecting his concentration.

"Evelyn? No, not possible," Terra said. "This BBTAY person has to be someone else watching him work in his office."

"Could it be someone watching him from a building across the street? A good set of binoculars and a room in line of sight with his office window would be all that was needed."

"But the person would have to be three stories up. Besides, Sean's office looks out over Odell Park, nothing but green space. No buildings from which to look into the windows of his office."

"Okay, so if we go with the idea that this person was involved in Sean's murder, and assuming that it could have been Evelyn, she would have had to hire someone to do it," Derrick said...again aware of the sensation he was missing something, something just out of reach in his memory.

"So maybe the flowers sent to Sean were from Evelyn," Terra said.

"What?" Derrick asked, startled out of his thoughts.

"Someone sent flowers to Sean the day he died. When I called Evelyn to find out, she said that she hadn't looked at the card, and assumed they were from me as we were having a little celebration that evening. Maybe learning Sean was coming home to celebrate with me was the final straw in her deranged mind," Terra said. "Oh God. How crazy is that?" she asked, her voice breaking, her fingers pressed against her lips.

Unable to stop himself, he put his arm around her, drew her close, consoled her, felt her pain as if it were his own. "I'm so sorry, Terra. So sorry for everything," he whispered into her hair, his heart flooded with memories of how good it had always felt to come home to her, to simply be with her, after a long day or a difficult case.

"This isn't you're fault," she said, looking directly into his eyes. A flash of connection, of sudden awareness floated between them.

"I was talking about—"

"About when we were together," she finished the sentence for him.

He nodded, holding her gaze, begging her with his eyes to understand. "I never meant to hurt you."

"You said all that before, remember?"

"And it's as true now as it was four years ago."

"Please don't do this," she said, moving away from him, resting her hands in her lap while her gaze settled on the computer screen.

Way to go, O'Leary. You're a total screw up when it comes to the one relationship that ever mattered.

He cleared his throat and tried to concentrate. "Okay. If it's all right with you, I'd like to take this flash drive into our computer people and see what they can tell us. I'll copy it to your computer for insurance."

"Can your tech people find out whose email address this is?" Terra asked, her voice suddenly clear and determined.

"We'll see. They're pretty good at things like this."

"Tomorrow I'm going into the office to spend the day with Evelyn, and I assume you'll be along at some point," she said, giving him a sidelong glance.

"What?" He glanced up from the screen where he'd been loading the contents of the flash drive on to her computer.

"Aren't you sending a forensic auditor into Cameron Industries tomorrow?"

He'd completely forgotten. *Where in hell was his head?* "Yeah."

"Tell them to watch out for Shamus. He's in a foul mood."

"Are you staying here alone tonight?" he asked, suddenly worried about her safety.

"I'm fine here."

There was sadness and defiance in her eyes, the woman he realized he still loved seemed so alone and adrift. What a fool he'd been to marry Marylou, a woman who tricked him into thinking she was carrying his child. He'd slept with her once after an evening of partying he couldn't even remember the next day, after he and Mike had solved a particularly difficult case. A few weeks later she came to his office saying that she was pregnant by him. He'd been torn between his responsibility for what he believed was his baby, and his fear that telling Terra about his betrayal would end their relationship. He'd gone with Marylou because he wanted to do the right thing by his child.

The night she admitted to lying about who fathered her child was rock bottom for him. He'd been duped, and in the process he had destroyed the one relationship that had ever mattered to him. He was to blame for what he did. Drinking too much was not an excuse.

Yet, he couldn't intrude on Terra's grief and tell her how he felt. He had no right to say anything to her. As he watched her struggle with her feelings he knew that no matter what happened in his life, this moment would be engraved in his heart forever. He would love her, and care for her and protect her any way he could. There would never be anyone else for him but her. "Terra, I'm worried for you."

"Please stop. If you must know, I can't be anywhere else but here right now. I tried staying at Carolyn's, but all I want to do when I'm there is to come back here. I know how weird that sounds, with everything that's happened in this house. But I have to be here. Sean would want me to be here. It's where we planned to spend our lives together." She gave him a clear-eyed glance. "But since you're worried and you came here so quickly, I'll call Carolyn and ask her to stay with me tonight. How's that?"

Again he was reminded that the woman he loved would not be stopped from doing what she wanted to do. "Goes to show some things never change."

She sat up straight in her chair. "Like what?" she asked.

"Like you're stubborn."

"And you're not?" She arched one eyebrow.

"You're right."

"Okay, I'll see you tomorrow," she said, walking ahead of him to the door.

"Be sure to put your security system on," he said, almost leaning in to kiss her as he'd done so many times, back when they were happy together.

"I will." She held the door, her eyes remaining on a spot beyond his shoulder.

He hesitated, hoping she'd look at him. As he waited the moment slipped away, leaving him no choice but to leave.

She closed the door behind him, leaned her head against the cool wood panels, and breathed slowly to regain her equilibrium. She'd managed not to let him see how hurt she was to find someone had been emailing her husband; had threatened him and had probably killed him. She'd been close to tears several times over what the emails had revealed. She'd clung to the notion that BBTAY might simply be a friend, maybe a business associate, but the content of the last email Sean had received denied her that solace.

She'd felt so vulnerable, so heartbroken that Sean had been in touch with another woman. Terra was hurt and embarrassed and needed Derrick now in a way she couldn't own up to. He'd seen the evidence of Sean's betrayal, yet he'd said nothing. What must he think of her now that he knew just how gullible she'd been?

Glancing at Sean's clock in the den she realized that it was after seven, and she hadn't eaten since breakfast. Yet she wasn't hungry. She wasn't really sleepy. She wasn't anything except lonesome and afraid.

Turning over what Derrick had said about Sean's secretary, she could only come to one conclusion. She would bet the insurance Sean had left her that Evelyn Thornton had nothing to do with those emails. Evelyn was not the kind of person to threaten anyone, and she'd been Sean's secretary for years. If she loved Sean as more than her friend and her boss, Sean would have said something.

It had to be someone else. Someone who had insinuated their way into Sean's life. Someone who was obsessed with Sean, who believed that Sean belonged to her. Someone Sean would have tried to disentangle himself from without embarrassing the person.

Sean was the kindest human being in the world. He would have wanted to let this person down easy without hurting them any more than was absolutely necessary. That could mean he wouldn't have told anyone about this woman's infatuation with him.

As she made a cup of hot chocolate she put a call in to her sister.

The phone continued to ring until it went to voicemail. This was the second time that Carolyn had been out in the evening the past few weeks. With all that had happened in the past few days she hadn't thought about it. But now she wondered if Carolyn had a boyfriend. Her sister had never been one to go out in the evening, not even to a movie. She left a message asking Carolyn to come over and spend the night with her.

Whatever was going on, she was certain her sister would call her back. In the meantime, she would put her dishes in the dishwasher, settle in and watch a little TV until Carolyn called.

Just after midnight, she called Carolyn's number again and waited for her to pick up. Carolyn must have a boyfriend, someone she was spending the night with. This was out of character for her prim and proper, by-the-book sister. Had Carolyn mentioned going anywhere the last time she'd seen her? If she had, Terra couldn't remember.

Whatever was going on, Terra felt too distracted and unfocused to make much sense of it. She would have to trust that her sister would call her when she got the messages she'd left. Exhausted, she went to bed in the guest room, avoiding the master suite whose door stood stubbornly closed.

Carolyn was entitled to her life.

Terra awoke the next morning, her neck stiff, her head pounding and she felt really nauseated. There was no way she could go to the office today. She needed to call Evelyn Thornton. She stood up, only to have her stomach heave dangerously. She eased back down on the bed and reached for the phone.

She dialed Evelyn's office number. "I'm home with some sort of flu bug. I won't be in today."

"Oh, you poor thing. That's awful. And of course I understand. Do you need anything? I could run it over to the house for you."

"Nothing for now."

"Call me later if you need me, okay?" Evelyn asked.

"I will," she said and hung up. She tried Carolyn's number again, and again it went to voicemail. *Where was her sister? And why hadn't she called?* Carolyn would know she was worried about her. An uneasy feeling mingled with her nausea.

She shoved the phone into the pocket of her robe and slowly made her way out into the hall. She was greeted by a flash of sunlight filtering from under the closed door of the master bedroom as she made her way to the bathroom. On her way back to her bedroom the phone rang. Kevin. "Hello," she said, her voice sounding hollow in her ears.

"Terra? What's wrong?"

"I think I have the flu."

"I'm coming over," he said.

"No. Kevin. I don't want you to get sick. Stay home."

"Wish I could. Something awful has happened."

"What?" she asked.

"Remember I told you that I'd been called in for questioning?"

"Yeah."

"I found out why."

"And?" she asked searching for a Tylenol.

"I went to Peter's house this morning, wanting to know why I was being questioned. He told me the police had to investigate everyone connected to you. He was getting pressure from the mayor. He was so distant with me. I asked him what was going on. I've never pressured Peter to go public with our relationship. Never. I've tried to understand his feelings around letting people know about us, but today I felt so hurt I got angry. He says he doesn't want to see me again. He's changing the locks on the condo. He will *allow* me to get my things out of the condo; that's all. He's sending his sister to meet me there while I pick up my things. Can you believe that?"

"No, I can't," Terra said, settling back against the pillows, feeling drained by Kevin's problem.

"His career means more to him than I do. He tossed me out because he's afraid. I know it. And the other thing he told me was that he had you interviewed as a suspect. Can you believe it? Detective Wilson wasn't simply trying to get at the facts. She believes that you killed Sean."

Terra sat up straight. "Why? I've done nothing but cooperate with the police. They're at Cameron Industries right now because I gave them access." She'd given Derrick permission to go into the office without a search warrant. "I haven't kept anything from them, and now you're telling me that the police chief thinks I had something to do with Sean's death."

"That's what Peter said." A long silence stretched out between them. "Terra, I hope that Derrick is working on a theory other than what Peter is suggesting. If he's not, you are in big trouble."

Terra swallowed against her fear. "Kevin, you know I would never harm Sean."

"Of course, but who would? That's the question we have to answer." He gave a long sigh before continuing. "Okay, let's think about this. Who would kill Sean? Shamus tops my list, followed or supported by his mother, then there's always Selena."

"Selena Shepherd? She's my housekeeper. I'd be lost without her."

"But she had access to the house. She knows everything there is to know about you and Sean, where you go and what you do. Can't rule her out without checking all the angles. But I assume that Derrick's looking at everyone, given what Peter said... And there is someone else...someone I just thought of."

"Who?"

"Carolyn."

"What! Not my sister! Kevin, stop this. You're being ridiculous."

"You know that as sweet as Carolyn is, she has always envied you. I was really surprised when she wanted you to stay at her house."

"Why would she envy me?"

"Because she doesn't have the glamorous life you do."

"My life isn't glamorous! That's crazy!"

"Not to Carolyn. You know I love her like she was my sister, but she is envious of your life."

"That can't be true. Sure. We've had our differences, especially when Mom was ill, but we've been pretty good sisters since then. And who in their right mind would be envious now?"

"Are you sure she's not?" Kevin asked.

She hadn't heard from Carolyn, not even a message. "Of course."

"I… She came to me for money a few months back," Kevin said.

"To you? Why wouldn't she come to me?"

"Pride, maybe. Anyway, she said she couldn't ask you. That your life was perfect, that you wouldn't understand."

"Stop this right now. Carolyn would never do anything to hurt me."

Kevin gave a long sigh. "Look. Sorry I said anything. I didn't mean it. I'm upset and taking it out on you. Sorry," he said again.

"It's okay. We're all upset and anxious. By the way, I didn't get a chance to tell you about the flash drive I found in Sean's desk when I was in the office."

"Flash drive? You're kidding me! What was on it?"

"A bunch of his emails between someone with BBTAY in their email address. The police are trying to figure out who the person is."

"Could this person have been stalking Sean?"

"No. No! Sean would have told me if he was being stalked. He would have gone to the police."

"Speaking of the police, any new leads?"

"I have no idea. Derrick took the flash drive with him to see if the technical people could find the identity of the person."

"And what do *you* think?"

"I'm so tired of all this. In my heart I can't help but believe that someone knew that Sean and I were home alone that evening. Only Evelyn knew about our evening plans because Sean told her. That night Sean locked the doors. I went to put the security system on and found the door off the patio downstairs open. They had to have had a key, and yet all the keys are accounted for."

Suddenly Terra was back in the moment when the man threw her on the bed and climbed on top of her. His smell, the anger in his eyes...his eyes. "Oh. No. Kevin, the man had blue eyes. Deep blue eyes. I've got to call Derrick."

"Okay, that's enough. I'm coming over. If you're starting to remember things you shouldn't be alone." The phone went dead.

She dialed Derrick's number and waited while it went to voicemail. "Derrick, it's me, Terra. Can you call me right away? I remembered something about my attacker."

Her hands were shaking as she ended the call. Agitated by the sudden memory and afraid to be alone, she waited anxiously for Kevin's car to pull into the driveway. She opened the door as he came running up the steps.

He hugged her close, took her hand, and led her through the hall to the kitchen. "What did Derrick say?"

"Nothing. I had to leave a message."

Kevin settled in on one of the stools at the kitchen counter, his large signet ring glistening in the light. "Okay, until we hear back from Derrick I want you to concentrate on every detail you can remember about that night." He kept her hand in his. "I'm here, and you're safe. Just try to remember."

"The ski masks made it hard to tell them apart. They were about the same size and height. The one who grabbed me was so rough. He stunk to high heaven."

Kevin leaned toward her. "Okay. He smelled awful."

"Yeah, like stale sweat, pizza and…beer."

"And what else?"

"He had been hiding somewhere behind me when I went downstairs that night. He moved so fast I didn't have a chance to run or scream."

"In good physical shape, maybe?"

"It's possible," Terra said, searching her mind, trying to remember more details.

"What else?"

"He was tall. His arms. When he grabbed me, it hurt."

"Keep going. Was he as tall as me?" Kevin asked.

"I'm not sure."

"Then let's do this. Stand up." He came around the table. "Pretend I'm him. I grab you from behind." He gripped her with so much strength it startled her. "Think Terra. What else did he do?"

"His arms hurt. I tried to scratch him. I tried to kick him. His arms tightened. I saw something on his hands. A ring of some kind….smooth…shiny. He picked me up off the floor."

"Like this?" Kevin lifted her off the floor, his powerful arms tightening around her body.

Suddenly she was back there, being held, frightened and shocked. She struggled to get free, digging her fingers into his arm. His arms tightened. Panicked, she screamed. "Let me go!"

"Oh! God! Sorry!" Kevin said, letting go of her and stepping away, a shocked look on his face. "What the hell got into me? I wouldn't harm a hair on your head. You know that."

He raised his arms over his head, rubbed his neck, a guilty expression on his face. "I must be losing it."

Terra took a deep breath to calm her nerves. Kevin had never done anything like that in all the years she'd known him. Was there something else going on in his life, something he couldn't share with her? The way he'd grabbed her made her wonder if he was really angry at something…or someone else.

"We're both under a lot of stress at the moment. You frightened me. It seemed so real." She rubbed her arms and sat back down at the table, feeling exhausted and worried.

First her sister behaving strangely…and now Kevin.

CHAPTER FIFTEEN

Derrick had sent the forensic audit team to Cameron Industries a day ago, and they'd been allowed in to talk to Shamus and the accountants in the office. He was really glad that Terra had the authority to allow them access to the accounting records. The whole issue of the missing money certainly gave Shamus one hell of a motive, if he was the person who'd taken funds from the company.

He was on his way to meet Mike Fenton after finally connecting with him on the phone this morning. Mike mentioned he wanted to talk, but not over the phone. They agreed to meet at the diner. When he pulled into the parking lot, Mike was leaning against his 1999 Subaru Legacy. Derrick noted a dent in the driver's door, and saw that its green paint had been scored by something sharp, a key perhaps.

Mike loved that car. Derrick thought it was a wreck, and he preferred to trade cars whenever his budget allowed. By the grin on Mike's face and the open enthusiasm in his expression he knew that Mike had something.

"What in hell kept you from calling me back?" Mike demanded.

"My partner, and I got a little busy. I was able to get into Cameron Industries, thanks to Sean's will."

Mike whistled. "So we have a rich, powerful widow to add to the mix?"

"We'll know more about the rich part when the auditors finish up."

"You think Shamus did it?"

"I think he ordered it."

Mike shrugged and spit a toothpick from between his teeth. "Same thing."

"So what was so important that you couldn't tell me over the phone and had to see me in person?" Derrick asked.

"Can't I just love your mug? Want to gaze into your soulful eyes?" Mike teased.

"Stop trying to come on to me and get to the point," Derrick said, enjoying the banter with his ex-partner.

"Okay, so here's what's got me all excited. You know we talked about Buddy and Lennie and what they might have been up to since we arrested them in the Pickering Case."

"Yeah. So?"

"So, I talked to one of my old snitches, and he says that Buddy Edson found a new form of employment. He's been working out of state, for someone probably involved in organized crime. But here's the good part. My snitch saw him back here a couple of weeks ago. Said he was here to help a friend. My snitch friend didn't know Buddy's friend's name, but it was a good enough friend to bring him back here."

"And you think the friend is Lennie Taylor?" Derrick smacked his head. "Oh! Damn!"

"What is it?" Mike asked his attention riveted on Derrick as they sat down in their favorite booth.

"Terra called me to the house the other day. She found a flash drive with emails on it, someone threatening Sean, someone whose email address was BBTAY. How could I have forgotten that? Dammit all to hell! These emails could have come from someone who was involved with Lennie Taylor. It would account for the 'TAY' in the email address."

"Possibly a friend, or wife, or ex-wife of Lennie—is that what you're thinking? That Lennie found out that BBTAY, whoever that is, wasn't happy with Sean—for whatever reason—and Lennie decided to join forces with Buddy and fix the problem?"

"I think it's a very real possibility. More likely the only plausible scenario we have at the moment," Derrick said as the waitress put full cups of coffee in front of each of them.

"Then you'd better get on it, find out who BBTAY is. It could be just a few letters in an email address to throw you off, you know that, don't you?"

"I'm not *that* Internet illiterate," Derrick said, standing up and putting money on the table. "I gotta go and check this out."

"If you're trying to pay me for services rendered, sweetheart, that's not nearly enough," Mike said, with a huge grin and a wink.

∽

Terra was rattled by Kevin's behavior, but he'd been so concerned and apologetic she'd decided to use what Kevin had just done, as scary as it was, and concentrate on what she could recall. "I remember my attacker was wearing a ring, Kevin. Do you think that memory is real? Or did I imagine it?"

"I don't know. All I know is that you need to talk to Derrick as soon as possible. If you can describe the ring a little better it might help."

"It was thick, with raised parts, a crest maybe?"

"Color?"

"Silver, maybe? I'm not sure."

"You said you thought someone close to Sean killed him. If that's true, why did they come in here and throw all his clothes around after he was dead? And why throw a rock through the window that night? I don't know Terra, this is more than we can work out on our own. Give me Derrick's number. I'll see if I can reach him."

"I'll do it." She dialed the number she'd memorized. "Voicemail again. Where is he?"

Kevin straightened his tie, a determined look in his eyes.

"Why don't you come with me and we'll see if we can find him?"

"What? Look at me. I'm a mess. I smell awful. I can't go anywhere. Besides I'm waiting for Carolyn to call me."

"Why don't you go over to her house and see if she's there?"

"I don't want to barge in on her, especially if she's got a date…who stayed all night."

"Speak of the devil," Kevin said seeing Carolyn approaching the house along the pathway in front of the windows facing the street.

Terra rushed to the door. "I've been worried sick about you. Where have you been?"

"I've been out." Carolyn peered at her sister, and touched her arm affectionately. "I'm sorry to have worried you. Everything's fine." She glanced at Kevin.

"My cue to leave," he said, turning to Terra, his hands outstretched. "Talk to Derrick, will you? I'll call you later."

"Where are you going?"

"I'm going to drop over to Cameron Industries, be your eyes and ears for a little while."

"When Shamus sees you he'll probably kick you out."

He gave her a thumbs up. "I'm Teflon tough."

They watched him leave. "I worry about him," Terra said.

Carolyn smiled affectionately. "Kevin can look after himself."

"I hope so."

"I haven't eaten. I'll microwave something and then I'll tell you where I've been."

"Can't wait to hear what kept you from returning my call," Terra said as she settled in to watch her sister in the kitchen.

To the low hum of the defrost cycle on the microwave, Carolyn began. "I've met someone. Someone really special. He asked me not to say anything to anyone because he's going through a difficult divorce. But I can't keep the secret any longer." The smile on her face was warm and dreamy. "He's lived here all his working life, and I didn't know he existed. We both love to write. He's actually working on a novel. I've shown him the children's book I'm working on. He thinks they're great. I just can't believe it. I met him when you were in the hospital. He was there with his Uncle Charlie."

"What's this guy's name?"

"Tim Martin."

"The reporter?" Terra asked, at once surprised and fearful.

"What? No. Not that Tim Martin. My Tim has his own import and export company. He took me out to dinner last evening." She took her cell phone out of her pocket just as the microwave pinged that the cycle was complete. "Here's his picture. The two of us together at Cymbals. We had a beautiful meal, and went back to his place afterward." She passed her phone to Terra.

The smiling face of the reporter made Terra want to throw up. She placed the cell phone on the table, pushing it as far away from her as possible. "That is the reporter. You must have seen him at the restaurant the day I met with Dennis Sparks."

"No. I left you to take a call from my editor. Tim wasn't in the restaurant."

"He was."

"Well I didn't see him."

"Carolyn, you can't be around him. He's been following me, calling here. He was at the Cameron mansion that day you and I went over there. He was at Kevin's place on the lake that morning. He's using you to get to me."

Carolyn gasped in surprise. "What are you saying? No. I'm sure Tim isn't a reporter."

"I'm telling you he is. We can go on the newspaper website and look him up if you like. You have to stay away from him. He's using you to get information about me, about Sean's murder case."

"That's not fair!"

"Carolyn, think carefully, did you talk to him about me?"

"Of course. You're my sister, and I love you. We've been talking so much. I feel so close to him. I want to share my life with him. I…I'm falling in love with him. He wouldn't hurt you or me."

Suddenly Terra remembered that night after Sean died…the tea…the exhaustion…the long sleep. Had Tim been at her sister's house that evening? Had he convinced Carolyn to put something in her tea, something to make her sleep, giving him the opportunity… Had he been in the bedroom where she was sleeping? Going through her things… Panic rose in her throat, making it impossible to breathe. "Carolyn, you've got to listen to me. He lied to you about what he does for a living. He's a reporter. He's after me. My story. You've got to stay away from him."

Carolyn's eyes were wide and glistening with unshed tears. "Can't you ever be happy for me?"

"Yes, but not about this." Needing to connect with her sister, to get her to see reason, Terra reached for her sister's hand.

Carolyn pulled her hand away, her lips pressed together, her eyes boring into Terra. "Why is everything always about *you*? What makes you think you're so special?"

Terra sighed and closed her eyes. The microwave pinged again. Carolyn yanked open the door and dumped the soup into the sink. Standing with her back to Terra, she said, "I came here so happy to tell you my news. But you couldn't leave it alone, could you? You had to make sure that everything is ruined for me."

Terra's stomach ached from the anger in her sister's words. If only she could hug her sister, tell her everything was okay between them. But she couldn't. There was too much at stake. "Who else did you talk about?"

Carolyn turned to her, her chin high. "We talked about you, about how much I worry about you. We talked about the horror of Sean's death. We talked about Kevin and what a good friend he is to you."

A warning bell went off in Terra's head. "Did you mention anything about Kevin's private life?"

Carolyn's chin went to her chest. "I might have." The sighing hum of the refrigerator was the only sound in the room. Suddenly Carolyn gave a huge sigh, gathered her phone, her purse and her jacket and started toward the door.

Terra followed, wanting to somehow stop her sister from leaving like this. "Carolyn, I'm sorry. If only you'd said something earlier I could have warned you about him."

With her hand on the doorknob, Carolyn turned her sad gaze on her sister. "I'm sorry too. I only wanted to be happy, to love someone. Like you and Sean. I want that. I've always wanted that. I've envied you all my life, grew up in the shadow of the great Terra. Mom and Dad's prized possession. The girl who got it right, every time."

"Carolyn, surely you don't envy me now; losing my baby, losing Sean. Please don't tell me you envy my life as it is now."

"No. I don't. When Tim showed up in my life, I truly believed it was my turn for happiness," she said, her tone cool as she opened the door and closed it gently behind her.

Tears burned hard tracks down Terra's cheeks as she stood watching her sister go down the walkway to the street. Carolyn had no idea what she'd done. What would Tim Martin write about her now that he'd found a source? And Carolyn hadn't said she'd stay away from him, which meant that he was probably waiting somewhere for her, to get more information about Terra and the case.

Kevin. She'd nearly forgotten about him. She dialed his number. He picked up on the first ring. "Kevin, Carolyn just told me something you need to know."

"You mean about Tim Martin? I already know. Peter called me to tell me about it. Tim called his office, said he had a source on the inside of Peter's personal life. The implication was clear."

"What are you going to do?"

There was a long pause, the soft roar of Kevin's Mercedes providing the background noise. "Peter and I are leaving town. He's turned in his resignation. We want to be happy, Terra. The only way that can happen is for the two of us to move somewhere else."

"Where will you go?" she asked, her voice shaking. "When will I see you?"

Another pause. "Peter is finishing some things in his

office. His resignation is effective the end of the month. We probably won't be out of here until sometime later next week."

"Why so fast?"

"It's the only way Peter can do it. He's had a job offer from the Miami-Dade County Police Force. He's decided to accept it. I'm going with him."

She'd never been without Kevin in her life. She couldn't imagine not hearing him at the door, bringing croissants while he talked about his designs. All the different ways their friendship had been fostered over the years meant there would be a horrible gap in her life if he should leave. "Please come over as soon as you can. I need to see you. After my fight with Carolyn, it's so lonely here. You're my best friend. Please." She gulped back the tears.

"I'm going to miss you too. We've been together forever, haven't we?"

"Yes! My life will be so empty without you. You've had my back as long as I can remember."

"Don't start crying," Kevin warned. "Or I will too. Let's just look on this as an adventure. You can always call me and chat, and come to visit us."

Terra wanted to convince him to stay, to reconsider. But Kevin loved Peter, and she understood how much he wanted to share a life with him. "It's not the same and you know it."

"I wish it could be different. But when Peter called and said he couldn't live without me, that we would make a new life somewhere else, I couldn't say no. You understand that, don't you?"

"Of course. Just say you'll stop by and see me today."

"I will. I'll call before I come. Talk soon, T-Bird," he said softly.

At the mention of his pet name for her she choked up. "Talk soon, Thunderball."

CHAPTER SIXTEEN

The Buddy and Lennie scenario was showing signs of promise. Derrick had had a call from one of the beat cops down on East Main Street. It seems that the bartender at the Lazy Susan said that two men came in the night after Sean's death, buying drinks and bragging about how they'd helped a friend put something right. They talked about getting back at one of the moneyed families in the town.

The other positive note this morning was that he and Meaghan had patched up their differences, and she had volunteered to check the emails and hurry the computer techs along to find the identity of BBTAY. She had also volunteered to interview the bartender at the Lazy Susan, and see if she could find any usable surveillance recordings for the night in question.

Meanwhile he'd had a call from the audit team and he was on his way to Cameron Industries. The cup of coffee he'd gulped down an hour earlier was playing havoc with his stomach. The coffee mixed with the excitement that he was about to learn a whole lot from the forensic audit, made him feel really positive that they would find Sean's killer very soon.

His gut hummed. Following the money was always interesting but in this case he was convinced the money trail would lead to answers about motive. He only had to wait to see what turned up.

He pulled into the visitors parking at Cameron Industries, got out of his car and started along the manicured walkway. Up ahead he spotted Shamus's wife, her face covered in tears, her blond hair bedraggled.

She turned, saw him and charged toward him. "Why do you hate my husband? He hasn't done anything wrong. He's a good man. We have a good life. What right have you to mess with it?" she demanded, blocking Derrick's path into the building.

"Ma'am, step back. You don't want to do this. You don't want to get involved in our investigation."

She stuck out her chin. "I am a God-fearing woman, and you will answer my question."

He didn't have the time or the patience for this craziness. "I'm not messing with your life, Mrs. Cameron. I'm conducting an investigation into your brother-in-law's death."

Tear slid down her cheeks. "You have no right. You're not welcome here in my husband's place of business."

"Where's your husband?" he asked as he moved to step around her.

She blocked him. "He's not here," she hissed, glaring up at him. "You and those people you sent drove him away."

"Mrs. Cameron, the police investigators are following my orders. They're here to do a job."

"You have no idea who you're hurting, do you? All you want is to give that…that woman a chance to tell more lies."

Derrick suppressed the urge to say something to set the record straight where Terra was concerned. He stood by his original thought—Bethany was terminally strange.

"Mrs. Cameron, please step aside."

She stared at him, her eyes narrowing. "Fine," she huffed, and with that she stomped off down the walkway toward the parking lot.

Derrick walked to the entrance of the building, having already forgotten Bethany's bizarre behavior, his attention on the case. As far as he was concerned the person most likely to want Sean dead was Shamus, and probably it was over the money, and what the PI had found.

But with these emails found on Sean's flash drive, it was also possible that someone else wanted him dead—someone who wanted a relationship with him. Terra was convinced that the email came from a woman, but Derrick had to keep an open mind. Meaghan had checked the cell phone, and found the same emails, and the chat room conversation didn't indicate whether the person disguised under the BBTAY email address was male of female. Regardless of gender, the threat in the last message had been clear.

On the way back from seeing Mike yesterday, he called in and asked Meaghan to pull everything they had on Lennie and Buddy. Knuckle draggers like Lennie and Buddy killed for money or revenge, and hadn't done an honest day's work in their lives. There had to be more information on the past criminal activities than he'd found so far.

He was about to call Terra and let her know he was at Cameron Industries when he realized he'd missed a couple of messages. He listened to Terra's first message, and was pleased to learn that she remembered the man's eye color and the second message was about a ring she remembered being on his hand that night. He'd call her back once he'd talked to Evelyn Thornton.

Minutes later he was in the reception area outside Sean Cameron's office. Evelyn Thornton came toward him. "The entire administration office is in turmoil over the audit. Is all this necessary?"

"It is. Where is Shamus Cameron?"

Evelyn frowned and glanced around anxiously. "He's left the building, I believe." She moved back behind her desk, her hands fluttering around her waist, her expression uncertain.

Was all this due to what was going on in the office today? The forensic audit? He didn't think so. "Mrs. Thornton—?"

"I'm not married. Never was."

"Evelyn. I need to ask you a few questions."

She sat down tentatively on the edge of her office chair. "What about?"

"What did you know about Sean's office life? By that I mean, was there anyone, any woman in the company, other than yourself, that was a close confidant of Sean's?"

"What are you suggesting by using the word 'other'? Are you implying that my relationship with Sean was something other than professional?" she demanded, the uncertainty gone from her demeanor.

"I'm asking what you know."

"Why? What reason do you have to question anything that went on inside Sean's office? I thought this investigation was about Shamus, not Sean."

Cool your jets, O'Leary. You need this woman's help and support. He pulled up an empty chair next to her desk. "Sorry to imply anything. Can I confide in you?"

She tucked her chin in, her short black bob flouncing around her cheeks. "Why would you want to do that?"

"We've discovered that someone, using an email address with letters BBTAY in it, threatened Sean the day he died. I'm interested in whether or not you've ever had an email come to you with BBTAY as part of the email address."

She frowned. "No. Why would you think that I'd be emailing with this person?" she asked. Her tone was glacier cool, yet her eyes were anxious.

This woman knew something, or suspected something beyond what she said. And that suspicion made sense, given that she'd worked there for years. She obviously liked her boss. Maybe she loved him and had joined the chat room to entice him into a relationship with her. And maybe when he didn't respond the way she wanted, she decided to hire someone to scare him. But why would she want him dead if she loved him? But, at the same time, if she expected him to choose her over Terra, maybe she was angry enough to have him killed. He'd have to check and see if she had any connection to Buddy or Lennie.

Still, Evelyn didn't strike him as the kind of woman who would do something like that. Becoming infatuated with her boss, possibly, but not to threaten him. BBTAY could have been used by anyone creating an email address, one set up to hide their identity.

"Evelyn, one of the emails made it sound like this woman could see Sean when the email was being written. Sean had been emailing with this person for weeks, and this person was making demands on him in these emails. I can't see how that could be, unless you have someone else working in this office. Do you have extra staff, someone who replaces you at break time, something like that?"

Evelyn carefully placed her hands on the desk palms down and looked at him. "No one replaces me on breaks. I put the phone on call forwarding to my cell phone if Sean isn't in the office. If he's here, he answers. If he's not, I lock the door to this office before I leave, whether after work or during the day."

"What you're telling me is that no one other than you could have been in a position to see Sean at his desk. The person who was sending the emails we found, the threatening one in particular, made it clear that they were watching Sean. Evelyn, if you're the only one in the position to do that, you need to come downtown with me."

Her mouth worked as if she couldn't breathe. Her hands fell into her lap, her sigh of resignation clearly audible. "If I tell you what I know, I could lose my job. I can't afford to let that happen. My mother is in care. I need the money. I can't afford to lose this job," she said again, this time with more force.

"Evelyn, what is it that you think you know? I won't tell anyone, and it may end up not being important. However it turns out, you have to speak up. We have to find Sean's murderer."

"But what I'm about to tell you doesn't make any sense. I may be helping you to draw the wrong conclusion."

Derrick leaned closer. "Let me decide that. Now, tell me what it is you think you know."

Terra hadn't been able to rest since Carolyn had confessed

her relationship with Tim Martin. *How had all this happened?*

If Carolyn insisted on dating Tim after he lied about what he did for a living, there was no chance that she and her sister could have a normal relationship. On top of that, she knew Tim planned to build on his reputation using insider details about the story of the sensational murder of a prominent businessman—using any means he could to get them. But would Carolyn not see what he was up to if Tim kept on asking questions about her and the family?

Terra wasn't sure Carolyn could resist a plea from someone she was in love with, no matter what was at stake. Searching to relieve the fear in her mind, she looked around for something to do, something mindless and mundane—the kitchen counters. She scrubbed the counters, the floor and emptied the dishwasher. When she finished she headed to the guest bathroom. Running the water until steam rose in clouds around her, she stepped into the large double shower. She scrubbed her skin until it stung, washed her hair and pulled a thick white towel off the heated rack next to the shower door. Feeling refreshed, her head clearer, she left the bathroom and went in search of clean clothes.

Just then the doorbell rang. Her heart jumped in her chest. It had to be Kevin though he said he'd call before dropping by. She'd actually expected him sooner but he probably had a lot to deal with as he prepared to leave town.

She'd let him in and then get dressed. Tugging the towel tightly around her body, she was about to head back down the hall to the front door when she heard it.

CHAPTER SEVENTEEN

Derrick stared at Evelyn Thornton in shock. The woman wasn't making any sense. There was no reason in the world for Sean to have allowed someone he seemed to have no real relationship with, to hang around outside his office. Had he felt sorry for her? Did he feel that because she was part of the family she had a free pass to Cameron Industries?

"Did she ever say anything to you as she sat there working on her laptop? You must have been curious?"

"She told me it was okay. She was a freelance writer. She'd always wanted to write for a magazine, and she had a contract to write a piece for the *Michigan Free Press*. Sean had agreed to be interviewed and had given her access to my office as part of the interview process."

"Did anyone else know?" Derrick asked, still trying to connect what he knew about this woman, passing herself off as a writer, and what Evelyn was telling him.

"I don't think so. And to be honest I wasn't very comfortable with it. She kept asking me questions about Sean and Terra, about their relationship. I found myself repeating the same thing. They were very happy together."

"And you never asked Sean about it?"

Evelyn shrugged. "What for? It was his sister-in-law

after all. None of my business. She wasn't unpleasant. When she came in she always brought me coffee."

"How long did it go on?"

Evelyn thought for a moment. "Just in the past week or so, maybe two weeks. To tell you the truth once she said she had Sean's permission, I just went along with it."

Derrick needed to make a call. "Thank you for this."

Evelyn Thornton gave him a distracted look. "You're welcome."

Derrick raced toward the elevator, his cell phone in hand. He dialed Terra's number, but it went to voicemail. He dialed his partner. "I need you to meet me at the Cameron house."

You're going to arrest Shamus?"

"No. Not that house. Sean's house."

"Why?"

"I know who wrote the emails. Get to the house as fast as you can. I need to talk to Terra and she's not answering her phone."

⌒〜〜〜

Terra's knees shook as she waited. Someone was opening the front door with a key.

It must be Carolyn. Her sister had left angry and upset, and might be returning to apologize. But her sister knew how much anxiety and fear Terra lived with every day since Sean's death. Carolyn had been the one trying to discourage her from staying here alone. Her sister would have rung the doorbell, or called first if she'd changed her mind and decided to return.

She clung to the wall as she eased forward down the hall toward the bedrooms as far from the front door as possible. She remembered what Derrick had told her. Get into a closet with the phone, call 911 and stay hidden.

Think! Where was the cell phone? In her panic she couldn't remember. *Was it in the bathroom?* No. She'd left it in the kitchen.

The landline phone was in the guestroom. She turned to

start back toward the bedroom when she heard something else—her front door opening and closing so quietly she wasn't even sure what she heard. In the same instant the door-ajar chime sounded on the security system.

Someone *was* in the house.

A scream rose in her throat. She choked it back. She needed to call 911.

"Terra?" a tentative female voice called out.

That wasn't Carolyn's voice.

"Who is it?" Terra asked, stopping in mid-stride.

"I'm sorry to bother you. It's Bethany. I came to see if you were all right. I suppose I could have called first, but I was in the neighborhood," she said to the chorus of her heels clicking on the marble floor.

Something was off. Way off. How had Bethany gotten a key?

She had to get to the phone. "I…I just got out of the shower. Can you wait while I get dressed?"

"Certainly."

Terra's hands shook as she entered the guest bedroom and hastily yanked on the clothes lying on the end of the bed. Seeing the phone on the table she scooped it up, her fingers trembling as she dialed Derrick's cell number.

Holding her breath she waited for him to pick up.

"Terra, I'm on my way over—"

The phone flew from her hands, cruising across the room and landing on the floor with a crash.

"Terra, my sister-in-law, I need to talk to you." Bethany smiled sweetly, a large butcher knife in her right hand.

Her eyes locked on the knife she eased away from Bethany. She had to stall the woman until Derrick got there. Her years of experience in the Emergency Room had taught her to remain calm, especially when dealing with someone mentally unstable, someone completely unpredictable and dangerous. "I don't understand. What do you want from me?"

A look of loathing flashed across Bethany's face. "Okay, let me tell you exactly what I want. We're going across to the master bedroom. I want to see the room where Sean died. I managed to sneak into your house the night he died and I got the envelope he left the office with." She rolled her eyes. "Sure enough, he'd hired someone to look into Shamus's activities at the office. But that's a whole other story." Bethany flashed the knife at her, motioning for her to go ahead of her into the master suite.

"Well, finally I get to see where he died without anyone interfering." She sighed with satisfaction, and tiptoed further into the room.

Terra watched in horror as Bethany knelt and prayed in the exact spot where Sean died, her words of confession, her cries for forgiveness an eerie sound. Terra looked away, unable to contemplate what was going on in front of her. Bethany was clearly mad, and had been completely obsessed with Sean.

Run! Do it now! Before it's too late.

"A cup of tea," Bethany said brightly as she rose quickly from her knees, slashing the air near Terra's arm. "A cup of tea, a chance to talk while we wait for my brother and his friend to arrive. Makes perfect sense to me. What do you think?"

Pointing the knife at Terra, she pursed her lips, a hard look in her dark eyes. "No. Forget that last part. I really don't care what you think."

Derrick hit redial. Terra's phone went to voicemail. He left her a reassuring message, asking her to call him back. The call had ended abruptly, leaving him worried. She could have simply dropped the phone, which meant that she would call right back. When it rang again, he answered to the sound of someone sobbing uncontrollably. "Terra?"

"No! It's Carolyn."

"Where are you?"

"I'm at the mall. I can't go home. I need to see Terra, but I'm afraid she won't talk to me. Derrick, I've made an awful mistake. I've hurt Terra. She's never going to forgive me. I should have known better," Carolyn cried.

"Is Terra alone at the house?" he asked.

"What! What difference does that make? I'm talking about me and my problems. I need your help."

"Calm down Carolyn, and tell me what you're talking about."

"Terra and I had a fight. I left the house angry with her. She said my boyfriend was dating me to get to her. I accused my sister, my only sister, of terrible things. I'm sorry," she sobbed. "I tried to call her, but she's not answering her cell or her home number."

"I'm on my way there now."

"You are? Why?"

Derrick didn't want Carolyn showing up when he and Meaghan told Terra about her sister-in-law, Bethany, and her obsession with Sean. "I'm following up on a lead, and need to talk to your sister. I'm sorry Carolyn, but I'm waiting for another call."

"Okay." She sniffed and hiccoughed. "Tell Terra to call me if she'd like to see me. Tell her I'm sorry."

"She'd probably like to hear that from you, not me, Carolyn."

He'd just hung up when the phone rang again. Mike's number appeared on the display.

"Derrick, how's it going?"

"I'm on my way over to Terra's house. I think I know who sent the emails."

"I found something, too. Bethany Cameron has a half-brother. You'll never guess what his name is?"

"Tell me."

"Lennie Taylor."

Fear blocked Derrick's throat. "Bethany's half-brother is Lennie? How did I miss that?"

"Because her single name was Anderson. Her mother, Helen, is Lennie's mother. I caught up with a friend of hers who told me that Bethany kept it quiet because she wanted to marry Shamus. She believed that Shamus wouldn't marry her if he knew."

"But Shamus would have known, wouldn't he? Surely he checked everything."

"Love's blind, I guess," Mike offered. "Derrick, that

means that Bethany could have gotten her half-brother and his friend to kill Sean. But why?"

"The emails. BBTAY is Bethany Taylor, the same woman who sat outside Sean's office the past couple of weeks pretending to write an article. She sent the threatening emails."

"You lost me."

"Catch you up later," Derrick said, hanging up and accelerating down the ramp onto the highway that led to Terra's home. He dialed his partner's number. "Meaghan, are you at the Cameron house yet?"

"No. I'm at the scene of an accident on Broadway Boulevard. I witnessed what happened. Didn't know you needed me there urgently. The ambulance and police are arriving now."

"I was hoping you were nearly at the house."

"What's wrong?"

"Terra's alone in the house." He went on to explain the rest of the story.

"I'll meet you there."

Where was Derrick? How much longer could she keep this woman calm? She pulled the screaming kettle off the burner and filled the teapot, steadying her hand as she did so. She had to keep Bethany talking until someone got here. She had to believe that Derrick would waste no time getting to the house once he realized she hadn't called back. But if he was going into the offices at Cameron Industries to see how the audit was going…all the way across town.

She took teacups out of the cupboard, filled the milk pitcher, found the sugar bowl and moved to the table, doing all of it as slowly as she dared. Bethany watched her, an eerie expression on her face. "Don't forget you're doing tea for four," she said, chewing on her thumbnail. "Why haven't you asked me how we did it, and why?"

"Did what?" Terra asked. She knew what Bethany had done, but she had to keep her talking.

"You know that Sean loved me."

Despite her fear, she looked straight at her sister-in-law. "No, he didn't. That was all in your mind."

"It was not!" She pounded the table. "I met Sean before you did. I was a waitress at the bar on West Main Street, Maddy's. Sean came in often. He was a good tipper, and so kind. Then I heard he was marrying you. Just like that. Out of the blue. You arrived in his life. After that, the only chance I had to be close to Sean was to marry Shamus. It took some doing, but I did it. I watched the two of you pretending you loved each other when I knew it was me Sean loved. You tricked him into marrying you. He was an honorable man who couldn't break his marriage vows. I understood that. I'm a Christian. I believe that what God has brought together let no man put asunder…" She rubbed her nose. "Or something like that."

Bethany started chewing the other thumbnail. "I sought forgiveness every day for having thoughts of another man other than my husband, but it didn't change how I felt. Finally I came up with a way to be near him while I figured out what to do."

Terra searched the face of the woman she thought she'd known. Bethany had always seemed so subservient, so out of time somehow… When their eyes met she saw the craziness there. Fear climbed her shoulders. She shivered. "Bethany, please tell me more. I didn't mean to hurt you."

"But you did. You hurt me so bad. Sean did too, in the end." She opened her jacket, displaying the one old shirt Terra had wanted from her husband's clothes. "I'm the one that came in here and got this shirt. I went through everything in his closet. I didn't want a suit. I wanted something that was special to him. I saw him one day in Daly's Hardware Store. He was wearing this." She fondled the collar of the shirt, her eyes closing for a few seconds.

Abruptly Bethany stopped, sat up straight and raised the knife in Terra's direction. "I had to have this piece of clothing." Her eyes narrowed. "And I hoped to scare you away from this house." She glanced toward the windows facing the backyard. "Lennie wanted to do something for me, something else after Sean's death. You didn't deserve to live in Sean's house. I did. He threw that rock for me. I'm not sorry, you know."

"About which part?" Terra asked, anger writhing around in her stomach, edging out of control at Bethany's callous admission that she had been involved in the incident that triggered the loss of her baby.

"When Sean wouldn't listen to reason, I had no choice but to take action. When I found out you were expecting Sean's baby I was so angry." She balled her hands into fists and pounded the table. "It was bad enough that you had Sean, but his baby? Never! You didn't deserve any of it, not Sean and not the baby. I'm not sorry for what I did."

Terra heard the woman's words as if from a great distance, barely audible. Everything that had ever mattered to her had been taken away by the actions of this....this *thing*...this killer. Her limbs felt limp. She could barely breathe. Even faced with Bethany's words she struggled to believe her. "You had my husband killed," Terra said as if in a trance.

"Like I said. I had no choice." Bethany gave a smug sigh as she looked around the space, turning her back on Terra. "But when this house is mine, when you are gone, I'll enjoy turning this house into something really pretty."

Life-giving air seeped back into Terra's lungs. She edged toward the corner of the counter, slowly moving closer to the woman as her fingers wrapped around the handle of the teapot.

She swung the teapot like a bat, bringing all her strength into the swing. Hot tea spewed across Bethany's shoulders as the china teapot hit its mark. Bethany screamed. The knife clattered to the floor. Bethany lunged at Terra, her hands reaching out for Terra, digging into her arm.

Fueled by blinding anger, Terra wrenched free and ran for the front door. She was on the concrete steps, running, when she was struck from behind. As she fell to the ground, her head hitting the concrete she saw two men coming up the walkway. She tried to get up, to call out, but the blinding pain in her head forced her back.

CHAPTER EIGHTEEN

Derrick turned sharply onto Terra's street, his lights flashing, the siren wailing. A few yards from her house he spotted a truck parked at the curb. Two men were walking up the walkway. He recognized them immediately—Lennie and Buddy.

Terra was on the front step. Bethany was standing over her. He slammed to a stop, shoved the gearshift into park, vaulted from the car and ran across the lawn. "Don't touch her!" he yelled.

Bethany and the two men turned toward him.

"On the ground," Derrick ordered, pulling his gun.

Somewhere behind him he heard another vehicle, and his partner's words of warning as she came up beside him, her gun trained on the three suspects. "Hands behind your back." Meaghan yelled.

"Got here as fast as I could," she said, moving to restrain the two men. More sirens wailed in the distance. "I called for backup."

Thankful that Meaghan was there, he turned his attention to Terra where she lay on the step. For a fraction of a second he thought she might be dead. Then she moved a little. Her eyes were unfocused when she opened them.

"We didn't do anything wrong, officer. My name is

Lennie Taylor. Me and my friend here, we came so I could see my sister, Bethany," he said, a whine in his voice.

"Don't say anything!" Bethany shrieked as a patrol car pulled up to the curb.

Derrick ignored all of them. "Terra," he whispered, crouching beside her and pulling her into his arms, cradling her head, touching her face. "Are you all right?" he asked.

He couldn't see any visible injuries. He looked closer: maybe a mark on her cheek. "Are you all right?" he asked again.

Her eyes met his. "You're here. What took you so long?" she asked, relief shining in her eyes. She reached for his hand. "Help me up."

"Not so fast." He touched her face, his fear pounding against his ribs. He could have lost her.

Her lips trembled as she managed a quick smile. "Bethany is crazy."

"Never mind her. She's going to jail. How are you feeling?"

"Okay, I think… Bethany must have hit me…"

"We have to get you to the hospital," he said hurriedly.

She didn't respond at first, just kept her eyes on him.

"Are you sure you're all right?" he asked.

"No." She shook her head and grimaced, her gaze returning to his face. "Why would Sean have had anything to do with that woman? Why was he emailing her? He only fed her belief that he cared about her. Why would he do that?"

Her words hurt him because she obviously loved her husband. He had no right to say anything, to expect anything. But he'd been the one protecting her. He was the one who figured what was going on. Derrick had saved her from those two goons. Yet her first thought was for a dead man.

Don't be a jerk! Of course her first thought would be about the man she loved.

Derrick cleared his throat. They'd probably never know why Sean Cameron had let Bethany think that he loved her. Maybe he hadn't realized that he was dealing with a deranged woman. Tech support, while going over Sean's laptop, had discovered that Sean had been on several chat rooms, talking to women. But Terra didn't need to know that. Terra believed in her husband and his love for her. She deserved to remember him as the man who loved her.

"We are pretty sure that Sean was trying to help Bethany. He allowed her to do an interview with him, to write about him for an article she was doing. She had no place of importance in anybody's life, no children and a husband who had his own issues. She was lonely and perhaps Sean believed he could trust his sister-in-law. Turns out she wasn't writing an article. Maybe when Sean discovered that, he tried to disentangle himself from her. But by then it was too late."

"Bethany was waiting here for her brother and his friend to come. She wanted me dead as well."

"Did she say that?"

Terra brushed the hair off her cheek, patted the damp spot of fresh tears just below her eye. "Yes. She wasn't the least bit sorry for what she did," Terra said, a soft moan starting somewhere in her throat and moving through her body. "How could this have happened? Did you know that she blamed me for Sean not loving her? She wanted him. She couldn't have him. She killed him." Sobs shook her body.

He was suddenly reminded of the old days when they were together. If Terra was upset, he would lie down beside her, hold her close and kiss away the tears. But that was then. Now, all he could do was hold on to her hand, and tell her the truth. "Terra I'm so sorry that you've had to endure so much these past weeks. But I hope you know that I'm here…if you need me."

Her eyes held his. When she did, he felt that old feeling of wholeness, of being a complete person once again. "Derrick, thank you for everything. I don't know what I would have done…"

If only she'd say something more, something he could hang on to. "No thanks necessary. You've had a really rough time, but maybe when you're feeling better you can call me and we can have coffee?"

"Maybe." She hesitated, then looked away. "I feel betrayed by Sean," she said biting her bottom lip.

And perhaps she had been. The tech people traced the email address to Bethany's computer. Sean hadn't discouraged Bethany from talking with him in the chat room. Sure, he didn't know who she was, but even when she threatened him he hadn't closed his chat room account.

They'd probably never know what motivated Sean to be involved in anonymous chat rooms when he seemed so in love with his wife. As Derrick sat on the edge of step beside Terra, he realized he really didn't care.

He met Terra's questioning look. All he cared about was Terra. She needed to hear the kind of words that would make her believe in her husband. He could do that much for her. "Just remember this: Your husband loved you." He shrugged, hoping his words worked their magic.

Her eyes met his…searching. He didn't move or pull away. She didn't touch him. She didn't lean into him. She simply sat next to him. And he was happy….for now.

"Thank you," Terra said, her voice clear and sincere.

EPILOGUE

One year later:

A breeze meandered across the open patio, sending stray leaves from the tree overhead scurrying ahead of it. The table awning above Terra's head fluttered, the sun warmed the air. She soaked in the moment, this new sense that life felt good for the first time since Sean's death.

Bethany, Lennie and Buddy had all been charged, and remanded for trial. She'd read that their lawyers were making all sorts of legal moves to prevent a guilty verdict. She didn't understand it and didn't want to. She couldn't waste her emotional energy on any of them. The only way to get past the horror of those weeks was to move on.

Carolyn had confronted Tim Martin, to discover that the man did intend to write a book about the Cameron family. He not only pretended to start a relationship with Carolyn, he had also befriended Terra's housekeeper Selena Shepherd looking for information.

With the Tim Martin mess behind them Terra and Carolyn had spent every Sunday putting together a cookbook of their mother's recipes. Tim Martin hadn't found a publisher for his misguided exposé.

Shamus had gone for counseling for his anger issues. He had worked this past year with Terra, the two of them forging a new way forward for Cameron Industries. They had cooperated with the police to uncover the two accountants in the head office who had stolen money from the company. Along with the accountants, two managers from the Midwest plants were facing embezzlement charges. Working side by side, she and Shamus had managed to reassure the banks that the company was financially strong. During those stressful months of working together Shamus grudgingly came to accept that she was a capable CEO. To be honest, she'd been surprised and pleased to be managing the company, and discovered that she had a head for numbers, something Sean had teasingly said she didn't have.

Despite loving her home, she was considering selling it. There were too many dashed hopes, too many plans destroyed, too many hurtful memories, to allow her to stay.

Oddly enough she was meeting Derrick here before the15K run that they'd both signed up for months ago. In fact running had brought them together during the horrible months after Sean's death. They were both surprised to see each other on the first Saturday practice run.

And the next Saturday after practice they went for coffee…more appropriately a green drink designed to build stamina. Mostly it tasted like a cross between raw carrot and some sort of oil to her, but it didn't really matter. They talked, and actually laughed together at one point. What they talked about didn't seem to matter, but they'd gone for that horrible green drink on ten different occasions.

She watched the people strolling along the sidewalk, many smiling, others walking with fierce determination. As usual she was early, but she liked these moments of anticipation. Over the months and weeks since that first Saturday meet she had slipped easily into sharing her thoughts with Derrick.

At first, sharing things with him had been very stilted and difficult, while he seemed somewhat constrained when he was around her, preferring to talk with other members of the running group. For her part she felt relieved that he didn't seem to care if she was at the practice or not. Then one day they found themselves alone at the meeting point for the practice run. He'd been attentive and caring, the way he'd been all those years before.

She was remembering those times when someone tapped her on the shoulder. She glanced up.

"Terra Cameron?" a handsome young man whose face was vaguely familiar smiled down at her.

"Yes."

"You probably don't remember me. I'm Al Butterworth the officer that came to your house the day Bethany Cameron was arrested."

She smiled in apology. "No, I don't. But thank you for being there. It was a pretty difficult day," she said, feeling a rush of memory around that day—all bad but one—Derrick.

He gave an easy laugh. "I've been in your neighborhood a lot this past year."

What was he saying? Had he been stalking her?

"I don't understand," she said, glancing around for Derrick.

He held up his hand. "Whoa! I didn't mean to make it sound like I was stalking you. I was following orders."

"Orders?"

"Well, not really orders. Detective O'Leary asked my partner and me to keep an eye on your house when we patrolled the area. He's been teaching a night course at the local college and we were part of the class. Ma'am, please don't be creeped out by this. He wanted to know you were safe, that's all."

Speechless she stared at the young man. "I… Thank you. I had no idea."

"He didn't mention it?"

All those evenings alone in the house, trying to piece her life back together, working well into the night on Cameron Industries business issues, surrounded by stubborn memories of the past, someone had been looking out for her. "No, he didn't."

Al's expression was one of apology. "Sorry. Don't tell him I told you."

"I won't," she said, wondering when Derrick had intended to tell her about this.

The young man smiled awkwardly and moved off, leaving her with her thoughts. When Derrick had left her house that day after Bethany and her two accomplices were taken into custody, she'd had only a couple of cursory calls from him. She hadn't seen him until they joined the same running group.

Lost in thought she didn't notice Derrick until he was sitting in front of her. "Oh!"

"Thinking of me?" he asked, a wide grin on his face.

"As a matter of fact, yes." She caught the sudden look of trepidation on his handsome features.

"Care to share?"

Did she dare broach the subject of their breakup? When he'd left her, she'd avoided anyone connected to him, didn't want to talk about him, all because she was so hurt and embarrassed. But now, after learning that he'd been keeping an eye on her, and what she'd experienced during the investigation into Sean's death, she had to know.

"Derrick, why did you and your wife divorce?"

Startled, he stared at her, a shocked frown on his face. "What? What's that got to do with anything now?"

"I need to know."

He rubbed his hands together, not meeting her glance. "This is difficult. I can't believe I could be so dumb. Me. A cop. Someone trained to be skeptical, to ask the difficult questions." He took in a deep breath. "I went out with Marylou one night, a stupid impulsive move. Woke up the next morning in her bed and with no memory of what happened. Three months later she comes to my office and announces she's pregnant. I was already feeling so guilty about what I did or almost did that I let her convince me that she was expecting my child. Turned out it was all a lie." His jaw worked. "It was the stupidest, worst time of my life. I hurt you. The last person I ever wanted to hurt. But I had no excuse for what I did. None. The only thing I could do was leave. You deserved better than me. And you found him."

The old ache pierced her heart. Tears threatened but she fought them back. "Why didn't you tell me? Why did you walk out and leave me to wonder if it was me? Why let me believe that I had done something? Why didn't you trust me? We were talking about getting married."

"I don't know. And I'm so embarrassed even now to be talking about this. I ruined everything between us. I divorced her the minute I learned the truth, but it was too late to make amends." His eyes met hers. The pain she saw there was genuine. "I was almost relieved when you met Sean. He was everything I wasn't."

"You were happy when I married someone else? That's the dumbest thing I've ever heard."

"Not happy. Just thankful that you were able to move on, to find love."

After he'd left her she'd sworn she never want to know anything about him ever again. Yet at this moment, knowing if he'd found someone seemed so important. "And you didn't find love, is that what you're saying?"

He stared up at the awning above their heads for a long time. She waited and waited and finally had to say something. "Look, I'm sorry I asked. It's none of my business. It's just that I met one of the officers you asked to watch my house. Unless you're a stalker, which you aren't, you must have had a reason for doing it. Were you trying to make amends?"

Derrick's eyes met hers. His hand reached across the table. "Yes. I had no right to ever come near you again, but I had to do what I could to keep you safe." He sighed, his eyes searching hers. "I love you. I've always loved you. I realize that my behavior didn't show that. I hurt you, and I'm so sorry." He pulled his hand back. "I've wanted to say those words for a year. When I saw you the night Sean died, I knew without condition that I still loved you. But I also knew my job was to help you anyway I could. I even had my boss questioning my ability to do my job where you were concerned."

He smiled that fantastic smile of his, tugging at her heart. "Terra, the happiest day of my life was the day you showed up for the run."

"You didn't rig that as well? Maybe talk to Carolyn about my plans to join a running group?"

"No. Never."

As she sat there with him, seeing the agony in his eyes, she knew he was telling her the truth. "And all those horrible green drink dates was your way of telling me you're here in my life, whatever that means."

He laughed. "Aren't they odd? But I've grown to like them." His gaze moved slowly over her face. "And yes, I'm here…. Always will be."

She could barely swallow over the lump in her throat, the longing for him, for what they'd had together, their shared belief in the possibilities life presented. All that had gone in a heartbeat of betrayal.

Could she trust him again? Could she bear to be hurt again by the one person who had destroyed her faith in what they had? But if they had a chance at happiness… These past weeks had been very happy for her, and it was because of him. Running was the reason she joined the group. Running was not the reason she stayed. Could she say what she really felt? Could she continue running in the marathon alongside of him if she didn't? "I want to try again. I'm scared you'll hurt me. It's as simple as that."

He leaned closer. "I promise I won't."

She fought the urge to slip into his arms, to feel once more the warmth of his embrace. "We've seen enough of life to know that promises can be broken, even when we don't mean to break them," she replied, her heart pounding in anticipation.

His gaze didn't falter. "Let's start out slow, give ourselves lots of time."

She saw the sincerity in his eyes, heard the caring in his voice. Yes, he'd hurt her. And yes, maybe he would again. But wasn't it worth the risk, if they could be happy together once more? "I'd like that."

"We are going to have the happiest life any two people

could have." He got up, came around the table and pulled her into his arms. "I love you, Terra. I always will."

She turned her face up to his. "Forever?"

He kissed her, a kiss that held so much promise. "Forever," he whispered against her cheek.

OTHER BOOKS BY
STELLA MACLEAN

Heart of My Heart, Harlequin Superromance

Baby in Her Arms, Harlequin Superromance

A Child Changes Everything, Harlequin Superromance

The Christmas Inn, Harlequin Superromance

The Doctor Returns, Harlequin Superromance

To Protect Her Son, Harlequin Superromance

Sweet On Peggy, Harlequin Superromance

Finding Mr. Wrong, Contemporary Romance

Desperate Memories, Romantic Suspense

Unimaginable, Romantic Suspense

ABOUT STELLA MACLEAN

Romantic suspense author Stella MacLean writes books populated with contemporary characters that will keep you reading well past your bedtime. Stella writes stories that are readable, relatable, and packed with emotional punch that will leave you remembering the story long after you finish reading the book.

Stella loves to hear from her readers, to learn what they enjoyed most about her books.

She can be reached at her website: www.stellamaclean.com.

Or you can find her on Twitter: @Stella_MacLean

Or on Facebook: facebook.com/stella.maclean.3

Made in the USA
Columbia, SC
17 September 2018